P9-CCJ-506

A SMALL AND INCIDENTAL MURDER

A SMALL AND INCIDENTAL MURDER

JOHN WALTER PUTRE

CHARLES SCRIBNER'S SONS
NEW YORK

Charles Scribner's Sons
Macmillan Publishing Company
866 Third Avenue, New York, NY 10022
Collier Macmillan Canada, Inc.

Library of Congress Cataloging-in-Publication Data
Putre, John Walter.
A small and incidental murder / John Walter Putre.
p. cm.
ISBN: 0-684-19139-3
I. Title.
PS3566.U86S64 1990
813'.54—dc20 89-10454 CIP

10 9 8 7 6 5 4 3 2 1

Printed in the United States of America

For Mom and Dad, who had to wait too long,
And for Helen, who, in so many ways, made it happen.

A SMALL AND INCIDENTAL MURDER

1

If nature had had a sense of humor, the island might have been shaped like an oyster or, failing that, at the least, like a crab. For the watermen who, for centuries, had harvested the bay, the shapes of oysters and crabs held meaning. It would have been as though the shoreline of Nantucket were configured in the profile of a whale.

But the winds and tides that sculpt the beaches leave the making of ironies to men. So it was that, in reality, the island's outline resembled nothing so much as a captured crayfish, held dangling by its tail from a harassing peninsula, with its twin claws reaching southward into the shoal waters of the Chesapeake Bay.

Doll remembered the island, though some years had passed since the last time he'd been there. He remembered its narrow back roads and its marshy ground and the houses and the mobile homes where the men who worked the water lived. The homes had seemed always in need of repair. He saw them again, in his mind's eye, with the hulks of disused automobiles and the scattered piles of rusting junk that, somehow, grew up around them, as inevitably as manicured lawns grew in the suburbs.

He wondered as he drove if that had changed.

He tuned the VW's radio to a D.C. country station. Outside, a rush of heavy spring rain drummed a competing tattoo on the metal skin of the car.

Ellis LeCates was a part of what Doll thought of as his kaleidoscopic past—kaleidoscopic not because of any special abundance of color, but because nothing in it ever seemed to last. The individual parts that fell into place as the cylinder turned looked stable enough by themselves: the Navy years, the Florida years, the last ten which he'd spent in the Delaware coast town of Lewes. Everything looked normal, except that nothing fit together. Relationships which he'd expected to last dissolved and slipped away until, somehow, all the continuity got lost, until nothing, anymore, seemed destined to endure beyond some finite definition of the moment. Doll took that as one side of the coin. The other was that the discontinuity gave him the gift of independence.

LeCates had come from the Florida time, when the two had made their living diving for a dredging operation. It had been a watershed year for Doll, the same that had been the first and the last of his marriage. LeCates had been no part of that nearly perfect disaster. He was five years' Doll's chronological senior, but utterly contemptuous of any kind of domesticity. Doll recalled him as a roisterous marauder whose nights were consumed in a perpetual search for bar fights and amenable women.

Circumstance, more than anything else, had thrown the two of them together. They did the same kind of work. The vagaries of a disinterested schedule had made them more than occasional partners.

They'd talked of insignificant things on the decks of the boats while they'd passed the time between dives. They'd drunk beer with the rest of the crew when the day was over. Conversation had meant football, or whatever was in season, interspersed with largely exaggerated tales recounting some of the livelier moments that, from time to time, happen in the trades subject to the capriciousness of the sea. As Doll recalled their relationship, there was nothing more to it than that.

So the phone call from LeCates the night before last had come as something of a surprise. It had not been the first call. There had been two before it: one five years ago, a kind of obligatory renewal of past fellowship when LeCates had first come north, and a second, a year or so back, that had brought the flat report that the owner of the Florida dredging firm had died. Both had been unemotional. Neither had carried any sense of urgency.

The third call had been different. Even over the long distance phone line, LeCates' voice had carried what Doll could only describe as an intensity. It sounded neither like anxiety nor anger, nor anything else Doll could quite place a finger on. He only knew for certain that he'd never heard the quality in anything LeCates had said before.

LeCates needed to see Doll—needed to talk to him as soon as possible. The meeting had to be in person, there, on the island across the peninsula where LeCates now made his living keeping a small general store. The matter was too complex, much too much so to be handled on the phone.

Doll had asked the obvious. Was LeCates in trouble? Did he need money? The reply had been that it was nothing like that.

The easiest answer for Doll to have given was no. The unilateral dictation of terms and LeCates' refusal to talk at all on the phone gave reason enough. But other arguments mitigated. April is early for diving work along the mid-Atlantic coast. The water temperature is still too cold and the seas of the winter haven't yet subsided. In another month, Doll would be working again, but now the accumulated boredom of the winter off was nearing its culmination. The second reason Doll came up with was curiosity. He couldn't resist the picture of the man he knew from Florida now turned placidly to managing a store.

Or so Doll told himself. But a part of his mind that somehow worked outside the rest kept coming back to the voice.

The rain streaked the windshield between the passes of the wiper blades and fogged the windows on the sides. The music became an annoying drone, and the pleasure Doll usually took from driving soured into a contest of endurance. He turned off the radio and shifted his attention to the landscape.

After Easton, the gentle roll of the low inland countryside flattened into marsh. Trees that had been distributed evenly over the land now grew clustered in rows or small patches, wherever the marginally higher ground would support them. And almost everywhere there was water, peeking out from the backs of fields, between the trunks of trees, or hovering, like a mirage, beyond the outer limits of the marshes.

There were more people, more houses along the highway than Doll remembered. The names of towns were familiar. They drifted by on signs set at the side of the road. Some were marked, as well, by small groupings of buildings. Others seemed arbitrarily fixed, with no discernible centers.

A village began to grow. Not a village like the others Doll had come through, but one that was larger and painted with the vividness of an artist's imagination. The houses were neat, colonial structures, well maintained, and finished in stains and antiqued paints. The center ran for several blocks. There were sidewalks with pedestrians in brightly colored rain slickers. The buildings were restored to evoke a sense of history. The stores had the look of the kind of establishments that people are fond of calling "Shoppes."

It was picturesque in a self-conscious way, the same way some towns on Cape Cod and in Vermont are picturesque. It was a town, Doll thought, that had made the buoying discovery that there could be very good money in "quaint."

The town also absorbed a large share of the traffic.

Beyond it, the highway was open. Even through the rain, the driving was faster. The island where LeCates kept his store wasn't far ahead. Marshlands encroached upon both sides of the road. Outside the marshes, open water began to pinch off the land.

Doll was driving down a narrowing neck. At its end, he came to a short, steep bridge. Up and down, it took only a second to cross it. He was on the island. He let himself think of what might be ahead.

The store was small, as Doll had expected it would be, small enough to fit comfortably in the first floor of a two-story house. The stock ranged from canned goods and soda to fishing line, cold preparations, newspapers, and combs.

The screen door banged shut behind Doll's back.

From a table at the end of the far left aisle, LeCates glanced up from his morning paper and coffee. Except for LeCates and himself, as far as Doll could tell the store was empty.

"Hey, Doll," LeCates said, standing. In a storekeeper's gesture, he wiped his hands on the front of his apron. "Damn you, it's good to see you. Even after we talked, I wasn't sure you'd see your way to make it. Sorry about the weather out there. Wish you'd had better. It's never what you think it's going to be around here."

Ellis LeCates was middle-aged.

It was something, Doll realized intellectually, that he should have expected. The last time Doll had seen him, ten years before, he'd been coming up on his middle thirties. Now he was somewhere close to forty-five.

His face was full and his waist thick—not to the point of obesity, but his weight, Doll guessed, was some thirty pounds or so more than it had been in Florida. His shirt, under the apron, fitted loosely. His pants were broadly cut and sagged in the seat and around the backs of the thighs. His hair was still black, but thinner. It was cut to a medium length and carelessly combed back from his forehead.

Doll shook the offered hand. At the same time, he wondered how the aging had happened. It wasn't an answer to say it came on gradually. There had to be an instant of revelation—a day, an hour, even a single moment, when you looked at yourself in the mirror and suddenly knew.

"Thanks for coming. Here, I'll get you some coffee." LeCates turned and started back toward the table. "Black, no milk, no sugar, unless you've changed." His walk still swayed, despite the years, to accommodate the roll of an absent deck.

"You've got a good memory," Doll answered. "Used to be you could never remember how much you'd borrowed from who."

LeCates chuckled and grinned. "Those days are long gone. You look good, Doll." He poured the coffee from a round glass pot he kept near the table on a warmer. "I would've known you on the street. You look like you did when we were working for Vicarias. That's a lotta years ago. I don't count 'em anymore. You work hard at staying in shape?"

"I run a little," Doll said, without being sure exactly what it was he was expected to acknowledge.

"You said on the phone you still dive. You still do it for a living?" LeCates put Doll's coffee on the table and motioned for him to take the opposite seat.

"Part-time." Doll sat and tried the coffee. It tasted stale, like coffee kept on the heat for too long, which, no doubt, was exactly what it was. "Enough to get by. The pay's too good. I'm spoiled for honest work."

LeCates shook his head and took his own chair. "Most honest damn pay you'll ever make," he said. "So honest I can't do it anymore. I near to drowned down there, Doll. So near that, when they got me up, they had to give me mouth-to-mouth.

My nerve is gone. I couldn't ever make myself go underwater again."

Doll shrugged. "As long," he said, "as you're happy with what you're doing now."

LeCates glanced out the window at the pavement of the island's main street and at the sheets of water that ran off into the sand and crushed oyster shells along the side. Doll looked too. The rain seemed lighter, the sky a little less gray than before.

"Part-time? You said you dive part-time," LeCates said. "Ain't no woman anywhere that'd let you get away with that. How come you never got married again? That first time, down there, was really so bad?"

"No," Doll said, though, even after ten years, the memories made the answer a very long way from the truth. He wondered how much LeCates knew about how it had been. "Do you mind if we change the subject, Ellis? Let's talk about how you like running the store. Or, better yet, why you had me come here."

LeCates picked up a plastic spoon and, to no evident purpose, stirred the surface of his cooling coffee. "Takes time to get it back together," he said. "I told you I needed to talk to you, Doll. I've got to get back to where I feel easy with you. I've got to know about who you are now—more than that you're a lousy advertisement for the holy state of marriage."

"Is that what this is about?" Doll asked. "I don't believe you got me over here to give you advice on getting married."

"Doesn't sound much like me, does it?" LeCates laughed and took a swallow of his coffee. He picked up the laugh again and let it trail off as he returned the cup to the table. "You asked about the store," he said. "Let me tell you something about that. You look around, you don't see exactly Neiman and Marcus. I don't clear fifteen grand a year here. But I can clear a little every year. I live upstairs, so the rent is free. Most of my groceries, I rip off from the store. Nobody hassles me, Doll. That's what's nice. People sometimes stop by just to talk. And the only way I'm likely to drown is if I get a little tight some night and fall off one of the docks into the bay."

"Sounds like you're mellowing out," Doll said.

"You're damn right I am. Forty-six years old this coming July. A man's got a right to. There're lots of worse ways to live." LeCates tapped on the table with his index finger for emphasis. "And it's all just like money in the bank. It's the kind of thing I'll be able to do right up to the day I die."

"Fine, Ellis, but you don't need my blessing for any of that." For a horrible moment, Doll saw himself at graveside delivering the eulogy over the casket of Ellis LeCates. He drove the apparition away. "And none of it," he added, "tells me anything about why I had to come over here."

The screen door opened. A girl came in, giving LeCates a further opportunity to postpone his answer.

She seemed to Doll to be somewhere in those confusing years that come just before the suffix "-teen" applies. She wore a patched pair of corduroy pants and a man's flannel shirt that served as an oversized jacket. She was neither homely nor particularly pretty, though she might have been more so had she taken the time to comb her hair.

LeCates met her at the counter and said good morning. She answered him by handing him a list. He wiped his hands on his apron again and began the task of collecting the items from the shelves.

"Something else?" he asked as he rang up the tally. "Last time your ma was in, she said something about needing pie tins."

The girl put some wrinkled money on the counter. For a second or two she stared at it, then asked LeCates if she had enough for the pie tins too.

LeCates did a fast count and shook his head. "But tell you what we can do," he said. "We'll give you the tins, but not charge you today. Next time, when your mother comes in, she can bring what they cost or else can bring the tins back if she wants to."

He added the pie tins to the bag.

"And you say hello," LeCates called as the girl started out. "Say hello to your sister and Farron. Don't forget your mother, too."

The screen door slammed.

"Not such a bad way to live," he repeated, as though to say to Doll that kind of thing was typical of what went on in the store most every day. He made his way back toward his coffee.

"These are decent people around here, Doll. You got to begin by understanding that. Nobody cheats you. Most don't lock their doors. After a while, they let you know them a little.

"That girl you just saw there was Dorothy Carrow. You wanted to know why I asked you to come here. It's because I think her father was murdered."

Ellis LeCates' story began with the explosion that had killed LeRoy Carrow. Officially, the coroner's inquest had ruled the death an accident, or, perhaps more accurately, had found insufficient evidence to determine that the cause of death was anything more than it appeared.

Accumulated gas leaked from a propane stove had ignited one morning when Carrow had tried to make coffee. The explosion wasn't big. It might have done no more than splinter the cabin and land Carrow in a corner with a few bruises and some superficial burns. Instead, that day the impartial probabilities of physics had dictated otherwise. The back of Carrow's head had hit the edge of one of the oyster boat's ribs. His skull had been fractured, his neck broken. Death, by determination of the medical examiner, was instantaneous.

"That's why I asked you to come," LeCates concluded. "I need you to find out if that's what really happened. You already know I think there was more to it than that."

"That leads to some pretty big questions," Doll said.

"I know." LeCates' lips tightened into a thin, straight line. "And I can't help you answer them. Or I won't. Maybe that's what I should say. I'm sorry, Doll, but that's got to be part of the deal."

"Then there's not going to be any deal," Doll said.

LeCates frowned and nodded. "I saw that coming. But you've got to hear me out. The first thing you're going to ask me is why I think what happened to Carrow was murder. How do I win at that, Doll? No matter what I say—right or wrong—it sends you off looking with something already there in your mind. I don't want you to know about what I think. I don't give a damn if what I think is right or wrong. I want you to find out what happened, whatever it was, and I want you to be able to say, when it's done, that nothing I did led you toward or away from it."

"Except to say, in the first place, you think it might be a murder. I wonder," Doll asked, "why you care about this at all?"

"I can't explain that either. Not without going back to why I think Carrow was murdered." LeCates began to reach for his coffee. He looked at it, hesitated, then apparently abandoned the idea of drinking any. "I told you I wanted to keep it objective, Doll. Can't we say, for now, that the only thing I'm after is justice?"

"It's the easiest thing in the world to say it," Doll said. "You can just about say whatever you like. It opens up all kinds of possibilities when you say beforehand you aren't going to back up the claim."

Doll shook his head and pushed his chair back from the table. "I'll tell you, Ellis, I don't like this thing at all. I didn't like it when you held back on the phone. I like it even less when you do it to me in person."

"Please, Doll." LeCates' forehead wrinkled, and his mouth turned down at the corners. It seemed less an expression of displeasure with Doll than it was discouragement at the position in which he found himself. "I know you don't like it. I'm asking you to trust me and giving you all the reasons in the world not to. But I'm asking you anyway. It's that important to me. Can't you see your way clear to do it, even as a one-time favor for a friend?"

"You're reaching, Ellis. I'm not even sure what you want me to do. What, specifically, is it that you've got on your mind?"

"Did you bring your tanks?"

"You said to. I brought them," Doll answered.

"Then I want you to do a dive on Carrow's boat. This afternoon. There are no tricks and no risks. It's right by the wharf where it was tied the morning it blew up. The bow is up. The stern is under a foot or so of water. But the water's so shallow there you could practically stand."

"What would I be looking for? Assuming I agreed to do the dive for you."

LeCates shook his head. "If you're asking me for something exact, I don't know. That's not holding back. I really don't. Anything that says the explosion maybe wasn't an accident. God help me, Doll, I don't know what that might be."

"What happens," Doll asked, "if there's nothing?"

"Whatever you want." LeCates offered a helpless smile. "How can I stop you, whatever you find, if you say that that's as far as you'll go? For God's sake, Doll, you're holding all the cards. Can't you see, I can't even make you do the dive?"

"Why come to me with this?"

"You're a friend. You're a friend and a diver," LeCates replied. "You've been around enough wrecks so you know what damage to look out for in a boat."

"When we talked on the phone, you asked me to come over here before you knew I was still diving."

"Did I?" LeCates looked confused. He seemed to try to recall the conversation, to grasp for some plausible answer. "Maybe I just figured you would be. Okay, you're right. It's more than that," he admitted. "I called you because I heard you do this kind of thing. You've done it before. I know a state cop from over where you live. Not all the way over on the coast where you are. He works the west side of the state. I brought up your name. I never seriously thought he might know you."

"And?" Doll knew what was coming next.

"The cop said he remembered you. He said that a year or so ago you were looking for a man who'd murdered some friend of yours. He also said that you'd killed a man who got in your way."

"It was self-defense," Doll answered.

LeCates nodded and said that the cop had said that, too.

"One more answer," Doll said quietly. "And, I'll tell you beforehand, Ellis, no evasions and it had better be the right one. Did you kill this LeRoy Carrow?"

"What?"

"Don't give me that 'who—me?' look." Doll didn't believe for a minute that LeCates was one-tenth as shocked as he appeared. "You think you'd be the first to come up with the idea of having someone who was supposed to be a friend check their tracks? You figure nobody before you ever had someone go over the ground to see what mistakes got made or what got missed?"

"I didn't do it. I didn't rig the boat. I swear that, Doll."

"You didn't hire it rigged? You had no part in it?"

"No. Nothing. I swear it. I'll swear an oath on anything you want."

Doll didn't reply at once. Instead, he gave LeCates a few seconds to rethink his answer. "I only hope that's the truth," he said finally. "Because, if it's not, Ellis, you'd be a fool to let me start this thing. If it's you, and I find that out, Florida's not going to make any difference. Whatever I find gets turned over to whoever ought to have it. And whatever happens after that is what happens. That's what comes on my side of the deal."

"I understand that. That's the way I want it," LeCates agreed. "Does that mean you'll do it?" he asked.

"It means," Doll said, "that I'll make the dive and look at Carrow's boat. That's all I'm willing to say for now. When that's done, we'll talk again. We'll see, then, where, if anywhere, we go from there."

2

The narrow channel that separated the island from the peninsula was only fifty feet wide at the drawbridge. In its effectiveness as a natural line of demarcation, the strip of water might as well have been a major continental river.

South of the channel, the scale of everything seemed downsized. Measured from tail to claw, the island was a fraction more than three miles long. Its greatest width scarcely reached a mile. Houses and trailers were scattered more or less evenly, wherever the land was solid enough to support them. But the northern end was where the community's business got done. LeCates' store, the elementary school, the inn, the gas stations, boatyards, and larger harbors were all compressed into an oval that a man could walk in less than twenty minutes end to end. The effect of the concentration was to give the impression that the island was even smaller than it was.

Doll walked beside LeCates along the main road. The rain of the morning had ended. The gray clouds were broken and moved swiftly overhead. Doll carried his diving tanks over his shoulder.

"The boat's a skipjack," LeCates said. "They're real beauties, if you know the breed. Designed for the bay to drudge under sail. Not many left anymore, less'n two dozen in all. Most of those are from here on the island. Somethin' to see when they sail."

Doll knew the bay's skipjacks. They were proud boats, with tall sloop rigs and high-arched prows—beamy and heavy, impossible to mistake for a yacht, but with an elegance and grandeur all their own. He also took passing note of LeCates' adoption of the local vocabulary. The warders of the English language decree that skipjack crews "dredge" for oysters. But those who have to haul for their living prefer to say that they "drudge."

"You said she's sunk. Do you know how bad she's damaged?" Doll asked.

"Not so bad from what I've heard." LeCates paused, perhaps to develop his assessment. "Sounds like she's holed below the waterline somewhere. The explosion likely blew something through. I mean somethin' must've sunk her. A lot of the cabin's torn away. You can see right down to the water inside. But she could sail again, Doll. I thought about that. I let it out a little that I might know a man who'd want to make her over."

Doll turned sharply toward LeCates. "Why do I think you're getting at something, Ellis? Is this something else I haven't been told?"

"I thought it might work out better if you were that man." LeCates either had a good sixth sense, or else he saw the flare in Doll's eyes. "You don't know how things are, " he rushed on to explain. "These watermen are suspicious old bastards. They don't trust anybody whose family ain't been here for at least a couple hundred years. I've been here for five, Doll. They'll talk to me, do business with me. But I'm still an outsider, and I'm always going to be one. You're going to have to deal with that. You start off right away by asking about Carrow, you'll be lucky if they talk to you at all, much less answer your questions."

"So we'll get them to trust us by lying to them. Good plan, Ellis."

Doll didn't think that LeCates was right; at the same time, he wasn't sure that he was wrong.

"It'll work. They'll accept you as a buyer," LeCates insisted. "And you got the perfect reason for making the dive." He clicked his tongue against the back of his teeth as though he were debating with himself whether or not to say any more. "It's a bad time for them now," he continued. "They're even more close-mouthed now than usual. You just can't know all the things they're up against."

"The oysters?"

"That's a part of it. Not all," LeCates conceded. "Things are getting pretty bad. The take they get off the bay gets smaller every year."

Everyone said that, especially the spots on the television news. The biologists and the politicians talked, while the watermen abandoned the bay to work as day laborers for anyone who'd hire them. The cry was that the bay was dying. No one but the politicians knew how to make it better. And they disagreed on what to do.

"You said that's only a part of it."

LeCates nodded. "The real estate market's the other. It's getting to the point where the water people can't afford to live here anymore."

Doll had seen that before, too. There were places on both sides of the shore where a buyer with the money could pick up a kerosene stove shack for fifty, sixty thousand dollars. Once the people who lived there got out, the renovations work started with a bulldozer. "But that kind of thing doesn't happen overnight," Doll said. "It's the kind of thing a person who looks ahead can see and plan for."

"It seems like it should be, don't it?" LeCates ran his hands over his shirtfront. "You're right, they won't go broke from it, Doll. In fact, startin' off at least, the ones who get out'll have a fair amount of money in the bank. The only thing is they'll be gone for good. There won't be anyplace for them like the island, and the island won't be like it is anymore."

Doll moved his tanks to the opposite shoulder. "The stuff it takes for survival changes," he said. "The rules stay the same. It's still a very Darwinian world."

They found LeRoy Carrow's skipjack as LeCates had said it would be. The boat lay alongside the wharf. Her bow, tied short, was pointed high. Her stern deck was under the water. The plywood sheeting that had covered the aft-portion of the cabin was ripped away, except for spike-shaped splinters that projected from the cabin's sides at the places where the roof had been attached.

Doll stared down into the opening that now was nearly filled with seawater. A sodden life cushion barely floated on the surface. The lid of a styrofoam ice chest drifted nearby. In the midst of the debris, a school of tiny fish inhabited the pool. Each sudden shift in their direction fired flashbulblike bursts of silver up from just beneath the surface of the water.

He walked the length of the sixty-foot hull. The skipjack was monocolored, white all over, except where her decks were worn gray and in the spots where the brown-red of rusting metal had stained her. Her only vanity was in the adornment of the trailboard under her bowsprit, which, by tradition, was decorated in bright hues of blue, red, and yellow.

As Doll turned away from the boat, he found that he and LeCates were no longer alone.

Five men stood in a horseshoe around LeCates, two in front, the three others behind. The front two were older. Doll's estimate placed them both a few years this or the other side of fifty. Age and the line of march implied that these were the captains.

They eyed Doll like two English lords come to examine a vagrant stranger trespassing on a posted estate.

The two were dressed pretty much alike, in oilskin overalls and rubber wader boots. The one to LeCates' left had a wiry look, the other a barrel chest and ample stomach that made the front of his overalls swell.

LeCates made the introductions. Doll, despite whatever reservations he had, became the man who had come to buy LeRoy Carrow's boat.

The barrel-chested man was introduced as Captain George Page of the *Betty St. James*. LeCates pointed across to the two skipjacks, berthed side to side against the opposite wharf. Doll had already seen the boats and the "For Sale" sign wired to the outboard skipjack's shroud lines.

Page nodded to Doll when LeCates said his name. His mouth appeared to carry the suggestion of a greeting. Doll watched the waterman's jaw work. The skin of his face was weather-toughened. His chin and cheeks were covered with a cactuslike stubble.

Ornan Atkins was the second of the captains. His boat, the *Winston B. Mills*, was rafted inboard of Page's. Atkins' greeting was cooler—so cool, in fact, that Doll wasn't sure that there had been any greeting at all. The expression Atkins wore seemed as fixed as that on a piece of statuary. His eyes were the color of stormclouds.

The others, as Doll had guessed, turned out to be members of the crew. They were Jerry Lee Godfrey, the mate from Page's boat, and Joely Edwards and Carroll Messick, hand and mate from the *Winston Mills*.

"So you're the man that wants t' buy LeRoy's boat." George Page looked thoughtful and shook his head, then spit a pea-sized pellet of tobacco and saliva onto the cracked shell cover at his feet. "I don't mean to be pryin', Mr. Doll—good Lord knows it's neither a' my business—but, you look across the water, there, you see my own boat's up for sale. Can't sell it, nohow. Nobody wants it. Don't mean to put my nose in, but just because it might give me some idea, I got to ask you what you think it is you're going to do with that ol' boat."

It had only begun and, already, LeCates' lie was getting too heavy to carry. Doll swore to himself. For the moment, though, he could think of nothing else but to add to it.

"I'm not interested for myself," he said. "I'm only here as the agent for a man from Baltimore."

Page glanced toward Atkins, then looked back at Doll. As best Doll could tell from the waterman's face, the answer seemed to satisfy him. Doll suspected that, on the island, a man could explain away a lot by invoking the eccentricities of the wealthy folk who came over from the cities.

"Bal'mer. Money, what else!" Page nodded and chewed at his tobacco. "So I take it that he won't be workin' her, then. What? Tear her down and strip her guts out? Make her into some kind of fancy yacht?"

Doll answered that he didn't know.

"Money!" Page repeated. "It sure must be a lovely sumbitchin' thing to have. Well, there's one thing I know. It's gonna take a lot of that." He turned to the younger man behind him. "Take a look at her, Carroll," he said. "You know the boat. You worked in the yards. Tell Mr. Doll what it's gonna cost."

Carroll Messick came from behind Page. He looked quickly to Atkins, then at Page, and then at Doll. He might, Doll thought, have been as easily a farmer as a waterman. He wore a plaid flannel shirt and jeans and a broad-peaked cap, the shadow from which turned his tanned face to a deep oak brown.

"Yard work always comes high," Messick said, glancing down at Carrow's boat. "You got hull work here." He shook his head. "Cabin's gotta be just about rebuilt." He shrugged to make it clear that what he was offering was only a very rough estimate. "Five thousand leastways, just to float her again. If you want t' convert her, can't help you much with that. That's as high as you want t' put into it. A hundred thousand? That's the low end. Man would be a fool t' get into it at all if he didn't want t' spend at least that."

"So that's a hundred thousand gets added t' whatever you offer LeRoy's widow," Page said as he scratched at the stubble. He paused, seeming to evaluate the bargain.

"Money!" he announced for yet a third time. He looked toward Atkins. "Think about all that damn money, Ornan. A man from out Bal'mer can put more than a hundred thousand into some ol' boat that'll just cost him more to keep up every year. How long'd you have t' work just t' see a hundred thousand? I ain't sure, if you put it all together—all the time I spent on the water—that I've made so damn much money as that in all my sinnerful life."

Atkins didn't answer Page's question, perhaps because Page hadn't really seemed to want an answer.

Doll asked if anyone knew any more about how much Carrow's boat had been damaged. "What I mean," he said, when no one replied, "was if any of you were here when the accident happened."

"We was all here. Keepin' the boats. Arsterin' season's mostly done. But what's that got to do with LeRoy's boat?" Page asked.

"It would help," Doll said, "if I knew how big the explosion was. Did it sound big enough to bust her open? How long did the fire last? How hot did it burn? Anything like that would make what I have to do easier."

"What d' you say, boys?" Page glanced around at the others. "Like I said, we was all here. All of us saw it. Jerry Lee, I reckon, was closest when it happened. He works for me," Page said, turning back toward Doll, "an', like you saw, I tie up outboard a' Ornan. Jerry Lee was in the bow. That was the end nearest t' LeRoy. Go ahead on, Jerry Lee. Tell Mr. Doll here what you saw."

Jerry Lee Godfrey was under six feet, but still the tallest of the five watermen. It seemed to Doll the only way in which nature had been kind to him. He was gangly and his movements awkward, though he was many years past the age when he should have learned to coordinate his body. To add to that, his lower jaw stuck out beyond the upper to a degree that made one wonder if the bone wouldn't have been better suited to an ox. As though in apology for his appearance, he stood with his head bowed and his hands crossed below the midpoint of his stomach in the attitude of a perpetual penitent.

He looked up at Page when Page addressed him by name.

"Didn't see nothin'. Nothin' at all, Cap'n. Heard the noise, I did, and right away I got myself down on that deck."

"You heard the explosion, Jerry Lee," Page said. "You heard what Mr. Doll said. Was it loud?"

"No, Cap'n. Not a lot," Godfrey answered, shaking his head.

"Did anyone actually see it?" Doll asked.

"Guess you could say I did," Carroll Messick offered. "I was for'ard on the *Winston Mills*, not that far from where Jerry Lee was. I saw a flash—low and quick. Then I saw the roof blow off, and I heard a kind of a pop. Jerry Lee's right. It wasn't real loud. Sounded about like a shotgun to me, maybe not so sharp."

Doll asked how long it was before Messick saw any fire.

"Right away," Messick said. "Big whompin' ball of it went right up with the cabin roof. After that first ball, there wasn't much. Most all a' what there was went up in that first shot."

"What happened then?" Doll asked.

Messick glanced around. No one else seemed anxious to volunteer. "Everythin' did. We all started runnin'. Joely got 'round to 'er first. He was workin' up on the dock when it went off."

"Yeah, I got 'round first," Joely Edwards admitted. Once he got started, the blush of reluctance appeared to wear off. "I jumped right on down there and got to LeRoy. I wasn't thinkin' at all about that damn ol' boat. I knew LeRoy was dead soon as I saw 'im. Poor son of a bitch. He was lyin' there with his head all off to one side like some damn bird that flew itself into a window. The skin on the back was all split open. There wasn't much blood. Just a little, leakin' out like it was some kind a' stupid red oil."

" 'Bout the boat?" Page said. "That's what Mr. Doll wants to hear. LeRoy weren't his affair. C'mon now, boys. Either body gonna say what happened next?"

"Somebody brought an extinguisher," Edwards said.

"Cap'n Atkins did," Messick picked up. "He got right on that boat behind Joely and gave what was left of the fire a couple good licks. Got it right out, he did; then he called me up in and told me to keep an eye for flash-ups. Didn' know where he was goin'. Cap'n Page'd gone to get an ambulance. It was only me and Joely and Jerry Lee."

"How long was it," Page asked, "do you think, before you got the fire out?"

Messick looked from Joely Edwards to Jerry Lee.

"Don't know. Maybe two minutes from when she first went up?" he said. "Could have been less. Seemed like it was. Things like that get t' movin' so fast. Time gets all mixed up."

Joely Edwards agreed. "Two minutes," he said. "It wasn't no longer. Wasn't that hot a fire, either. Mostly, I was watchin' LeRoy, but I don't remember seein' Carroll hittin' either flash-ups."

"No, I didn't," Messick remembered. "If they'd a' happened, you'd sure think I'd a' seen 'em. Don't know, though. I wasn't thinkin' too good. I didn't even realize that damn boat was sinkin' till Cap'n Atkins got back with that electric pump."

Page nodded. " 'Bout it, Mr. Doll. That's just 'bout like I remember it happ'nin'. The bilge pump, I think—what was she, Ornan?—five gallons a minute? Somethin' like that. Eitherway, if it helps you t' know, it weren't enough to keep that ol' boat up."

"Propane loose is nasty stuff," Doll said. "That's the only thing I don't understand. The gas is scented. They make it smell like rotten eggs so you can tell if there's a leak. With that much around, Carrow had to smell it. It doesn't make sense that he ever struck the match."

"Seems like that, don't it?" Page wore a thin smile that seemed to Doll to be deliberately sardonic. "But LeRoy never smelled no gas. LeRoy's nose weren't no good since either body on this island can remember. LeRoy couldn't a' smelled a twelve-pound polecat sprayin' piss on his shoes from downwind."

Doll swam easily along the surface. He kept his face down in the water and used his snorkel to breathe. His legs provided the momentum. His arms, to streamline him, drifted close to his sides. In his right hand, he carried a waterproof lamp.

He covered the short distance quickly. The stern of Carrow's sunken skipjack loomed up like a great white ghost at the limit of Doll's vision. He dove and began his inspection at the bottom.

To do the job right, to let it confirm what he thought he knew, he had to approach the inspection as though he knew nothing. That meant he had to put out of his mind all that LeCates and the watermen had said. It meant taking time to look for things that logic told him weren't going to be there.

He started with the side of the boat against the wharf.

Near the surface, there was no space between the bulkhead and the hull. At the bottom, there was a narrow tunnel, barely large enough for Doll to wiggle into at the stern, not nearly wide enough for him to make his way through to the bow.

Methodically, he drew the beam over the planking. The port quarter of the hull showed no evidence of abnormality. There was no hole. The seams looked tight. Doll ran the light over the mud of the bottom. No one had been careless enough to let a superfluous stick of dynamite or any other commercial explosive slip over the side.

Doll swam around the stern, passing under the keel of the skipjack's push boat, which floated above him, still held in place by the lines from the davits. The stern itself appeared as solid as a granite wall. He came out of the push boat's shadow and up along the starboard quarter of the hull.

Again, there was no hole, or, to be more precise, no hole in the obvious sense—nothing, for example, that Doll could have put his fist through. But the wooden hull was ruptured, nevertheless.

The water pressing from the outside had strengthened the planking and taken a lot of the force from the explosion. What remained had mostly expended itself in the easier route, straight upward, ripping away the much weaker roof of the cabin. Still, there had been enough power below deck to spring more than a dozen planks free of their fastenings. The seams had split where the planks had been screwed to the ribs. Individually, the openings seemed insignificant. Cumulatively, Doll was sure, there was more than enough area to admit the water needed to sink her.

He came to the surface and pulled back his mask and took a minute to hang from the gunwale and breathe the fresh air. Then he went back to work again. This time, he knew, the quarters would be closer. Diving in wrecks in however much water had never been a job for claustrophobics.

Doll hand-walked himself through the elbow-deep water that covered the stern deck. When he came to the companionway that led down to the cabin, he stopped to take off his swim fins.

The cabin took up less than a quarter of the boat's length and not much more than two-thirds of its width. There were generous exterior decks on both its port and starboard sides. A normal skipjack crew numbered four hands plus the mate and captain. For any three men, the quarters would have been adequate—assuming that nobody wanted to sleep.

Doll stepped down onto the cabin sole. The water reached his chest. He put back his mouthpiece, squatted, and turned on the lamp.

In the enclosed space, the beam seemed much more powerful than it had outside. The first thing it fell on was a small, cast-iron coal stove, with a vent pipe that rose toward the surface in imitation of a submarine's periscope. Opposite, on the port side, was the skipjack's propane cook stove.

The space was small and the water clear enough that Doll had no difficulty examining the details. He found where the gas line entered the cabin, then traced the route of the tubing toward the stove. The metal showed no cuts or compression damage and only a minimum of aluminum oxide rust. It ended at the back of the stove in what Doll recognized as a flare and hex nut fitting. Doll tried to twist the fitting with his fingers.

It moved. In fact, it moved quite freely.

He got his face mask as close to the fitting as he could. It took him some time to find the proper angle, but, from a particular vantage, a series of short, sharp, closely spaced grooves marred the smoothly planed surfaces around the circumference of the nut.

Finally, Doll moved the inspection along. He searched the cabin lockers, opening each in turn. He found rope, blocks, and assorted spare parts, shovels, rake heads, and the like—no greasy cans to suggest the presence of gasoline, no paint thinner, no alcohol, nothing more volatile than the remaining cans from a six-pack of beer.

One locker held a collection of handtools, all neatly arranged in stacked plastic trays like the kind people use to store kitchen utensils. Doll's involuntary reaction was to shudder. Orderliness in any wreckage reasserts the human dimension of disaster. In that confined space, under the water, it seemed as though, at any moment, LeRoy Carrow might return to use them again.

Doll closed the locker and decided that he'd seen enough. He climbed back up and out through the companionway. He knelt on the deck and spit out his mouthpiece, pulled back his cowl, and swallowed greedily at the air.

3

"All right, Doll. You're gonna make me ask for it. You didn't like the story about coming here to buy the boat. And you're pissed 'cause there are things I don't want to tell you. You figure, now, you got the chance, and you're going to turn the tables over on me."

LeCates' patience, by Doll's watch, had lasted through some eighteen minutes since Doll had finished his dive on Carrow's boat. The duration LeCates had filled with a random sequence of frowns, muffled grunts, and not-so-furtive sideways glances. Now, Doll was being told straight out that the storehouse of endurance was exhausted.

He saw no point in telling LeCates he'd wanted the time to set the pieces of evidence together.

"Okay, let's take the bad news first," he said. "You told me you thought Carrow was murdered. That means you think the explosion was deliberately set. You want to know if it was or not. The safe answer is, I don't know."

"Safe answer? What the hell does that mean?" LeCates stopped walking and turned toward Doll. "That's bullshit, Doll. What the hell did you bother to come here for? If all I'd wanted to hear was some damn-fool waffle, I could've just read the damn inquest report in the first place."

"Then maybe that's what you ought to do!" Doll answered

quietly. "Nobody waffles on the easy stuff, Ellis. You want pat answers? Don't ask the tough questions. You want any answers at all, back the hell off my ass."

The coffee back at LeCates' store was hot and freshly made. LeCates was subdued, his anger spent—or perhaps only muted by the knowledge that what Doll chose to tell him wasn't under his control. He stared off into the middle distance.

"No-co Man. You ever heard of that?" he asked.

Doll shook his head and wondered what LeCates was trying to get at.

LeCates smiled thinly. "You remember Pietros?"

"The tank man? Vicarias's nephew? The one who used to get our tanks filled and keep track of the equipment?"

"You never knew him, did you, Doll? I mean outside of that. He was a funny little shit. I used to take him with me some nights. He could come up with names. I was George Washington. He never told me why. Vicarias was Geeseball. That came somehow outta Greek and bald and the way his head went back and forth when he walked. And you he called the No-co Man. Used to say when you found yourself drownin' one day, you still wouldn't make no commotion."

"I never heard that," Doll said. In Florida, he'd kept them all at a distance. He felt a twinge of discomfort at the realization that the distance hadn't always worked both ways. "Do you want to hear what I found down there, Ellis? You couldn't seem to wait out on the road."

"I want to hear," LeCates said. "If you're ready to tell me, go ahead."

"The first thing," Doll began, "is that I'm satisfied the explosion really was caused by the propane."

"Only now?" The tone of LeCates' voice was careful. It asked for explanation, rather than offering argument. "I never even thought it might not be. With the coroner's report and the way that Page and them all described it. . . . Whatever made you even think it might be something else?"

"You did. You said you thought it was deliberate," Doll answered. "Loose propane isn't the easiest or the surest way to blow up a boat. It's a whole lot simpler to wire it with some commercial explosive. Maybe not what you want to do if you thought you could make it look like an accident, but at least worth looking into. That kind of thing isn't hard to spot. Anyway, it didn't happen. But, if it had, you'd be more than halfway there. You'd have a *prima facie* case for murder that no police authority anywhere could afford to walk away from."

"But as long as it's the propane, you don't," LeCates concluded.

"There's more evidence than just the gas. But it's a whole lot chancier," Doll said. "The cause of the leak—at least the one I found—was a loose fitting between the propane line and the stove. Combine that with plier marks on the connection and a tool drawer loaded with open-end wrenches half an arm's distance away."

"I don't follow." LeCates' eyes narrowed and searched Doll's face uncertainly.

"The tools?" Doll said. "The fitting's a hex nut. What would you use on that? Even an apprentice mechanic knows better than to use a pair of pliers. Especially when he's got the right tool in a locker no further away than his elbow."

"That's pretty skimpy, isn't it?" LeCates asked. "Just those two things together—a loose nut and some plier marks. Fittings come loose all the time. It's the kind of thing that's got to happen a hundred times a day by chance."

Doll nodded. "Probably a lot more often than that," he conceded. "But let me flesh it out a little for you. Suppose we say, for a minute, your hunch is right—then somebody got on board the boat and rigged that gas line. He couldn't have done that kind of thing just any time. It had to be when nobody was there to see him do it. That means, most likely, he did it at night. And that would almost have to be the night before the morning that the boat went up."

"I guess," LeCates agreed uncertainly. "I still don't see where you're going with all that."

"He's got to use a light, and he's got to be quick before somebody sees it. The last thing he's got time to do is try matching sizes of open-end wrenches. So he grabs the first tool he finds that he knows will do the job."

"It would be like that, wouldn't it?" LeCates' eyes grew at the prospect. "You're beginning to believe it, aren't you, Doll? You're beginning to believe that LeRoy Carrow was really murdered."

"Or," said Doll, "he was like a lot of guys, sloppy about the way he did his job. He didn't check the fitting, and the nut worked itself free. We don't know when those plier marks got on there. Maybe back to the day that he put the stove in. Or maybe the thing had come loose before, and he'd used the pliers then to tighten it."

"No," LeCates said. He tried hard to say it with conviction, shaking his head like a man who'd already heard the truth he wanted and didn't want to hear it retracted.

"Nothing's as clear as you want it to be," Doll said. "That's what I meant by what I said out on the road. I can't tell you for certain that LeRoy Carrow was murdered."

LeCates stared out the window as though his mind was working over something. A minute passed. Then nearly two. And then, without warning, he returned.

"Doll, I want you to talk to someone," he said. "I want you to come with me to see Elaine Carrow. I want you to tell her what you found."

"Sorry, Ellis, I'd just as soon not. That's the kind of thing I'd go a long way out of my way to avoid."

"Please, Doll. Elaine isn't like that. I promise it won't turn into anything emotional. I told her about you. The truth. Who you really are and why I asked you to come here. She knows you're here by now. You can guess how news travels around this island. You've got to come, Doll. If you don't, she won't know how to take it."

"And where does it go from there?" Doll asked.

"I'll leave it all up to you," LeCates answered. "Just like the dive. After you talk with her, if you want to go, you go. If you stay, I don't expect something for nothing. I'm willing to pay for whatever you do. I don't know what you get for this kind of thing. But, if you're willing to stay, I'd expect to pay you for your time."

"But you want to know more than 'if' LeRoy Carrow was murdered," Doll said. "If he was, you expect me to find out by who. And then what, Ellis? Do you all dress up in sheets and take the guy out back and lynch him?"

LeCates swore it was nothing like that. "You'll see that," he said. "You'll see that yourself when you talk to Elaine."

Elaine Carrow was tall even in her flat-soled, canvas shoes. She was dressed in a pale, floral-patterned housedress that fitted loosely and came to below her knees. Her waist was slender, in contrast to the almost masculine breadth of her shoulders. She wore no makeup that Doll could see. Her muddy-blond hair was cropped to a functional length.

She said hello, then bowed her head so deeply that Doll wasn't able to see her eyes. After an awkward silence, she turned away and went to lower the fires under her cooking.

"You'll stay for dinner, Mr. Doll? You too, Mr. LeCates?" she said without looking back.

"I can't, but thank you. I still have some things I have to do," Doll said.

"No, no. Not me," LeCates replied, scratching at the fleshy bottom of his ear.

"Then something to drink. A beer or a soda?"

Again both men declined.

Elaine Carrow ended her business at the stove and turned away. She went to the kitchen table and, tugging the skirt of the dress down as far as she could, she sat in one of the chairs. She waited with her feet on the floor, staring off through the window, avoiding everyone's eyes for as long as she could.

Outside, the day was approaching its end. As the sun sank toward the water, it sent out its yellow-orange rays in streaks across the blue of the Chesapeake Bay.

"Elaine was born in this house," LeCates said.

"Is that true?" Doll asked. Not that he doubted it. The topic wasn't particularly comfortable. Its single great advantage was that it felt less awkward than the one that everyone knew would have to come next.

Elaine Carrow replied with a fleeting smile and nodded. "It was my father's house," she said. "That was Edgar Mills. It was his father's, too. My great-grandfather helped my grandfather build it. That was Winston Mills. Cap'n Atkins' boat is named for Cap'n Winston."

"There's a kind of a rule here." LeCates laughed as though he hoped to make them all a little less self-conscious. But, as far as Doll could see, the effort accomplished only the opposite. "If you're new, you don't say anything bad about anybody. They've been here so long, they're all related somehow. Keeping your mouth shut's about the only way to stay out of trouble."

"I like knowing everyone," Elaine said. "It's like a big family. Everyone helps. There's a proverb. It says, 'Many hands make light work.' "

"That's true." LeCates nodded supportively, as if he thought it was important that Doll be convinced. "That's what's kept them all going these past few years."

"They haven't been easy times," Elaine agreed. " 'Specially with the sickness in the oysters. Sometimes I think it isn't fair that people have to work so hard to get so little."

"I know it's been bad," Doll said. "Ellis told me that. So did some of the men down at the wharf."

"Cap'n Page and Cap'n Atkins," LeCates explained. "Doll's met them both. They were down there along with Carroll, Joely, and Jerry Lee. They came over when they saw us. I told them what we said I would, that Doll was maybe going to buy LeRoy's boat."

Elaine nodded and then shook her head. "I wish there was somebody who'd buy it."

"Doll went all over it, inside and out," LeCates said. "Much better than I could have done. Don't expect too much, though, Elaine. You can't expect too much from the one dive. But let him tell you, himself, what he found."

She looked over at Doll. He tried to read her face and found in it an expression that implied more trust than Doll had placed in anyone for a great many years. At first, it seemed an almost childlike naïveté. But the eyes suggested something more. A keen and mature intelligence was buried somewhere beneath. The trust she gave Doll was willed and not innate. Doll had no idea at all of what he might have done to merit it.

"As Ellis says, it's not very much," he began. "All I can say is that it could have happened either way. I can't tell you if your husband was murdered. But, just as strongly, I can't tell you that he wasn't."

"Tell her about the stove line," LeCates prompted.

Doll did, and then went back to review carefully the dual interpretations that could be placed on what he'd found.

When he'd finished with that, Elaine Carrow sighed. "I'm sorry. I can't help you," she said. "I see what you want me to tell you. But I don't know how careful LeRoy would have been—about the gas or anything else. A wife will think the best of her husband. I always believed he took good care of his boats."

"We can ask Farron, so long as we don't tell him why we're asking." LeCates turned to Doll. "Farron's the son. You remember. You heard that. I told Dorothy to say hello to him this morning. Farron doesn't know about what's going on or why you're here. But he did sail with LeRoy sometimes. As regular crew for a while."

"Did your husband have a regular crew?" Doll asked.

"Not for the year since Farron gave it up," Elaine replied. "He said he couldn't make it pay to keep anybody on regular. So he worked, when he worked, with who he could afford. There were days when he even worked the boat alone. That's very hard work, Mr. Doll. In the old days, they always worked with six—a captain, a mate, and four men on the drudges."

LeCates moved his arm to see his watch.

"There's more we have to do," he said. "And you all will be wanting supper soon. Elaine, it's all got to be up to you. You've got to decide what you want Doll to do."

"To do?" Elaine looked doubtful. It might have been that she hadn't anticipated the question, but Doll's guess was that she still hadn't made up her mind on how to answer.

"Remember, Elaine, we talked about this," LeCates said. "We know a little more now, but not all that much more than we'd guessed before. Doll can go further if you want him to. He can ask questions, maybe find out more. But only if you want him to."

"I couldn't pay him. I don't have any money," Elaine said.

"That's all right. It's taken care of," LeCates said. "He'll do it for me. He owes me a favor." Making sure he was out of Elaine's field of vision, LeCates winked across at Doll.

He lied with an utter innocence that made Doll wonder if the truth meant anything more to LeCates than a matter of personal convenience.

"Then what do you want me to do?" Elaine looked to LeCates.

This time LeCates shook his head. "I can't tell you," he said. "I can't help you with that. All I can say is that I have my reasons. Someday I hope I'll be able to tell you what they are."

There were footsteps on the porch outside, followed by the crash of a door. The noise stopped the discussion cold. Farron Carrow came into the kitchen.

His hair was that same tint of dirty yellow. In length, it was about the same as his mother's. His height was the same. But his skin had an oaken tan, the kind that comes from outdoor work, especially outdoor work around water. His face was young. He looked from Doll to LeCates. His eyes were, at once, remote and, paradoxically, filled with anger.

"Joely Edwards came into the station," he said. "If it wasn't for that, I'd be down there yet. Is this the one who wants to buy the boat?"

"This is Mr. Doll," LeCates replied, though Farron's question had been more directed to his mother. "He's the man who was down by the wharf to look at it today."

"Then why didn't you tell me? Why didn't you tell me so I could be there? Why didn't you tell me so's I could be here now? Wouldn't be if it wasn't for Joely. Don't even get off for another half hour yet." This time what he said was fiercely meant for LeCates.

"Nobody meant to leave you out," LeCates said.

"No?" Farron eyed LeCates viciously. "You know what my father'd say, if he was here? He'd a' said you can't trust no man who makes his money just markin' up the price a' what he sells t' others. He'd a' wondered if you thought, maybe, my mother wouldn't know how much that boat is worth."

"Farron, no. That's not fair." Elaine waited, saying nothing more until her son showed her the respect of turning to meet her eyes. Then she spoke quietly. "These men never talked about money to me, Farron. And I never would've sold the boat without talking to you. I think you want to apologize to Mr. LeCates."

Farron Carrow nodded in LeCates' direction, but that was as close as he came to an apology. Instead, he turned to Doll.

"What do you want the boat for, anyway?" he asked. "Joely said something 'bout you lookin' at her for some rich guy up in Bal'mer."

"Mr. Doll," LeCates said, "is what they call an agent. His job is to find out what kind of shape the boat is in. He has nothing to do with the money."

" 'Cept," Farron answered, "that whatever he says is gonna set the price on what his friend from Bal'mer is willin' to pay. Well, what d' ya' say about that, Mr. Doll?" He looked sharply at Doll for a second time. "What kind of shape you say that boat is in?"

"She's sprung," Doll answered evenly. "Along the starboard side, abeam of the back end of the cabin. She needs to be refastened. Maybe that means she has to be sistered. That's the worst of it. The rest of the work looks fairly routine."

The appraisal seemed to catch Farron off guard, as though the boat had come off better than he'd expected and he wasn't sure if he ought to argue, or maybe just leave well enough alone. He reminded Doll of the cabin roof and the water damage from the time that she'd been on the bottom.

Doll shook his head. "Those are costs to you, if you want to raise her and work her again. They don't apply if somebody wants to convert her. The cabin and the whole interior are parts you'd want to be replacing anyway."

"I wish I *could* raise her," Farron said wistfully. "If that was all there was, I'd borrow the money, whatever it took."

"Farron's looking for something else," Elaine said. "He's got a job at Fuller's station now, but Mr. Fuller's selling the property to someone who won't be keeping the business. It's like most things here. Nothing seems very permanent. Farron told LeRoy a year ago that there wasn't any future for him on the water. I don't know which of the two of them it was worse for."

Farron looked away. "All right, Ma, they don't care about that." He turned to Doll. "Sounds like maybe you know your business, Mr. Doll. What y' say 'bout the boat sounds fair—fairer than maybe I thought it'd be. Y' know, ya can't always trust folks that get themselves tied up with folks from the cities. Maybe it's you I maybe should be apologizin' to."

"No," Doll said. He left it there and resigned himself to feeling hypocritical. He cursed both himself and Ellis LeCates for that.

At Elaine's urging, Farron began to leave to wash for dinner.

"But we've got a couple things we'd like to ask first." LeCates glanced deferentially toward Elaine. "If that's all right with you, Mrs. Carrow."

"What questions?" Farron said warily.

"You sailed with your father after you got out of school?" LeCates asked.

"You know I did," Farron answered. "I sailed with him then and whenever I had time off all the years before that."

"Then you know how he worked, how he kept up the boat?"

"How he worked? I don't know what that means, Mr. LeCates. I don't know what you think you're talkin' about."

"I mean was he careful . . . about keeping the boat up. How would you compare him to, say, Cap'n Atkins or Cap'n Page?"

"Who wants t' know? What you tryin' to make it out now? That it was his fault that his boat blew up?"

"Mr. Doll wants to know," LeCates said. "You said before that what he said about the boat was fair to you. Don't you think he's got a right to the same? Don't you think he's got a right to know how well the boat was kept?"

Inside Doll steamed. In the context, there was nothing he could do.

"Better than Cap'n Page's any day," Farron said. "Good as Cap'n Atkins'—least as good. You can put Cap'n Atkins' boat against any other skipjack on the bay, and you won't find a better kept boat around."

"You're sure?" LeCates persisted.

Farron visibly bristled.

Elaine broke in. "Mr. LeCates doesn't mean to be saying anything against your father."

"No, Farron, I don't." LeCates backed away.

"Now go. Dinner'll be along." Elaine Carrow got up from the chair and looked into the pots on the stove. "You've heard it all. There's nothing else that's going to be said. There's nothing for us to do but to wait and see what Mr. Doll's man from Bal'mer decides."

"You haven't put us up an offer," Farron said, addressing himself to Doll. "You gotta know we'll sell that boat in the meantime if we can."

Doll nodded.

Farron returned the nod curtly and left.

"He's so protective," Elaine said when he'd gone. "Protective of me, of LeRoy's memory. It's a stage I think they all go through when they start to think of themselves as men. He's a good son; I don't like not having told him the truth."

"You need to decide what you want to do," LeCates said softly.

"I know I do," Elaine replied. "I suppose I should want to know about LeRoy, but do I? I ask myself what good, what harm would come from my knowing." She looked at Doll. "Ellis says he can't help me. Can you?"

Doll drew in a breath and let it out. He meant it to show his own discomfort and, at the same time, that he understood the decision Elaine faced was a hard one.

"If you mean can I put myself in your place, I can't," he said. "If it were up to me, I suppose I'd say that justice had some social value. I won't tell you it's going to help anyone. I won't say it's going to be comfortable. Once something like this starts, nobody knows what will come out. Everybody has skeletons. Everybody gets anxious."

"Well, then . . ."

"Before you say that . . ." Doll held up his hand. "There's something else you have to think about. Ellis, here, wants you to tell me to go ahead. He won't say that himself. I don't know why he wants that. I don't even know if what he wants or what he doesn't want should concern you. But I thought I had to tell you before you made up your mind."

Doll turned to LeCates. "And you have to know something, too," he said. "From here on out, if this goes beyond where it is now, Mrs. Carrow's the one who calls the shots. If she's the one who's got to start it, then she runs it for as long as it lasts and however it goes. You're not any kind of middleman, Ellis. You've got to understand that."

"That's fine with me," LeCates answered. "But what happens about the money? She told you she can't pay you. What about the favor for a friend?"

"That's just what it's going to be," Doll said. "The favor you said I owe you goes over to her." His stare warned LeCates against pushing the subject any further.

Elaine looked from LeCates to Doll. She shook her head a final time and appeared to make up her mind. "I don't understand this. I don't know what the right thing to do is," she said. "But whatever you plan to do, Mr. Doll, I suppose—if Ellis thinks it's right—you might just as well go ahead."

4

As a rule, Doll avoided introspection. It became too easily a mental narcotic, a form of self-indulgence more disabling than it was instructive. There were times, though, when he felt the need to take a limited accounting, and, at those times, he tried to be honest with himself—ignoring the cautions that said it was impossible to be. The most consistent positive value Doll was able to find in himself on those occasions was that he was a better than average judge of human character.

The result of that discovery was that he'd learned to trust his instincts where assessments of people were concerned. In the case of Elaine Carrow, he chose to trust them again. Nothing else let his decision to help her make sense.

Outside the house, Doll declined LeCates' offer of a ride and a bed over the store. He walked, instead, through the darkening night to the inn, which numbered among the island's most heralded landmarks.

A gentle but chilly breeze drifted in off the water. The clouds of the day were nearly all gone. The moonless sky gave itself over to a brilliant field of stars.

* * *

The back of Millman's Inn faced the water on the eastern side of the island. The front overlooked an enormous lawn that interposed itself between the inn and the island's principal road.

The two-story building rambled like a huge New England farmhouse, though the expansive lawn and white façade carried, as well, the suggestion of a nineteenth-century Southern plantation. A glass-enclosed porch ran along the right side front. The incandescent light inside conveyed an ambience of warmth and welcome.

Millman's was, foremost, a sportsman's inn. If the location hadn't told Doll that, its decor made the proclamation unmistakably. The walls were hung with pictures of game birds and enough examples of piscine taxidermy to make an avid conservationist nervous. What space remained was given over to framed and laminated newspaper clippings with stories and pictures of gleeful anglers displaying their more spectacular catches.

In season, Doll decided, he couldn't have gotten a room without a reservation and would have had trouble affording the rate on the doubtful chance that one had been available. But April was a slack time, too late for gunning and a good six to eight weeks too early for any kind of decent fishing. This time of year, the pace at the inn was slow. Except for the locals who came for the bar or the advertised Thursday night "twofer" dinners, Doll got the impression he had the place pretty well to himself.

The man in the small office was seated at one of the two desks behind the counter. He looked up, inspecting Doll curiously as Doll closed the door. The name plaque on the desk said "Wesley Mowen." Hung on the wall behind the desk was a larger, etched metal plate which bore the inscription "Wesley Mowen—Innkeeper."

"Weren't expecting you t' come by here," Mowen said. "Figured you'd be stayin' down at the store with Ellis."

"Ellis snores," Doll replied.

"Does he, does he? Nice thing t' know." Mowen nodded his head, apparently in appreciation for the insight. Lethargically, he got up from behind the desk, found a registration card under the counter, and slipped it across to Doll. "Hear ya come some distance t' here. You're from somewhere over east, they say," he said conversationally.

"Lewes," Doll answered as he filled out the card. "Seems like I might just as well be back where people know me, for the way everyone around here seems to know who I am."

"Around here?" Mowen laughed. "Why, son, you're the biggest news in town today. I've been half expectin' that they'd send out one of them reporters from up at the newspaper just t' have a look at ya. You give this place a real test a' conscience is what you do. 'Cept that nobody wants t' make the Carrows' hard luck any worse than it is, you'd have 'em beatin' down the doors to sell you boats."

"Captain named Page half offered me his."

"That'd be George. Yeah, he'd like to sell 'er to you, all right." Mowen took the filled-in card from Doll, examined it without embarrassment until he was satisfied, then, in his slow-moving manner, filed it away. "Skipjacks goin' cheap right now. Shame, 'cause those boys deserve to get what their boats is worth. Not that it's somethin' that matters to me, but—what d' you think?—your man from Bal'mer gonna buy the Carrow boat?"

Doll shrugged to say he didn't know.

"She in that bad shape?" Mowen asked.

The hull, Doll said, was partly sprung. He left his evaluation at that.

Wesley Mowen slipped Doll's room key across the counter.

"Second floor, back," he said. "Outside 'round the front to the right as ya go out the door, then up those stairs there by the light. Got a nice view of the water—not that there's all that much to look at this time of year. Mostly the charter boats along the dock. Nice skipjack out on the end if you want t' look it over."

"No, thanks," Doll declined the offer. "I've seen all the skipjacks I need for one day." He took up the key and put it in his pocket. He turned toward the door, then, as though in an afterthought, he turned back toward Mowen. "Maybe you could help me on one thing, though. You must have known LeRoy Carrow pretty well. Do you know how good a captain he was? What I mean is, before the explosion, did he take the trouble to keep the boat up?"

"LeRoy?" Mowen scratched contemplatively at a small indented place in his cheek. "Well now, from what I hear," he said slowly, "ya spent some fair amount a' time down there today. You had yourself a good look at the boat. I'd a' thought it would've told you what you needed. Didn't it, though?"

"There's always more to know." Doll found himself recalling LeCates' insights about the practiced distrustfulness of the islanders. Wesley Mowen was careful and smart enough to weigh his answers before a man he didn't know. A lot, Doll thought, like the other people he'd met on the island, and a lot like those he'd met everywhere else.

"You look at a boat, you see things that have to be done," Doll went on. "Some things you miss. It helps to know how much you miss if you know how good the guy was who kept up the boat."

Mowen scratched at the dent again, this time nodding as he rubbed it. "LeRoy was a right good waterman, al'right. And I ain't sayin' that just to speak no ill of the dead. He maybe raised a bunch a' people's hackles, but there's nobody I ever heard t'say he didn't take care of his boat."

"Doesn't that make the accident hard to understand?" Doll asked.

"Does a little, maybe," Mowen agreed. "But then, you already heard, I guess, that LeRoy couldn't smell. Still, you got a point. I don't see 'im lettin' that profane gas get around. He knew that gas was dangerous stuff. 'Specially since his sniffer was bad."

Mowen's stare wandered over the counter past Doll. The innkeeper seemed to choose the moment to wax philosophical. " 'Strange to man are the ways of the Lord,' " he said. "That's what the preacher preached when he spoke the last words over LeRoy."

It seemed to Doll a safely enigmatic thing to say. He asked if, in Carrow's case, the words had any special meaning.

"Strange that the Lord allows men so young to be taken from their families is what he meant, I guess." Mowen shook his head as if to say that his conclusions were no more than that. "Strange 'bout LeRoy and his sniffer. Strange maybe, too, that LeRoy didn't like to see things change. And now, the way things got worked out, he ain't gonna have to see it. *Is* strange, indeed, the way the Lord works sometimes, Mr. Doll. Ain't, for sure, neither a doubt 'bout that."

And stranger still were the ways of His people, Doll decided. He didn't say that to Wesley Mowen, though. Instead, he asked directions to the bar.

Doll sat by himself at one of the tables in the public room. At the other tables and along the bar, there were, in all, a dozen men and maybe half as many women. The room could have held four or five times that number before it got to the point of crowding—another reminder that the inn's business was seasonal.

He tried his first swallow of his ale, tasting the smoky richness of the malt and the tangy edge that unaccountably reminded him of autumn leaves and evergreen trees. The taste had a ritual familiarity that relaxed him. He checked his watch. The time was after eight. Some minutes more than thirteen hours had passed since he'd started his drive to the island that morning. It seemed, somehow, as though it had been a lot longer.

The thought was interrupted by the smell of something biting in the air. The acrid odor of cigarette smoke invaded the space about the table.

A man with the cigarette in his mouth stood across from Doll, holding a whiskey over ice. He wore an emerald-green sports jacket—large and loose fitting—a beige shirt, and gray slacks. His tie was a deeper shade of green than the jacket and patterned with a flock of brightly colored mallard drakes.

"You must be the one they're calling Doll," he said. His voice was a deep, froggy baritone. Between the whiskey and the cigarettes, he seemed to Doll a reasonable candidate for a bout with esophageal cancer. "You're the one who came here about the boat. You're the guy who's been looking at LeRoy Carrow's skipjack."

Doll acknowledged that he was.

"Fine boats. Those are fine boats," the man said, nodding to underscore his assessment. "Mind if I pull up a place at your table? Take a load off my feet and sit down?" He held out his hand. "My driver's license says Richard D. Vaughn, but everybody around here who knows me calls me Ardee."

Doll said he was called Doll and pointed toward a chair.

"Less than twenty of 'em now, I think," Vaughn continued when he'd sat. "Less than twenty that actually work the bay. That number's fell off a lot in the recent years. When you get down to that few, seems like every time you lose one it's a lot."

"I guess so," Doll said.

"Be a shame, when the last one's gone. Grand old boats. The ones they're sailing now, the actual boats, have been on the bay for seventy, eighty, some a hundred years or more. Problem is it's getting so you can't make any money with them. They say you're not a waterman, that you don't intend to work her?"

"The way word gets around here, I figure you also must have heard that I wasn't looking at her for me. What's your stake in this? Do you broker boats? Is that where all of this is leading?"

"Broker them? No. What would make you think that?" Vaughn ground out the remains of his cigarette, but incompletely, so that a thin whisper of the sharp, white smoke continued to trail up from the ashtray.

"You sound like a broker." Doll watched while Vaughn took down half his whiskey at a swallow. "You talk about the boats like you seem to know about them. You don't sound or look much like a waterman."

"A waterman! God, no. I suppose I don't." Vaughn laughed. "Good for you, Doll. You've got perception. You notice things in people. I am a broker. That's how close you are. Not boats, though. They're only a hobby. My business is real estate."

"Here?" Doll asked.

Vaughn tilted the palm of his hand back and forth. "Not here on the island mostly. Though I handle a property here every now and then. My office is a couple miles the other side of the bridge. My own business. For twelve years, proud to say it. Now my son works for me. It pays a decent living."

Doll poured a new portion of ale from the bottle until he'd refilled his glass to the one-quarter mark. "I understand the land business is pretty hot right now," he said.

For a moment, Vaughn stared at Doll. "How exactly do you mean that?" he asked. His voice sounded suddenly mistrustful. The expression on his face suggested that his mood was on the edge of turning belligerent.

"That people are interested in buying out here," Doll answered and waited.

"Well, that's true," Vaughn acknowledged cautiously, his anger still held in tentative abeyance. He took a swallow of his whiskey and reached for another of his cigarettes. "You see, that's kind of a tender point around here, eh . . . Doll. It's the kind of thing that people can get really riled about. Happens all over, but here, right now. . . ."

"The people who want to develop wear the black hats. I understand how that can work," Doll said. "I'm not here to take sides."

Vaughn lit the cigarette, exhaled a cloud of smoke, and nodded his head elaborately.

"You can't know how good it is to hear you say that," he said and drew on the cigarette again. "The last few years, I guess I've heard myself called every name there is in the book. Most of them by your good friend, LeRoy Carrow."

Doll tried another swallow of the ale. "No particular friend of mine," he replied and left it at that.

"Well, anyway," Vaughn went on, "you're right enough about that black hat thing. You'd think I ought to have a cape and a mustache to curl. The truth is, Doll, I make my living the way I can, just like everybody else. I go home at night to a wife, a dog, a son who ought to get married, and a fifteen-year-old daughter—God help me—who I pray every day isn't going to have to be. But as far as the land goes, the market makes the rules, not me. I'm only the one who gets buyers and sellers together, and who comes off looking like the villain of the piece.

"Did you see that movie, *Grapes of Wrath*?" Vaughn seemed to warm to his subject. "You know that scene where they bulldoze the guy's house under? They make the realtors look like the guy on the 'dozer. Next thing you know, we'll have invented MSX. For the liberals and the news reporters, this kind of stuff is mother's milk."

"This is all LeRoy Carrow talking?" Doll asked.

"He was the center. I'm telling you, Doll—he could play all the right chords when he wanted. A goddamn demagogue, that's what he was. A damn vicious son of a bitch."

"But the market's the market. What could he have changed?"

"Not much, that's true," Vaughn admitted. "He could maybe have slowed things down for a while. A sale or two here and there. Can't hold back the tide, though. Nobody can. Not very much, and not for long.

"I'll tell you, Doll, now's the time to buy in. In twenty-five years, you won't know this place. It could go a couple ways or maybe two combined. There could be condos or some real top-dollar private housing. Little shops selling suntan oil and bathing suits. And rooms in this inn where we're sitting now? Year 'round, Mowen won't be able to keep up with the waiting list."

"Where do I sign?" Doll asked, with just enough of a touch of a smile to put the skids to Vaughn's salespitch.

"Sign? You don't mean you've actually sold something, Richard?"

The voice by itself, apparently, was enough for Vaughn to identify the woman who'd come up behind him. He spoke before he turned his head.

"Rachael Teal," he said, "this is Mr. Doll. Mr. Doll represents a consortium of Japanese bankers. Actually he's just agreed to transfer funds to buy up the entire island."

"Mmm, I've heard." Rachael Teal smiled and extended her long arm toward Doll. "Starting with all the sunken skipjacks he can lay his hands on."

Doll shook the offered hand. Her eyes met his. Her grip was firm and assertive. Her hair, by contrast, was soft. Maple brown in color, it fell with the grace of a gentle waterfall to just above her shoulders. She wore a pale green blouse and a straw-yellow business suit. Her eyebrows were dark and swept up at the ends. The expression they produced made it seem that she was always on the point of raising a question.

"Join us," Vaughn invited. "And for godsake, my name is Ardee. When are you going to stop calling me Richard? Call him Doll. That way we'll both know when we're supposed to answer."

Rachael took one of the two remaining chairs. Vaughn ordered drinks all around—an ale for Doll, another whiskey for himself, and a light Scotch and soda for Rachael.

"Why can't a man ever be called what he's named?" Rachael mused aloud. "It must be some kind of rite of passage. Do you all have formal rechristenings or something?" Then she abruptly changed the subject. "I understand from the talk around town that you're here to buy LeRoy Carrow's boat, Mr. Doll."

Doll answered that he was on the island to look at the boat. He was just the hired help, he said. Any decision on buying the skipjack wasn't his.

"Well," Rachael replied, "someone should buy it. I'm sure the family must need the money. I don't know the first thing about boats, but I'm sure for every day it sits on the bottom . . . well, whatever its value is has got to go down."

The bartender brought their drinks to the table. Vaughn had the tab added to his bill.

"Doll and I were talking," Vaughn said after he'd taken the first swallow of the fresh whiskey. "I told him how unfair it is that we're always the ones who get tagged as the villains."

"You do. Not me, Richard, dear." Rachael smiled too sweetly, making the smile into a mockery of innocence. She turned to Doll. "I've told Richard that he ought to change professions. Being a male, in his situation, can be a major disadvantage.

When men get mad at men, they all have to be macho about it. I can do all the same things that Richard does, but when a man gets mad at me, all I have to do to quiet things down is look helpless."

"When, in fact, she's anything but. You have to look out for her," Vaughn said. "This one's the ERA's answer to Fiske and Gould. Watch out, or she'll steal your undershorts without ever taking your pants off."

"Hardly true, Richard, but, if you find that the image excites you . . ." Rachael laughed at the uncompleted thought and washed the laugh down with a sip of her Scotch and soda. "He means that I'm the real pariah," she expanded. "Richard sells a lot or a house for twice what the people around here think it's worth, and he gets come down on like he'd struck a blow to apple pie and motherhood. But I'm the one they really ought to be worried about."

Vaughn reached for a cigarette, but Rachael put her hand on his and shook her head. For an instant Vaughn frowned, but then he withdrew his hand from his pocket.

"I work for a syndicate of Washington investors," Rachael continued to explain. "Don't think, for a minute, Mr. Doll, I'm telling any tales out of school. What I'm telling you is what you might call an open secret. Richard knows it. So do most all the people around here who've got a financial stake in things."

"Except that the secret's open and it's not," Vaughn said.

"Absolutely true," Rachael agreed. "The difference is that, while Richard sells his odd house here or there, I'm quietly buying up options. Nobody cares about options because nothing seems to be happening. Nobody moves out; nobody new moves in next door. It all happens down the road somewhere—whenever the people I'm working for decide the time is right to pull the string."

"You make it sound like a pretty cold-blooded business," Doll replied.

"But is it really? That's the whole point I'm making." Her dark eyes fixed on Doll. She held him with what seemed a practiced intensity that made Doll feel she was used to holding people like that. "That's the face that people put on it. But change here on the island is inevitable. I'm sure that Richard has already given you his little soliloquy on the inescapable dictates of the market."

"I recall hearing something along those lines," Doll acknowledged in what he mentally conceded was one of his poorer attempts at irony.

Rachael smiled and then turned back to being serious. "Well, he's right in that, " she said, "for as far as it goes. But, if change is going to happen no matter what, then the least we can do, if we act intelligently, is to make the change desirable. Don't you see? That's the difference between Richard and me. Richard's change is disorganized and haphazard. With the group I represent, the change that happens is controlled."

"From that," Doll said, "I gather that you were also one of LeRoy Carrow's bugbears. Or would it be more accurate to say that it worked the other way round?"

"I never had a problem with LeRoy Carrow," Rachael answered, smiling again. "Does that sound a little disingenuous, Mr. Doll? LeRoy was a Jeremiah, a voice, in this case, quite literally crying out in the wilderness. He was a tail trying to wag a dog. Did my name get used? It did. Not as much as Richard's." She cast a sideways glance at Vaughn. "But it came up in LeRoy's invectives every now and again."

"That didn't bother you?" Doll asked.

"Bother what? My reputation? My business? My God, Doll, it was advertising. People pay good money for that!"

"Ardee," Doll said, "says the media people are all on the other side."

"Always." Rachael Teal curled the corner of her mouth in an expression of disdain. " 'To afflict the comfortable and comfort the afflicted,' wasn't that what Mencken said? But don't make the mistake of romanticizing this. And don't make fools out of practical people."

"She's right, Doll," Vaughn agreed, putting down his glass after another ample swallow of his whiskey. "The only property I can sell is a piece that somebody who owns it wants sold."

"That's what Carrow's real problem was. He couldn't compromise." Concluding her case, Rachael folded her hands on the table. Her nails, Doll noticed, were lacquered in a shade of red that matched her mouth. "He couldn't accept change and let it make the most for him. He tried to hold on to a past that couldn't be held on to. People who make up stories love romantics. The real world is seldom as kind to them."

Vaughn's glass was nearly empty. Doll's ale wasn't yet half gone, but his turn had come to call for the next round of drinks. Rachael declined. She'd barely tasted her first Scotch and soda.

"I still say that Carrow was one mean-mouthed bastard." Vaughn's hand worked quickly. He managed to get out a cigarette and light it before Rachael Teal was able to stop him.

5

Doll slept until past eight o'clock the next morning without once managing to dream of Wesley Mowen, Ardee Vaughn, or Rachael Teal, or, for that matter, of the Carrows or Ellis LeCates. He woke in that pendulous, surrealistic silence that so often cloaks the shore towns on out-of-season Sundays. A shaft of bright yellow sunlight fell across his pillow as it streamed through the curtain seam into the room.

From the window he looked down on the water and the dock, lined with its small fleet of unattended charter boats that Mowen had promised would be there in hibernation for the winter. From habit, his eyes picked out the navigation marks. He followed the channel toward open water as it twisted first to the right close by the shore, then cut sharply back upon itself in its serpentine path to the bay. Across the bay, Doll could see the opposite shore. The water between was quiet and empty.

He began the day with an hour's run, south along the island's main road to its end at Tall Pine Point, then back along the same road to the inn. The sun on his skin felt warm. A light breeze evaporated the perspiration from his face and neck.

As he ran, he did his best to clear his mind of all but what his senses presented to him—the sights, the smells of the island, and the steady, untiring rhythms of his body.

The exercise was mental at least as much as it was physical. It afforded Doll an intermission, taking him out of a world of complexity and compromise and leaving him in a simpler one that gave him the space to be alone. Doll had heard others try to relate the same sensation. He'd heard it described in words like "mystical" and "transcendental." To Doll it was another reward that came from honest, physical sweat—and that was exactly all it was.

Back at the inn, he showered and dressed and picked up a *Post* on his way to breakfast. The rest of the morning he spent alternating between the newspaper and the Sunday morning news shows on the four channels that his room's thirteen-inch black-and-white TV provided. It was nearly two in the afternoon before he got to LeCates' store. He'd expected to find it either open or closed. In fact it was neither—or both.

The main door was open, the screen door held shut by only its spring. Any customer who wandered by was free to walk in and search among the shelves for what he wanted. LeCates sat outside on the porch in a patio chair. His face was toward the sun. At his side was a round umbrella table minus its umbrella. His legs were stretched out across a worn-out wire crab pot. On the table by his elbow was an open can of beer and a mostly consumed bag of corn chips. A radio, tuned to an Orioles baseball game, droned on at a medium volume.

LeCates pointed toward the screen door.

"Get yourself a beer from in the cooler," he said.

Doll did and took the straight-back chair on the opposite side of the table.

"Your timing's not too bad. Only top of the second. Orioles down two to one," LeCates reported.

Doll popped open the snap tab on the beer can, took a swallow, and tilted the chair so it rested on its back legs with its top against the wall. A Yankee batter went down on strikes. LeCates asked Doll how he'd slept.

"It's going to be a slow job," Doll replied.

LeCates shifted his position, apparently to capture a better angle on the hot spring sun.

"Don't tell me your problems. Tell Elaine," he said. "You made the point clear enough last night when you said you'd be working for her."

"And you said that was fine," Doll reminded him.

"It is. It is." LeCates seemed to gauge his expression to say that he didn't very much care one way or the other.

"Then you got what you wanted, didn't you?" Doll made the question rhetorical. "So how about a little cooperation, Ellis? Even making allowances for what you don't want to talk about, I'm beginning to think there are all kinds of things you could tell me."

"Like what?"

"How about motive? Now why do you think anybody around this island would want to kill off a peaceable man like LeRoy Carrow?"

"How should I know? You're supposed to be the detective." As though to reemphasize his indifference, LeCates chose that moment to rummage through the bag for another portion of corn chips.

"Would it clear things up if I told you I met Ardee Vaughn last night?"

"Might," LeCates allowed. He looked over at Doll. The disclosure apparently perked up more interest than he was able to hide. "What did old Ardee have to say?"

"You know damn well what Ardee had to say," Doll replied sharply. "Because Ardee doesn't work too hard at keeping what he thinks a secret. You could've told me all that, Ellis. You had to have known it. According to Vaughn, Carrow had enough to say so nobody for three counties around could've missed it."

"So it couldn't've been that hard to find out," LeCates answered. "You don't need me. You just proved it, Doll. You found out for yourself about LeRoy's . . . What's the word for it? . . . Compulsion? . . . Obsession? Anyway, you don't need me. You found it out for yourself the first night you were here."

"That doesn't answer why you couldn't've told me."

"And what? Have someone say later on down the road that I was the one who put you on to it? Thanks, Doll, but no thanks. I told you before that wasn't what I wanted."

Doll asked why. LeCates replied angrily only that it wasn't because it wasn't, and that was all Doll had to know about that.

"What about Rachael Teal?" Doll asked.

"What about her?" LeCates, seemingly despite himself, began to look interested again.

"Same thing as Vaughn? Did Carrow get in her way too?"

"What did she tell you? Or did you get it all through Vaughn?"

LeCates seemed to Doll to be a man in a contest with himself, drawn between his grudging desire to stay silent and his equally impelling impatience and curiosity. Doll tried to make the most of LeCates' dilemma. He fed out the little he'd managed to learn in very small portions.

"She says he didn't bother her as much."

LeCates shrugged. "Not as much? I guess it comes down to what you mean by 'much'—in dollars?—in agreements?—in just calling names?"

"She didn't say which," Doll replied.

"She's a hard one to know. She keeps to herself." LeCates languidly stretched his neck, then faced back toward the sun and closed his eyes. "But no matter what you say about that, you got to admit she's a goddamn decent-looking woman."

"She seems to have Vaughn pretty well wrapped up."

"Ardee Vaughn! That's no big deal. If a snake had hips, Ardee Vaughn would try to screw it. If he could toss her the commission that comes from a couple-hundred-thousand-dollar sale, then maybe, just maybe, the poor bastard would have half a chance."

"Suppose he could throw her something else. Something of value other than money?"

" 'Something?' What does 'something' mean?" LeCates' eyes were open again. He looked at Doll, his brow as furrowed as a newly planted field. "What the hell are you talking about, Doll?"

"I'm talking about two people with a common interest," Doll answered. "The interest in this case being LeRoy Carrow. Or, let's be more specific: an interest in getting LeRoy Carrow off of their backs."

"You mean kill him?" LeCates pushed himself upright in his chair. "Christ almighty, Doll. Do you really believe that? You believe that Teal and Vaughn got together and killed him?"

"I don't think Rachael Teal went around loosening any propane fittings. I'm really just asking questions, Ellis. Vaughn doesn't hide how he felt about Carrow. All I'm suggesting is what could have happened if Rachael had offered him a little added inducement."

"Christ, Doll. Holy Christ." LeCates shook his head. "You got yourself one hell of a mind. I mean—picking out Vaughn was logical enough. But I never saw, as a part of it, him gettin' into that Teal broad's pants."

"That's why I'm asking," Doll replied. "I don't know if he did or not. He doesn't seem like the kind to stick his neck out on his own. I don't see him as hard-boiled enough to have done it for just the money alone."

LeCates sat pensively back in his chair and set about performing a series of long and nearly toneless whistles.

"I don't know," he said, at last abandoning the entertainment. "One minute I see it. The next I can't. It fits together. It makes a neat picture. Then I laugh because no matter how hard I try, I can't see the two of them in the sack together. I'm not saying yes. I'm not saying no. I'm no way saying it couldn't have been."

"Then who else is there?" Doll asked.

"That's the whole point. We're back where we started." LeCates frowned and fingered his beer can. "You've got to keep on looking, Doll. If you want to know people who wanted Carrow dead, your problem's not gonna to be making a list. Start with Vaughn's son Gerry. He's just one more example. The way I hear the story he damn near killed Carrow in public view one night over at the inn."

"And the others who should be on the list?" Doll said. "I hear you saying I ought to be looking for something more along the size of a herd."

"You look. Go see what you find. Don't you see what I'm telling you, Doll?" LeCates said with the air of a man growing tired of explaining what was obvious to him. "There are two ends around here. You must see that yourself, so I don't see what harm comes if I help you to fill in the spaces. Vaughn and Teal are on one end. Carrow's on the other. But everybody else, everybody you talk to, is someplace in between along the same line. You talk to them and they're all on Carrow's side. But where do they put their bankbooks, Doll? That's another thing altogether, and a whole lot harder to know."

"Where's yours, Ellis? Where do you put your bankbook these days?" Doll asked.

"I could say it's none of your business," LeCates said and smiled a smile of benign indifference. "But it's nowhere, Doll. Not yet anyway. I'm not screwed to the wall like the rest of them are. The store makes enough to keep me alive, so I don't have to make any right-away choices. I guess that just about puts me in the catbird seat for now."

Doll stayed for two more beers and enough of the rest of the baseball game that the Orioles were down seven to two going into the ninth. It was four-ten when he left LeCates and started walking back down the main highway toward the inn.

He felt in a vaguely self-congratulatory mood. The talk with LeCates, all in all, had come off better than he'd expected. He was basking in that modest success and, at the same time, enjoying the ebbing afternoon, when he noticed a pickup truck coming north along the road.

The truck was sun-bleached and dirty enough so it no longer had a distinctive color. It ambled through the limited speed zone, its pace such that not even the most punctilious traffic officer could have regarded it as a candidate for a citation. Doll couldn't hear the noise of its engine, but the raspy blare of a radio and the boisterous echoes of masculine laughter preceded it as it approached him, slowed further, and finally stopped.

Captain George Page leaned out of the right side window. His hammy fist held an open can of beer. Jerry Lee Godfrey sat beside him. Captain Ornan Atkins was at the wheel. Carroll Messick and Joely Edwards sat in the bed in the back, on opposite sides, with an open case of beer and the stereo portable blasting out its music between them.

"Damn it t' hell, Carroll," Page turned and shouted back through the cab's open rear window. "Turn that goddamn radio down." With the volume lowered, he turned back toward Doll. "Right fine afternoon, Mr. Doll," he said. "Reckon you're comin' back from Ellis's store. How you doin' with ol' LeRoy's boat? 'Cordin' to Farron, you gave her a pretty fair report."

"It's coming," Doll said.

"Comin' how?" Page raised an eyebrow.

Doll had foreseen the question. "Some things I might need to look at again. See if I can tell if and how much she needs to be sistered."

"Mmm. Yeah." Page set his jaw to work on his tobacco. "I recall now," he said as he chewed, "Farron sayin' you said about that. Where you headin' now, Mr. Doll? On your way back to the inn?"

Doll nodded.

Page wrinkled his nose as though it itched and the movement was a substitute for scratching it.

"You the kind a' man who takes a drink now an' again before his dinner, Mr. Doll?"

On the opposite side of the cab, Atkins' gray eyes looked straight ahead. Whatever he saw or thought was impossible to guess. He seemed to take no notice of Doll. Jerry Lee stared down at the can of beer he held balanced between his knees. In the back, Carrol Messick and Joely Edwards drummed lightly on the walls of the truck bed, keeping approximate time with the music from the radio.

"That an invitation or simple curiosity?" Doll asked.

"Invitation, naturally." Page grinned. "We don't hold right with too much curiosity 'round here. Invitation's good, anyway, so long's you got the money to pay for your own."

"I'll pay my own way," Doll said.

"Then hop up back," Page called. "Jerry Lee, reach down behind the seat there an' fetch Mr. Doll out a jacket. Gets cold back there once the truck gets t' movin'," Page said, turning back to Doll. " 'Specially after the sun goes down. Carroll, damn you, keep that goddamn radio down and fetch Mr. Doll out a beer."

* * *

Page was right. It was cold even before the sun went down, and the icy can of beer in his hand only made Doll feel all the colder. Messick and Edwards, though, seemed none the worse for the weather. They finished their beers and had started two more before they lobbed the first cans into a basket. The two of them worked as a team against Page. Carroll made sure his attention was elsewhere, and Joely, in increments, turned up the volume on the radio.

Doll worked at his beer. The can was still half full when they offered him another. Doll shook his head and involuntarily shivered.

"Shit! This ain't no kind a' cold," Carroll shouted as he laughed. "This kind a' weather's the kind you pray for come January out on that damn bay."

"That's the damn truth. You tell 'im, all right, Carroll," Joely chorused.

"Cold enough for me," Doll said and meant it. He remembered Ellis LeCates and wondered momentarily if the inside of the body went before the outside started to go. The thought of the cold made him shiver again. Irrationally, he took another swallow of the beer.

"Turn that sumbitchin' radio down. Last goddamn time I'm gonna tell ya!" Page yelled again from the front.

Messick did and this time left it there. Doll asked where they were going. Messick answered with a street name Doll didn't know, then expanded the answer to the name of a tavern in the postcard town Doll had passed through.

"Like to show 'em, now an' again," Messick said, "what the men from out the island are like."

Joely Edwards laughed. "Showed 'em damn good last time we was in there. Maybe have to show 'em again afore they let us back in the damn place."

"Did you do this with LeRoy, too?" Doll asked.

"Yeah. Now an' again," Messick said, with what sounded to Doll like a trace of uneasiness. "He used t' come along sometimes. Farron sometimes too."

"Hey! Hey!" Joely Edwards shouted, staring out over the tailgate at the road behind them. "Ain't that Covey Wallace's car comin' up there?"

Doll followed automatically as Carroll Messick turned his head. A car a half mile or so behind them was closing at a moderate but steady rate. Doll could make out nothing more than a low, gray silhouette. Carroll Messick and Joely Edwards strained their eyes to see more.

"Easy back there, boys," Page called back from the cab. "Don't want t' hear neither a' you two hotheads startin' no trouble."

"Who's Covey Wallace?" Doll asked.

"Tonger," Joely Edwards said without taking his eyes off the advancing car. He said nothing more and apparently thought that the single word was answer enough.

The car was no more than a hundred feet behind them by then. It was close enough for Doll to see inside. The driver was short, hardly able to see over the wheel. His jaw was set. His face seemed to have the texture of tree bark. He looked to Doll like an angry Christmas dwarf. Doll assumed he was the one that they'd called Covey Wallace. Beside him was a second man, with two more in the rear seat. The men from the car stared ahead at the truck as intently as Messick and Edwards stared back. The car suddenly veered into the left lane, accelerating rapidly to pass.

Ornan Atkins held the pickup to a steady course and speed.

As the car came alongside, Doll could see that the right side windows were down. The next thing he knew, a beer can whistled past his head. From the corner of his eye, he saw Joely Edwards and Carroll Messick duck.

The can hit the opposite side of the inside wall and fell to the truck bed. Beer spewed out onto the floor. Another crash followed. More beer spilled. Doll realized the men from the car weren't throwing their empties.

As though on signal, Edwards and Messick stood and returned coordinated fire. A ringing metallic pong recorded the single hit. There was no time for a second volley. By then, the speeding car was out of range. As it curved back in front of the truck, three fists with extended middle fingers rose from the windows into the air. Edwards and Messick, still standing, answered in kind.

"Casualties? Prisoners?" Page called back from the cab.

"Bitchin' tongers," Joely Edwards swore. "Carroll an' me, we didn't start nothin', Cap'n."

"Know you didn't," Page answered amiably. "Either man's got the right to defend himself, boys. How 'bout you? How you holdin' on there, Mr. Doll?"

"I dropped my beer in all the excitement," Doll said. "If I'd known before what the game was about, I could've used it for covering fire."

"Terrible waste either way," Page replied. "Boys, y' make sure Mr. Doll's got another. Damn tongers ain't got no sense a' humor."

Everybody laughed except for Ornan Atkins, who just kept up the steady pace of his driving.

There were two sides to the tavern in the postcard town. Each served the same food and drink. The difference between them came down to a matter of emphasis. The room on the left was where you went for dinner and maybe had a beer on the side. On the right, there was a bar as well as tables and videogame machines. And the priorities were precisely the reverse.

Page brought the first round of drinks over from the bar and distributed them around the tables the other watermen had pushed together. Talk began with the hands taking turns at being the butts of the captains' jokes. But once the barbs started, the razzing got generalized, with the hands who weren't the target of the moment cannibalistically joining the captains in the attack.

Joely Edwards caught it first for the length of his hair, then Jerry Lee for his inept approaches to the hookers in the Baltimore strip bars. Carroll Messick, it was held by common agreement, could Jonah any race boat with a crew that was foolish enough to take him aboard. By that time, they were into their third round of drinks, and no one, as yet, had even suggested the prospect of eating.

For Doll's benefit, Page explained that to call a man a Jonah was the same as calling him a jinx.

"Ain't no Jonah. Never was," Carroll Messick objected.

"Next year, maybe, we let you race with the tongers," Joely Edwards roared.

"Yeah. For ol' Covey Wallace, maybe." Jerry Lee nodded his approval and giggled.

"Now you just let ol' Covey alone," Page said. "He's had himself enough hard luck." Page turned to Doll. "Ol' Covey from the car back there—like you heard—he's a tonger. Always a bit a' feudin' between the tongers and the drudgers."

Doll didn't have to wait for Page to go on to explain.

"Tongers say the drudgers rake their beds." Page winked at Doll. "Likely, now an' again, some do."

"Nobody we know." Jerry Lee laughed again.

"Course not. Nobody we know," Page agreed. "Wouldn't do that. After all, we all got tongin' licenses ourselves. Anyway, them tongers is watermen, too. The times is hard for them just like us. That's really why ol' Covey's so sore. He decides t' get out an' sells his place. Gets a contract on it an' all. Looks out the next day, an' everything's brown. Well's gone all salty. Believe it or not, some sumbitch has gone and salted 'is land."

"So the contract's no good," Doll said.

"Shit, no," Page replied. "Place ain't livable no more. Drinkin' water's all gotta be brought in."

"Sucks." Carroll Messick nodded. "Even t' happen to an ol' tongin' bastard like Covey Wallace."

"Sucks." Jerry Lee Godfrey nodded in turn.

"And Wallace thinks it was done by a drudger?" Doll suggested.

Page looked surprised. "Not that I know," he said. "What'd ever make you think a thing like that?"

"There are some, I hear," Doll answered, "that don't like to see the places on the island sold."

"You talkin' 'bout LeRoy? Then I'd say that you'd be a long ways out a' line," Page said. "You got no call to talk 'bout LeRoy like that."

"Only what I hear from Richard Vaughn."

"Which ain't no more than a greedy man talkin'." Page's face was as cold as the biting wind in the back of the pickup. Nobody else around the table spoke. Doll felt the menace, like a bad shift in the wind, in the silence that suddenly prevailed.

"You don't wanna go around believin' all a' what some men tell ya, Mr. Doll," Page said with exaggerated evenness. "Course, we all heard 'bout that—your talkin' to Vaughn an' all. We heard you talked to Wes Mowen, too, 'bout LeRoy bein' a good enough captain."

"Then you probably heard I asked Farron Carrow the same thing."

Page smiled, but the smile held no humor. "We did hear that, as a matter a' fact. That's all part a' your job, I guess. Reckon we can't fault you for askin'. As for Ardee Vaughn, well, we all know he's just a natural talker. But I'll give ya some free advice, Mr. Doll. A man don't want t' go talkin' 'round 'bout folks that he don't know. An' he don't want t' be askin' too many questions."

Doll looked around the table, from Atkins to Messick to Godfrey to Edwards and, finally, back at Page. What he found in the faces was what he'd expected. The humor was gone. All eyes were on the outsider. He gave LeCates credit for having been right about that. There wasn't even a hint of a potential ally in the crowd.

"You know, now," he said, "if we start counting up the numbers, maybe this is going to seem a little foolhardy to some of you. You see, I know I can't stop whatever interest makes you keep a log of who I talk to. But I intend to go right on talking all the same. And it'd be a real mistake for any of us to walk out of here today thinking I felt myself accountable to any of you."

Doll never moved his eyes from Page's. "And you tell Jerry Lee," he added, "that if his hand moves another inch closer to the neck of that bottle, I'm going to have to break his goddamn arm."

For seconds, no one at the table spoke or moved.

Finally, Page chose to end the stalemate. He grinned.

"Okay," he said, "maybe you're right. Maybe we all got ourselves off on the wrong foot there for a minute. I take all the blame on myself, Mr. Doll. If I made it sound as though we all set the dogs on ya, the truth is that, on a place like the island, ya just can't help being told things that happen."

Doll poured some beer into his glass and nodded. The tension ebbed a little more.

Page's grin broadened further. "Other truth is," he said, "if I was twenty years younger, myself, I'd a' put up with Ardee Vaughn or the devil for just the chance a' meetin' up with that Rachael Teal."

Amid the laughter Jerry Lee giggled.

"Ya like bein' out on the water, Mr. Doll?" Page asked. "Reckon ya must, or ya wouldn't earn your livin' like ya do. Ya got balls. Whatever else ya got, I gotta give you that. When we take out the skipjacks, or even the small boats, if ya ever wanted to make the trip, I, for one, would be pleased to have ya come aboard." Page glanced up along the table. "I'm sure, for his part, Cap'n Atkins would, too."

If Ornan Atkins would, Doll noticed, he didn't bother to say so.

6

The next morning's sky was a wash of gray. Lower, toward the east, its color turned to a robin's egg blue, then bleached to a hazy white along the horizon. Beneath the rim of the world, the orange sun seemed to wait, poised for the precisely right moment to keep its appointment with the new day. The cool, damp air was still. The quiet water from the bay slapped gently at the hulls of the boats along the wharf.

Doll stood beside the *Winston Mills* and looked across toward LeRoy Carrow's crippled skipjack. Fatally crippled. The wonderful irony of pretense, he thought, was in how easily it could bounce back on and fool the pretender. To play the boat's savior, Doll had made himself believe that somewhere, somehow, there might actually be one. He admitted now, in the silence of the predawn, that he knew there wasn't going to be.

He was tired, and his head throbbed—not from too many beers, though, if asked, he wouldn't have denied he'd had his quota—but from the cigar smoke that, as the evening had moved along, the watermen had taken to generating in densities approaching those of a Maine coastal fog. The smoke combined with the lack of sleep. When Doll had gotten back to the inn, his watch had shown the time as two in the morning. He turned his attention to the peace of the gulls and the empty expanse of the bay. He waited, though he had nothing more than his own instinct to suggest that the one he waited for would come.

Ten minutes later, Ornan Atkins' colorless pickup truck rolled off the main road and onto the gravel and shell ground cover of the wharfside parking area. The door swung open, and the captain got out, dressed in his working attire of oilskin overalls and thigh wader boots. He was alone. Doll had guessed that he would be.

Atkins paid Doll the courtesy of nodding to say good morning, then started to climb aboard his boat.

"Cap'n Atkins . . ." Doll called after him.

Atkins turned, but so slowly as to make it clear that Doll's interruption was a distraction and that any further conversation wouldn't be of Atkins' choosing.

"Ain't goin' out today. Just here t' put in some work on the boat. If you'd asked last night, could a' told ya that then. Saved ya the trouble a' gettin' up so early in the mornin'." Atkins turned back toward the *Winston Mills*.

"I didn't come here to sail," Doll said.

Atkins glanced back toward Doll without offering any further encouragement.

"I came because I wanted to talk," Doll said. "I figured after all the hoopla last night it was going to be a late morning for everybody else except you."

"Boys 've got a right t' their fun now an' again. Got my own work t' do. Reckon we all do." Atkins shook his head as he grabbed a shroud line and swung himself up onto the deck. "Reckon you got work a' your own to do, too."

"Not a thing. I'm on my own time," Doll answered.

Doll counted on the power of impertinence. The reply offered enough of a challenge so that Atkins wasn't able to ignore it entirely. He gave Doll an admonishing scowl, then set about opening the hatchway that led down to the cabin.

"I won't make it that easy, Captain," Doll said. "I'm not just going to walk away."

Atkins took a moment, then turned from the hatchway. He stuffed his hands into the pockets of his overalls and walked with no evident hurry across the deck to the point nearest to where Doll was standing. From the vantage of three feet above Doll's head, Ornan Atkins looked down.

"You've made a mistake, Mr. Doll," he said. "Seems t' me like you're under a wrong impression. You think that, on the other times we met, I didn't have neither thing to say 'cause there was others a' the boys around? Not so, Mr. Doll. Not the way I am. Ain't either thing I got t' say t' you this mornin' I couldn't a' said last night if I'd a mind to."

Pulling a toothpick from out of his pocket, Atkins jabbed at a space between his teeth. "That's, maybe, the difference between you an' me," he said, without relenting in his attack on the offending particle. "What I got to say, I kin say t' everybody—else I ain't got it t' say t' nobody a'tall."

"Then you live in a simpler world than I do, Captain. Or else you just close your mind and your eyes to a lot of what goes on."

Atkins stopped picking. For a moment he only chewed at the toothpick. His facial expression didn't change except for a very fleeting instant when, Doll thought, he caught the smallest hint of humor in the eyes.

"You're an insolent little puffer, ain't ya?" the captain said at last in a tone so neutral that Doll found the meaning impossible to comprehend. "Last night I guessed maybe it was the beer that made ya cocky. Now I guess, maybe, it's deeper than that. Trouble with you, boy, is that nobody ever learned you respect."

"Farron Carrow says you keep a good boat—as good or better than any of the others on the bay. He said his father kept his boat as good—at least as good, maybe better than yours."

"Farron's a good boy," Atkins answered, taking the statement at its most superficial level. "Nice thing that he takes some pride in the way his father kept things. That's maybe a part a' what I was sayin'. Respect, you'll remember I said."

Doll ignored the implicit rebuke and pointed toward a metal tank mounted on the stern of the *Winston Mills*. "That a propane tank? You carry a stove on board? How often do you check the fittings, Captain?"

The only reply Atkins offered was a return to a silent, expressionless stare.

"Once a week? More often than that?" Doll prodded. "And you could smell a leak, couldn't you, Cap'n Atkins. How often you figure LeRoy Carrow used to check his?"

But Atkins refused to be provoked.

"You know what I'm asking, Captain," Doll persisted.

"Course I know. Don't mean I gotta answer," Atkins said.

The response was direct, as Doll realized he should have expected. The problem was that he wasn't used to being told quite so openly that whatever he might think didn't very much matter. The only reply Doll had was lame, and he knew it.

"That only raises more questions," he said.

Atkins' eyes narrowed. His mouth curved ever so slightly at the corners. It was the kind of smile that Doll had thought was under limited copyright to IRS agents and lawyers. "Questions? What'd that raise questions about—from a man who goes around sayin' that he's only here to buy a boat?"

Involuntarily Doll looked away. He caught himself much too late to hide the impulse.

"Let me tell you what you're really askin'," Atkins went on. "You want me t' tell ya all 'bout my neighbors an' my kin? Mr. Doll, I sail an' I live with these folks. I've known most of 'em since they was born, or since I was. I've seen 'em christened; I've seen 'em married; an' I've helped haul up their drowned bodies out a' that damn bay. Now what the hell is it makes you think I'm gonna answer either questions 'bout those good folks just t' please you?"

Ornan Atkins' expression soured. He stared down at the deck of his skipjack as though there were something he was suddenly ashamed of. "Now go 'way, boy," he said, " 'cause you see ya make me talk too much. Didn't mean to ruffle y' feathers none. But, it's the best part a' my nature to be blunt in what I say."

The exchange with Atkins had temporarily drawn Doll's attention away from the ache in his head. Now, as he walked along the highway, all the fatigue and the throbbing returned—not only returned, but redoubled. The progress that he'd hoped to make seemed only to have taken him backward. If not beaten, he'd come away battered. He took a shortcut diagonally across the lawn from the main road toward the stairs to his room at the inn.

The sun was up, warm already, a harbinger of the steambath days of July and August ahead. Doll was only vaguely aware of its heat. He wasn't conscious of the motorcycle that turned into the driveway or of its stopping halfway between the main road and the inn. The first sound that caught his ear was that of his name being called across the intervening distance.

He looked up and saw the cycle and Farron Carrow half sitting, half standing, astride it. Doll altered his direction toward the bike. Although he walked quickly, his headway seemed slow. The lawn in itself was bigger than it had looked. To have someone waiting made the crossing of it seem to take even longer. But by the time Doll could see the look on Farron's face, he wouldn't have minded had the lawn been twice the size that it was.

It seemed to Doll to be a bad morning on the verge of turning rapidly worse. He did his best at a casual greeting, knowing before the words were out that any effort at lighthearted conversation wasn't going to work.

Farron didn't say good morning. All he said was that he hadn't figured on Doll's getting up from bed this early. After that, he went straight to the point.

"What did you decide 'bout my father's boat?" he asked.

Doll went back to the lie about it not being his decision.

"Or anybody else's?" Farron said. "You know what they're saying about you, don't you, Mr. Doll?"

"I don't even know who 'they' are," Doll temporized, and waited to see which "they" Farron had in mind.

"Then you maybe ought t' start with Cap'n Page. Or any a' the other drudgin' boys you was out with last night."

"What do they say, Farron?" Doll asked.

"They say that you're a goddamn liar. That's what they say. They say you don't care a turd in hell 'bout buyin' up my father's boat."

"They're right," Doll said. "I was never part of any deal to buy your father's boat. The whole story was a phony from the start."

So the lie broke—with all the suddenness and finality of a springtime thunderstorm. Doll had expected to feel a mixture of emotions. The only one that he felt in that moment was relief.

"Why!" Farron Carrow demanded.

"You're entitled to know," Doll answered, "which is going to make it hard to understand why I'm not going to tell you."

Farron called Doll a son of a bitch. The oath, Doll thought, was the smallest due that he had coming from LeRoy Carrow's son. But Doll also had other commitments. Whatever else Farron might learn was going to have to come from his mother.

"I said you're a son of a bitch," Farron challenged. Now that, for him, the worst seemed realized, his anger called for something more substantial than words.

Doll, meanwhile, was prepared to do whatever he had to to avoid the altercation. The question came down to how best to do it. Doll had seen enough fights start to know that backing away was, as often as not, exactly the wrong way to avert one. He took his chance, knowing there was no way to be sure if the choice that he made was the right one.

"Did you ever think," Doll said in a slow, conversational voice, "what a mistake it is to pick a fight when you're hung up across the seat of a motorcycle?"

The observation succeeded at least to the point that it seemed to catch Farron by surprise.

Doll pressed the advantage. "All the other guy's got to do," he said, "is kick the damn machine. After that, you wind up under it or using all your muscle to try to keep the thing from going over. Either way, the guy's got all the time he needs to get a damn good start on cracking your head."

Farron started to move, then seemed to realize that, if what Doll had said was true, it was already very much too late for that. He stared at Doll uncertainly, then carefully settled himself back down into the seat.

"Is it true," he said, "that my father was murdered?"

"Where did you hear that?" Doll asked, trying to sound less dismal than he felt.

"Drudgers say you think he was. They say that's what you're really here for. They say Ellis LeCates brought you here for that."

"I told you all I can say," Doll answered. "If the time comes when I can tell you more, I will."

"They say that's gotta be why you're here because a' the kind of questions you been askin'. Folks around here look out for one another. You better know that now, Mr. Doll. I been to school with Carroll and Joely. Me and Jerry Lee were closest friends right up to the time that he went into the Army. Ain't nothing gets said in front a' them that ain't gonna get back to me."

"What are you saying, Farron?" Doll asked.

"That I could help you, Mr. Doll. You said before yourself that I got a right to know. The way things get around, ya gotta see now that I'm gonna find out anyway."

Doll shook his head and studied the spokes of the wheel of the bike.

"I know there were plenty who thought my father was crazy. Nothin's new in that—no newer than the fights I been gettin' into since around when I first started high school. He wasn't crazy, though. He was different, sure enough, 'cause he didn't measure everything in money. But different ain't crazy, Mr. Doll."

"No, it isn't crazy," Doll said.

Farron nodded as though even the token agreement helped. "Took the time to teach me all he knew 'bout the water." He kept his attention divided. As he talked, he polished the bike's speedometer with the sleeve of his jacket. "Had his faults, sure enough. Did some things he shouldn't 've. We had our fights. Doesn't make him crazy, though. The man never did nothin' so bad it deserved to get him killed."

"Give it time," Doll said. "Meanwhile, I'll promise you this: I'll tell you all there is to tell just as soon as I can."

The offer, for some reason, turned out to be enough for Farron to accept. He looked up at Doll and nodded, then walked the bike through a clumsy half-circle and stomped the engine into life. "All right, Mr. Doll. I know I don't know all a' what that means, but, for now, I'll trust you as far as holdin' yourself to what you say. I'll be back, though, 'cause, sooner or later, you gotta tell me. You said I got a right to know, and I sure ain't gonna let you get away."

Farron engaged the cycle's gears.

Doll watched the motorcycle kick up gravel as it swung from the drive and turned north onto the main highway.

* * *

Doll managed the rest of the trip to his room with some difficulty. His head beat a cadence loud enough for the crew of a Roman galley to keep stroke. He wanted to take two aspirin and sleep, but he made himself change to his running clothes instead. The first mile was nothing less than torture, but then, slowly, his sweat glands opened up and the accumulated poisons began to leak away. He ran for a long time, pushing himself in windsprints and then backing off. The pain of the exercise became more insistent than that in his head, and then the pain in his head was gone. The dragging weight of fatigue left him. His muscles grew tired, but his body worked itself into life.

Back at the inn, he showered and, finally, let himself sleep. The time was just after noon when he awoke. He was rested. The twin disasters of the morning were behind him. He even felt mildly hungry after the nap.

Lunch at Millman's Inn was served in either the dining room or, less formally, at the smaller tables scattered about the bar. The dining room was large and, on this day, empty except for a family of four who, by their own choice or the wisdom of the hostess, were seated along the outside wall at the farthest possible distance from the public room. The man and woman, together with two neatly groomed, preadolescent children, were dressed in those smartly casual outfits that are the standard advertised fare in the pages of the better Sunday supplement magazines.

By contrast with the overabundance of empty tables in the dining room, unoccupied tables in the bar were few. Watermen in jeans or overalls sat beside local businessmen. The tables were crowded with sandwiches and burgers, jars of mustard, and bottles of ketchup and beer.

Wesley Mowen served as maître d' and part-time, help-out bartender. He found Doll a table and promised him a waitress would come by. He started to leave, then changed his mind and turned to sit in the chair opposite Doll's.

He looked at Doll oddly for a moment. The waitress came over.

"Yours is an ale, if I recall right," Mowen said. He ordered an ale for Doll and a beer for himself. "Hair a' the dog what bit ya," he said. "Ya have to answer one question for me, though. You really offer to take on all them boys from Page's and Atkins' boats all t'gether?"

Doll decided he must have begun to adapt. He no longer felt surprise at how fast and how thoroughly the little bits of everyone's news got around the island. "Nobody ever got real serious about it," he answered.

"Still and all. . . ." Mowen clicked his tongue. "I reckon maybe ya could say that Page and Atkins might be just a little past their primes. But Messick and Edwards—I dunno—seems to me that either a' them could pretty much go his weight if he'd a mind to."

"Like I say," Doll repeated, "I didn't think anybody was all that serious. Besides, I wouldn't do that to you, Mr. Mowen. I heard for the real fifteen rounders you have to come here."

"Here?" Mowen's voice took on a defensive edge, as though Doll had implied something that might serve to damage the inn's reputation.

"LeRoy Carrow and young Gerry Vaughn," Doll said to explain.

"Oh, that one." Wesley Mowen smiled sheepishly. "Yeah. Guess that did make the local headlines," he admitted.

"Anybody get hurt?"

"No, no. Well, somebody could've," Mowen admitted. The waitress brought the bottles and glasses. "On the house," Mowen said. He poured for both of them and took a swallow of his own before going on.

"Started right in here. Quiet night. Downright quiet up till then. Ol' LeRoy," Mowen said, pointing, "he was sittin' right down there, 'bout midway down along the length a' the bar. Weren't but a dozen or so here when it happened. News, though, went out around the island 'bout like wildfire."

Doll asked how it got started.

Mowen nodded, remembering. "Could say 'bout like wildfire, too," he said. "Like I told ya, LeRoy was up at the bar. Guess I'd served him four or five. That weren't a lot a' beer for LeRoy. Not for most a' them other water rats neither. Now you, I served you four or five, I'd have to watch ya. LeRoy, he's spent a lot a' years in practice. He could a' drunk easy that many yet again."

"The Vaughn kid was here, too?"

"No, no. He don't drink much here. Guess maybe that's 'cause him and the island folks ain't all that close when it comes to gettin' along. He likes a place up in the big town. Not where you guys went t' other night. That's almost all a watermen's hole. They'd kick his ass hell to breakfast if he ever showed his neck in there."

"So what made him come here?"

"LeRoy Carrow! That's what made him come. Damn kid come in through that door there like gangbusters." Mowen pointed out the direction again, this time with the neck of his beer. "Stomps right up to where ol' LeRoy's sittin'. Grabs 'im by the shoulder. Spins 'im around on that ol' stool. Starts to call him a sumbitchin' sumpin' or other. But that's jus' about as far as he gets afore ol' LeRoy comes 'round with 'is fist an' busts young Gerry right square in the mouth."

"Should've slowed him down some," Doll said.

"Should've. Should've." Mowen nodded emphatically. "But that Vaughn kid, he had himself a head a' steam up. He was pissed an' he was drunk. 'Tween just you an' me, I don't know what else he might a' been. Well, LeRoy sent 'im backward into that table jus' 'bout where those two guys with the fried chicken is. I mean he went pitch-ass backwards right over the top. Got right up. Don't think he even felt it. Don't think he felt Leroy hit 'im neither. Don't think that damn kid felt nothin' at all. He got right on up, an' he went after that ol' boy LeRoy like a madman."

"You said LeRoy was sober."

"Yeah. Sober enough." Mowen agreed. "Don't mean he could stop a buzzsaw. That Vaughn kid went after him swingin' everything he had just like a pissed off ol' tomcat. Took three guys to pull 'im off. Me an' another t' hold back ol' LeRoy. Both of 'em wanted to go at it again outside. Regular fight, I might even a' let 'em. Not that night. Not those two, though. Believe one of 'em would a' killed the other, sure."

"Do you know," Doll asked, "what the whole thing was about?"

Mowen shook his head. "Couldn't tell ya, Mr. Doll. I know what I see, an' 'bout the rest, I don't ask questions. All I could say you gotta know by now. No love got lost 'tween ol' LeRoy and those Vaughns."

"I sort of heard that from the father," Doll said.

"Yeah, well, you can depend on it," Mowen said, taking another swallow from his beer.

"Who else had it in for Carrow?" Doll asked. "That first night here, the night I checked in, you said something about him raising a lot of people's hackles."

"Did I? Did I say that?" Mowen seemed to think back, as though he were trying to remember what it was he might have meant. "Least ways, we know for sure," Mowen said laughing, "he raised the hackles pretty good on Gerry Vaughn."

"What about the others?" Doll pushed.

"Others. Well, now. . . . Let's see, Mr. Doll, you've already talked to Ardee Vaughn, and ya talked to that Rachael Teal lady. You talked to Ellis LeCates. I gotta figure that. An' ya spent a bunch a' time talkin' t' George Page an' some a' the watermen. Now ya want me t' tell you somethin' ya haven't heard so far from all a' them. Tell ya the truth, Mr. Doll, I'm not so sure I want t' do that."

"It's all off the record," Doll said. "I'm not gonna be saying Wes Mowen told me this."

"No, I'm sure ya won't. Just, all the same. . . ." Mowen smiled. "Tell ya what I can do, though. There's a guy who maybe could help ya some. Couldn't hurt ya eitherway t' meet 'im."

Turning in his chair, Mowen waved an invitation to a man across the room.

"This'd be Andy Dowling," Mowen whispered confidentially, returning his attention to Doll. "Andy represents us simple folk when it comes t' makin' all them laws up in Annapolis. Makes it his business t' know folks pretty good."

"Andy Dowling." Mowen repeated the name by way of introduction when Dowling got to the table. "Ya can talk t' him, Mr. Doll, 'bout what you want. Like I say, our Andy knows. An', Andy, Mr. Doll here's from outta town, so there ain't no point in your tryin' to politic his vote."

With a sudden expression of annoyance, Mowen glanced around the bar. "Damn waitress," he grumbled. "Where the hell'd she go? Mr. Doll, lemme get ya somethin' from the kitchen rustled up afore they decide that it's time that the damn place got closed."

7

Andy Dowling stood beside the table, exhibiting no special grace, except for the consummate skill with which his left hand balanced a saucer and cup nearly filled to the rim with coffee. He wore his hair short, in a flat-top style that was popular in the late nineteen fifties. From what Doll could guess of his age, he might have been wearing it that way ever since. He wore a tan jacket and a striped blue and red tie. The jacket's lapel was adorned with a pin in the design of a miniature American flag.

With the completion of the introductions, Dowling's chubby face lit up with the glow of recognition.

"Oh, Mr. Doll." The smile he presented was broad enough to show a line of pristinely white teeth. "I've heard a lot of talk about you. You're the man who's here to buy LeRoy Carrow's boat."

Doll didn't bother to deny it. Instead, he accepted Dowling's outstretched hand. Mowen, meanwhile, used the excuse of the kitchen to free himself and leave the two of them alone.

"I hope you'll be able to see your way to giving the family a decent price," Dowling said as he sat down. "Of course I know business has to be business. But they're good folks, Elaine and the family. I'd like to see them get all they can of what's coming to them."

"I'd like to see that, too," Doll said. It was strange, he thought, the way a thing could be the truth and a lie at the same time.

A waitress appeared with a crab salad sandwich on rye that Doll hadn't ordered. Wesley Mowen, it seemed, had taken the matter of what Doll was having for lunch upon himself.

"Wes is a kidder. He's got me always drumming votes," Dowling said heartily.

Doll said nothing.

"The real truth," Dowling went on, "is that I've hardly ever drummed a vote. Course, come election time's different. That kind of flesh on flesh is what people expect. But here, like today, when I talk to folks—that kind a' thing ain't drumming. A man that goes into politics has got a feeling for people. Likes to hear what folks got to say. Can't rightly call that drumming, can you, Mr. Doll? But that's just ol' Wes's way a' having his fun."

"I don't think he means any harm," Doll said. He passed on the opportunity to offer Dowling any firmer reassurance.

Dowling, meanwhile, had learned enough in politics to know when it was time to take what he could get.

"Oh, no. I'm sure he doesn't," he agreed. "Wesley's a good man. Hard worker when it comes to that. Different kind a' work, of course, than most around here do. Not the same as pulling up oysters up from the bay. But hard, too, worrying about a big place like this. No, Wesley Mowen earns his money. Everybody on this island earns his bread."

"All one big family," Doll said.

"Well, yes." Dowling nodded uncertainly as he seemed to consider the point. "I can see how a man might say that."

"Except for LeRoy Carrow."

"LeRoy? Oh, because he's dead, you mean." Dowling shook his head somberly. At the same time, he spread his fingers flat on the table as though he were getting ready to kick up into a handstand.

"Ahhh!" he sighed. "What a tragedy that was. A good man with a God-fearing wife. Three fine children. Two of 'em girls not even grown. Hard thing to see a man like that cut down. 'Specially so with the senseless way it seemed to happen—for a man like that to die in the act of lighting a stove."

"Bad luck," Doll said, "about the gas getting loose and Carrow not being able to smell it."

Dowling looked uncertain again. He shrugged vaguely as though to imply reserved agreement.

"Then again," Doll said, "maybe the picture isn't so friendly as we'd like to make it be."

The uncertainty deepened in Dowling's face. Doll didn't wait to be asked to go on.

"Let's be honest with each other, Mr. Dowling. That 'one big, hardworking family' pitch I'm sure sounds great on the floor of the state house, but the truth, between the two of us here, is that the neighborhood hasn't been all that cordial. As a matter of fact, there are some around here who feel a whole lot more cordial now that good ol' LeRoy Carrow's got his final patch of ground."

"I don't believe that." Dowling looked sternly at Doll. "I believe there might be some who disagreed with him. I believe there could've been a lot like that 'cause LeRoy Carrow was the kind of man who spoke his mind. Some folks, naturally enough, disagreed with what he said. Doesn't mean that they looked on him with any kind of vengefulness for that."

"Covey Wallace?"

"Despicable thing to happen to anyone. To salt a man's land is a lower act than stealing money from his wallet. Almost as bad as slandering the dead, Mr. Doll. LeRoy denied any part in what happened to Wallace's land. He was never charged, certainly never convicted. Unless you know for a fact that I'm wrong, I think I'll forgo your insinuations and go on taking the man at his word."

"Gerry Vaughn disagreed with Carrow so much that, if he hadn't been pulled off, he would have killed him."

"Talk." Dowling shook his head again. "Talk's what it mostly all is. Fights are like whiskey around here. Every one I've ever heard about seems to get better with age. The Vaughn boy's anger was misdirected against LeRoy, but that's not to say it had no legitimate cause. He was the agent for the Wallace property sale, obviously something else you knew already."

Doll wondered if it was that connection that Wesley Mowen hadn't wanted to make. For the moment, though, Doll put the issue aside and went back to Dowling.

"Where do *you* stand?" he asked. "Fox or hound, Mr. Dowling? Which side do you run on these days?"

Dowling paused to taste his coffee. He frowned at the cup. Doll guessed from the face he made that it was cold.

"Meaning LeRoy's or those who'd like to see increasing development? I like to try to see it from both sides," he answered. "The watermen are an institution here. No man respects them or their place on the shore more than I do. I stand aside, Mr. Doll, to no man, anywhere, in that. It doesn't mean though, that I, more than anyone else, can alter the course of events in the natural world. Only the things of God's heaven are permanent."

"You're saying," Doll suggested, "that Carrow didn't understand things had to change."

"No, I'm not. You're saying that." Dowling reached into his jacket and came out with his wallet. "LeRoy wasn't any man's fool, Mr. Doll. You're wrong if you try to make him out one. The only thing he didn't see was that the new time was already on us. Every farmer up an' down these parts can tell you there'll be a first frost next winter. That doesn't mean he can tell you the day that it's going to come."

"They must vote you in by landslides," Doll said dryly. "You've got a real nice way with words."

"And you for asking questions, Mr. Doll. I can see now why you've raised the local eyebrows. You do a very thorough look-around for a man whose only interest is buying a boat."

Andy Dowling chose that moment to smile. He took out two single dollar bills, folded them, and tucked them neatly beneath the lip of the saucer.

"Do you really want to know what's going on here?" he asked. "If you do, there's a zoning meeting day after tomorrow. They hold 'em in the evenings right across the road there at the school. If you're as concerned as you say, you ought to come by. You'll see that most folks have heads on their shoulders. You might even find they don't need LeRoy or anybody else when it comes to making up their minds."

Dowling pushed himself back from the table.

"And now," he said, extending his hand again, "I have things I have to do, Mr. Doll. You may not think so, but for me this little talk has been helpful. Maybe we'll see you at the school, or maybe we won't." He started to go and then turned back. He smiled. "You know," he concluded, "there are those around who take a dim view of strangers on the island. I, for one, don't. If the devil's going to be among us, I say that a man's a whole lot better off to know his face."

The politician in Andy Dowling laughed enthusiastically at the joke.

LeCates stood behind the counter next to the cash register. He glared at Doll. His nostrils flared. He gave the impression of a bull in the act of pawing the ground before charging.

From Farron Carrow to Ellis LeCates, Doll decided, the day hadn't been one of his best, measured in terms of endearing himself to other people.

"And what the hell is Elaine supposed to say?" LeCates demanded. "Good for you, Doll! Your conscience is clear. He's not your son. How come you're the one that gets to be holier-than-thou? Once you're out and over that bridge, nobody back here is gonna mean two pieces of crap to you."

"It didn't work, Ellis. The story didn't work," Doll said. "That's all there is, and that's what you don't want to hear."

LeCates' face reddened. "So you jump ship, and nobody else matters. Doll saves Doll, and the rest of the world can go screw."

"Don't fool yourself, Ellis. Elaine Carrow's a damn strong woman—and maybe a whole lot better at handling things that go bad than you are."

The last part seemed to hit LeCates hard, harder than Doll had thought or intended. LeCates took immediate refuge in a furious silence.

That was the opposite of what Doll wanted. He set himself to the task of mending fences.

"Let's forget the part about the boat. If I was right or wrong, it doesn't matter. It's behind us. What's important is that I need you, Ellis. If it got lost in the other argument somewhere, we still want the same thing to come out of this in the end."

"So?"

Any answer, even that, Doll knew, was a partial compromise. The edge in LeCates' voice was there, but the tone had sufficiently softened so as not to make the response combative.

"I need background, Ellis. I can't work without it. I've talked to a lot of people since I've been here. I need your opinions, your impressions. Whatever you can tell me. I need them if I'm going to get anywhere."

"What people?" LeCates asked guardedly.

"Rachael Teal. The Vaughns." Doll listed them off. "Anyone else you think I should know about. Somebody I heard called Covey Wallace."

"Wallace is a tonger." LeCates kept the petulance in his voice.

"That's the one," Doll said, ignoring it. "The way they say 'tonger' seems like it has some special meaning—like fathers ought to set loose the dogs and lock away their daughters."

LeCates didn't laugh, but he looked to Doll as though he had to struggle not to. Doll was willing to settle for that. Coming close was enough.

"Only means you were with the drudgers when you heard it," LeCates said. "Drudgers and tongers both dig for oysters. Drudgers use the skipjacks. Tongers got these rakey things on poles." He demonstrated the mechanism by meshing his fingers, then opening and closing his hands while he kept his arms together at the wrists. "When you figure it out in shares, a man makes about as much one way as he does the other. As best I can see, the difference comes down to temperament. Drudgers like company; tongers don't mind working alone."

"I heard some of that from Page and the others," Doll agreed. "Seems to me there was more than that, though."

LeCates nodded. "The law assigns special grounds to the tongers where the drudgers aren't supposed to go. Which is not to say it doesn't happen sometimes when the marine police aren't too close around. It's been going on for as many years as anybody can remember. A skipjack, in a single pass, can drudge up a whole mess of tonging oysters."

"This tonger Covey Wallace, he's also the one who had the trouble with his land being salted."

"Yeah, I thought you'd get around to that." LeCates glanced over at Doll. "I saw the land. No question but it got salted all right. For the rest, nobody talks about it. That mostly means that, whoever did it, nobody, except for maybe Covey Wallace, wants to know."

" '*Maybe*' Covey Wallace?"

"I figure," LeCates replied, "that maybe Covey Wallace already figures that he knows."

"And Gerry Vaughn?"

"Same thing."

That was right, Doll thought. So far, he knew, it was all familiar.

"Okay, let's try it from another angle," he suggested. "Forget the developers and forget Covey Wallace. Let's say that Carrow was killed for some other reason, something that's altogether away from the problems with the land."

"Other reasons?" LeCates looked doubtful.

"Something that Farron said this morning," Doll explained. "Something vague. Something about something his father did wrong. It could have been Wallace's land, but I don't think so. It was something that seemed to have bothered Farron more particularly, something that seemed to have happened more than once."

LeCates bit at his lip and looked away. "Stay away from it, Doll. It's not what you want. It's got nothing to do with what you're trying to find."

"What doesn't?" Doll stopped himself, barely. He'd come a needle's width away from climbing all over LeCates. "Damn it, Ellis, don't you see you can't know?" Doll pleaded. "Nobody can. That's why it's all got to come out."

"This is dirt, Doll. It's soap opera crap. The last time I heard, you weren't into that kind of entertainment."

"That's the problem," Doll shot back. "A man is dead. Somebody killed him. This damn thing isn't entertainment."

"No. You're right. It isn't," LeCates, accepting the chastisement, replied quietly. He pursed his mouth, postponing his answer, and then he let it all come out.

"LeRoy was getting his ass laid up in Baltimore. Farron found out." LeCates looked away from Doll. "The two of them had what you might call some words about it."

"A fight?"

"One time," LeCates said, nodding, "it wound up like that."

"You're telling me LeRoy had a woman that he went to regular up in Baltimore?"

"Not that way. The whores in the strip bars," LeCates answered distantly. "It's as much the rule around here, as the exception. A couple crews'll get together, go up, and make a night of it every now and then. Farron knew about the custom well enough. He just never saw his father getting into anything like that."

"Elaine?"

LeCates shrugged. "Probably she knew, if she let herself admit it. We're such damn fools sometimes—men are, I mean. Don't know when we got it good, so we piss it away. That's not it, Doll. It wasn't Farron. And it damn well wasn't Elaine."

"If that's true, we're back to the land again." Doll went on talking, more to himself, though he nominally spoke to LeCates. "You were right the last time, Ellis—what you said about where people's bankbooks are. Anybody on the island—anywhere else!—could have had some financial reason. Wesley Mowen and Andy Dowling don't like to say it, but the way they go at it comes down to the same thing."

"You make it sound hopeless," LeCates said tiredly. "All of it comes down to nothing in the end." He gazed out across the empty store, through the screen door, and into the azure distance beyond. "I mean, if we go back to what you first said, we're not even sure if it was even a murder. That's the bottom line, isn't it, Doll? When it comes down to the two big questions, we really don't even know that."

"It's the one thing that we do know," Doll said. For the first time that afternoon, he permitted himself a trace of satisfaction. "Those fittings didn't come loose by themselves. I didn't get much from Ornan Atkins, but I've got his silence to testify to that."

Doll left LeCates in the store. He walked along the road, passing the houses, catching the occasional aromas of evening dinners cooking on the stoves. It wasn't the time of day to go calling, but then, he knew, the visit had to be made.

When, finally, he stood on the step, his emotions were mixed. A large part of him wanted to get the thing over; the rest hoped that Elaine Carrow wouldn't be home.

"Mr. Doll, I didn't expect you." She held the door open, obviously flustered by his presence.

"I know. I should've called first," Doll replied. "I'm sorry. May I come in?"

She stepped back from the door and closed it behind him when he'd entered. Doll listened for the sounds of the girls and heard nothing. Farron's motorcycle, he'd noticed, hadn't been parked in the driveway.

"Are you alone? I know it's a bad time," Doll said. "I'm sorry if it is. I can come back."

"No, it's fine." She shook her head and averted her eyes to the floor. "Please sit down," she invited, and gestured toward a kitchen chair. "The girls are on a school trip today. They won't be home until after dinner. It's Farron's late night at the station. Now, let's see—I offered you soda or a beer before. The last time you didn't want it. I can offer it again."

"No. Thank you." Doll felt anything but comfortable. He rejected the chair in favor of standing. "Look, I came to apologize. Farron came to see me this morning. He asked about me buying the boat. It was a bad story. I never should have used it. I had to tell him it was a lie."

"I know. He called me to tell me," Elaine Carrow said.

"Oh," Doll muttered. He tried to catch her eyes, but she kept them turned away, and so there was nothing for him to meet. "That's all I told him. I didn't tell him you knew anything about it. I didn't tell him anything about what might have happened to your husband. Not that it matters very much. He's started hearing rumors. Anyway, I didn't confirm or deny them. The last thing I meant to do was leave you in an awkward spot."

With an obvious effort, she made herself look at him, as though, despite her own discomfort, she felt compelled to help him. "It wasn't that awkward, Mr. Doll." She smiled weakly. "He told me what you said, and about why people are saying you came here. He asked me about LeRoy being murdered. I told him I knew you hadn't come about the boat and that the rest, for now, was just what you called it. Only rumors."

"He wasn't angry? He accepted that?"

"His pride was hurt. He knew it was only a part of an answer. He's at the age where he wants to be included in everything he thinks of as being adult. He's resentful now, not really angry. In a day or two, he'll be over it, and he'll be fine."

Doll wondered if she was right, or if she really believed herself what she'd said, or if she'd said it only to make the moment easier for him.

"I'm sorry," he repeated.

"It's nothing." Elaine Carrow shrugged it away. "It's not your fault. It isn't anyone's but mine. I'm the one who made the decision to keep things from him. You couldn't have done that yourself. I had to agree. Maybe he's right and I was wrong. Maybe he's past my deciding what's good for him. It's the kind of thing that mothers do and have a hard time stopping."

The smile stopped, and her face turned down again.

"But it tells you something . . . the rumors and all." She turned completely away from him, with an abruptness that surprised Doll, and made a sudden fetish out of doing something with a jar of fresh-cut flowers next to the sink. "Mr. Doll," she said with her back still toward him, "before you take this any further, there's something else you really have to know."

Doll waited.

She turned from the sink and faced him squarely, as though she thought it was an important thing for her to do.

"Ellis LeCates . . . and me," she said quietly. "I suppose you must have heard that just about everyplace you've been."

"Ellis and you? In what way? No, I haven't heard anything."

"Then I can only believe," Elaine Carrow said, "that you're very discreet."

Doll left it open for her to continue or not. He gave her time. In his mind, he conceded the double standard, knowing that he wouldn't have given the same leeway to LeCates. If Elaine declined to go further, he'd move on to any topic he could find that seemed innocuous. Now that she'd begun, it would have to be finished. That didn't mean it had to be finished now.

"Not what you might think," she whispered, trying to explain. "I wouldn't want you to think the worst of me. Please believe me that there was never, never, anything physical between us. Neither of us ever spoke to each other about what there was. But people talk. Oh God, yes, they talk!"

"I'm sorry," Doll said. "I don't mean to pry. But I thought, at first, you were saying one thing, and now I think—I'm not sure that I follow." Then Doll saw the blush in her cheeks, and, all at once, too late, he understood.

"I was married to LeRoy," Elaine said as though the rules that followed from that were clear and forever unassailable. "I was his wife for twenty-three years. I was never unfaithful to my husband, Mr. Doll. Never. I couldn't have been. More than that, I loved him. God, I'm so confused. In so many ways, I still do."

"What you had with Ellis was platonic?"

"I'm afraid I don't even know what that means," Elaine said. "One day it was just there. I went into his store to buy something unimportant. I saw Ellis there, and—God, don't ask me how—I knew that he had feelings towards me. And in that same instant, I knew that I had feelings for him too.

"I never said anything. Neither of us ever did. But it was there, shared between us, and I know we both knew it—at least I think he knew it too. Love and guilt and shame, all wrapped up in one, Mr. Doll. Other people must have seen it. It isn't the kind of thing that gets missed."

"No one's said it to me. Not even a hint," Doll told her.

"Well . . ." She found a tissue and touched it to her eyes, then used another part of it to blow her nose. "Then I'm glad I got it out. I had to tell you. But, please, please don't ever say that I said it. I could never admit to anyone else that the gossip was true."

"Ellis? There are reasons that he has to know."

"Oh, God," she exhaled. "If you have to, yes. I told you, I'm sure that he knows already. But go ahead. Do whatever you have to, Mr. Doll."

Outside again in the failing sunlight, the first thing Doll had to get over was the inconceivable assertion that any woman could find herself in an extramarital infatuation involving Ellis LeCates.

After that, things got harder.

In a world where people regularly take obscene joys in willfully inflicting pain upon one another, what Elaine Carrow had told him sounded to Doll like a confession in search of a sin. By any common standard, it seemed an absurdly small transgression. Or was the guilt that each individual felt the truer scale for the purpose of comparative morality? In the end, Doll rejected the question as unanswerable—and, even if it could be answered, worth less than the effort.

8

It was seven that evening by the time Doll got back to the public room at Millman's Inn. Instead of a table, he took a stool along the bar. The woman who took his order had thin purple lips, a puckered face, and gray-black hair set in curls so tight they gave the appearance of turned wire. She brought the ale and poured it, took Doll's money, and left him alone.

Doll was glad for that. He hadn't come for conversation. For a while, he wanted time to think—time to try to fit into the puzzle the new piece that tied together Elaine Carrow and Ellis LeCates.

He brooded over the ale. He didn't know for how long. The steel-haired woman came by again, and Doll had to test the weight of the bottle to find that it was still half full. He shook his head and tried to empty the remainder into his glass, but found he hadn't drunk enough for the glass to hold all of what was left—which made him all the more surprised when the woman placed a second bottle at his elbow.

In reply to the question she read in Doll's face, she glanced across toward one of the tables. Her mouth turned down in a frown of contempt that left no doubt of her feelings toward fancy-dressed women who went around buying drinks for men.

Rachael Teal waved at Doll from the table.

She was alone, by her own choice, Doll was certain. He was

now, he gathered, expected to remedy that. He took the bottle of ale that she'd bought him and joined her.

"I had to snap you out of it," she said, smiling up at him. "I've been watching you for the past ten minutes. Sitting up there all by yourself, you looked like a man who'd saddled himself with all the most terrible problems of the world."

Her soft brown hair shimmered as she spoke. She let the arch in her eyebrows turn the statements into questions.

"It's the trouble with drinking alone," Doll answered and sat across from her. "There's no stimulation. It makes me sulky. I'll do better now. You can take that as a promise."

"I don't need a promise." She grinned and sipped at her Scotch and soda. " 'Doll.' " She tested the name on her tongue. "I've tried to make it sound right. It fits you in some ways. In others, it's totally wrong."

"It's short and easy to remember," Doll said, but Rachael seemed hardly to hear his reply.

"Even Ellis LeCates calls you 'Doll,' and he's supposed to have known you forever. The word is that the two of you used to work together."

"We used to dive together," Doll replied. "That was a few years ago now. But a long time less than forever."

"It's hard to see LeCates doing anything that physical." Her eyebrows made it a question again. "He looks like packing out cans on the shelves is about the extent of what he could handle."

"Diving's like that. You have to keep at it or else you lose your edge. It takes a lot. Some divers, when they give it up, give up on all the rest as well. When that happens, after a while they lose it all."

"But you keep it all up," Rachael observed.

Doll answered that he had to, that the work he did required it. She asked what the work was. He told her it was mostly underwater construction.

"I take it, then," she said, "that you used to be in the Navy. That's the place where people get trained for work like that."

"Not the only place. But, yes, that's where I got mine."

"And it's also demolition work? It has a lot to do with explosives?"

She let the connection snap shut with all the impact of the steel jaws of a trap. She hadn't closed the circle, quite. The expression she wore remained a mask of casual curiosity. But Doll had no doubt about where the talk was heading. On the small chance he might be wrong, he made a halfhearted attempt at an evasion.

"A lot more oxyacetylene cutting. Most of it's getting rid of wrecks or debris that's blocking the use of somebody's channel."

"In what you do now," Rachael readily conceded. "But in the Navy it's different. You blow up obstructions and things like that. I remember from back in college, one of my roommates went out with a man. . . . Well, that's all ancient history, isn't it? The point is, though, a man who'd been through training like that would know a lot about how and why things explode."

"Things like?" Doll stared across the table, his eyes daring her to make the final point.

"Boats, for example," Rachael Teal said smiling.

Doll twirled the amber liquid in his glass and took a swallow. "Why do I feel like I ought to check to see if I'm still wearing underwear?" he said. "What do I attribute it to—high-level reasoning, or is it just that you've got a few good ears to the ground?"

"A little of both," she said, displaying a measured degree of pride. "I mean, my God, Doll, if you're supposed to be buying Carrow's boat, what are you still doing here? Why all the questions about Carrow—who hated him, who didn't? You don't need to know all that if all you want to do is buy his boat. I can believe curiosity up to a point, but you press the role beyond any possibility of belief."

"Thank you," Doll replied.

"Now don't get yourself all into a funk," she said. "Actually, all that I've said so far is so obvious that it's more or less general knowledge. What I take credit for is the demolitions part. All I had were the two parts I took as fact: one, that you were an accomplished diver, and two, that you were here about something besides Carrow's boat. The rest, the demolitions and the Navy, I put together myself. C'mon. Be fair. You have to give me high marks for that."

Doll tipped the rim of his glass in Rachael's direction.

She smiled again and saluted him back with her Scotch and soda.

"Thank God," she replied. "I was so afraid you were going to be tiresome and insist on denying it all. Then I would have had to be persistent. It could have gotten ugly, and that would have been bad for an acquaintanceship that's only just getting started."

Doll thought about saying that that would have been a shame. Instead, he refrained and let Rachael Teal have her moment.

"So you're here to find out who killed LeRoy Carrow." She pressed her lips together, giving the impression that the revelation had only now started her thinking. "I wonder if that matters to me. I suppose that whether it does or it doesn't all depends upon why."

"Why?" Doll asked. "I mean what's the 'why' that makes the difference?"

Rachael Teal understood and had no difficulty making the clarification. "We both know the answer to that," she said. "If you're here on some odyssey of personal honor or justice or revenge or whatever, the truth is, Doll, that I don't care and I won't get in your way. I have no reason to do anything to stop you. I might even help you if the right time came and I felt in the mood."

Doll noticed that her face no longer held a trace of humor. Her eyes were cool and even. They seemed to collect each nuance in Doll's expression and manner with all the ravenous intensity of a jungle predator that had gone a long time between meals.

"I take it, then," Doll said, "that you didn't have a part in what happened."

"What? To Carrow—assuming he was killed? Do you mean was I in on it with whoever killed him? What's wrong with you? Are you crazy, Doll? Do you really believe that I'd get myself involved with anything as insane as that?"

If Rachael Teal was acting, Doll decided, she was good enough at it to give consideration to changing professions. On the other hand, those who would swallow murder were unlikely candidates to strain at the need to cover the deed with a lie.

"But going back to what would matter to you. . . ." Doll took his turn at smiling and returned, he hoped, the sense of being played. "If why I came here somehow affected your business. . . ."

"Exactly," she answered without an instant's hesitation. "If it's business, if you intend to use Carrow's death or murder or whatever to pick up anywhere near where he left off . . . then I'll show you a piece of demolition work that will make the kind you're used to look like stepping on an anthill."

"You told me the last time we talked," Doll said, "that Carrow didn't do you that much damage."

"Carrow didn't. Maybe you could," she answered. "And listening to all the arguments again is something I'd just as soon not have to get into."

"I told you before," Doll said flatly. "I've got no interest in the economics."

"But you came up with all the right buzzwords—or the wrong ones, depending upon the point of view. But all right, Doll. I'll take your word." She sat back in her chair. The softness was back. Her moods changed capriciously, as though in response to a sudden touch on some unseen button. "Frankly,

I'd be glad if you're not the enemy. You're fun. Handsome even, in an offbeat kind of way." Her dark eyes measured his reaction. "I hope the small dose of flattery won't give you too big a head."

The talk between them stubbornly refused to end. Neither Rachael nor Doll seemed to press it forward, but somehow, almost despite them, it seemed to run on. Rachael had snorkeled once in Florida, and another time in the Bahamas. She remembered species of colorful fish and tried to describe them for Doll to identify until the exchanges turned themselves into a game.

They moved from the fish to the topic of coral, and from there, through a certain intrinsic logic, to shipwrecks and treasure. They argued the merits of the ideological war between the treasure salvors and the underwater archeologists and met on common ground in agreeing that, once the government got into anything, whatever depended on initiative thereafter stopped.

The time slid by. The background noise in the bar got louder. The tobacco smoke got thicker. Or perhaps those were only the excuses that let them find another place to talk.

Doll waited by the head of the dock behind the inn. From where he stood, looking landward, he could see the darkened windows of his room and the soft glow of the yellow light that filtered out through the curtains of the dining room. Twilight was gone. The sky had turned black from east to west. He could barely make out the hazy pinpoints of the stars. The early night still held the warmth of the day. On a bench beside him were two snifters of double cognacs and a small teapot of steaming hot water. The cognacs, the teapot, and the setting all had been Rachael's ideas.

He watched her as she appeared on the path in the mist of the halogen lights around the far side of the building—a graceful, slender shadow in slacks, unmistakably Rachael Teal. As she came close, color emerged. The slacks were gray, the turtleneck sweater a deep shade of blue. Her brown hair appeared black against the night. The contrasting white of her throat and the crimson slash of her lips drew his eye.

"Hello," she said. Her voice took Doll by surprise, as though he hadn't heard its richness before. It was soft and mellow, with a textured, Karen Carpenter resonance.

She glanced down at the bench, then back at Doll. She bent from the knees and swept up the two snifters, then led Doll out along the dock to the far end where the skipjack was tied.

When they both were aboard, she went to the stern. She sat with her back against the wheelbox and made the serving of the cognacs into a ceremony. Pouring the contents of one snifter into the other, she warmed the inside of the empty glass with the steaming water, then, reversing the process, warmed the second glass and divided the cognac between them.

"This is better. Yes, much," she said. She handed Doll one of the glasses. "Breathe it first, then talk to me. I want to know all that's worth knowing about you."

"Uh, maybe I'm wrong about this," Doll said as he glanced around, then looked back at Rachael Teal. "But isn't this somebody's boat?"

"You mean somebody else besides me?" She smiled. "A captain from back toward Easton owns it. He looks like a bear, but, really, he's a pussycat. He buys me a few drinks now and then, and we talk. If it'll make you feel better, I'll tell him the next time I see him that we were aboard. But I can tell you right now, he's not going to mind."

"You don't have a room here at the inn." Doll let the glass of cognac wait for another moment. "Do you want to tell me how you managed the change?"

She blinked and looked around at the night, deliberately taking time with her answer. Putting the rim of the glass just beneath her nose, she inhaled the strong bouquet of the liquor. She rolled a few drops across her tongue, breathed more air across it, and finally swallowed.

"I want to talk about you," she said. "But I'll answer your question on the condition that, after I do, you answer mine."

"Within reasonable limits," Doll agreed.

Rachael seemed to think over the answer and finally shrugged. "I stay at a place that's miles from here. Worlds beyond that wretched little drawbridge. As for the change in wardrobe . . . it's all in the van. The company gives me a van to use. It's full of all kinds of useful things. Soil maps, aerial maps, measuring tapes, a surveyor's transit, all the useful tools of the trade—and clothes suitable for most occasions. I've got the windows curtained, so it makes a satisfactory, if not exactly lavish, place to change. There, now, you see. I hold nothing back. I've been completely open with you. Now you have to tell me everything."

"You really work at the business part," Doll said.

"I do work at it," Rachael answered flatly. "One thing I decided a long time ago was that I wanted to make money. A lot of money. Is that all right with you?"

"How much is a lot?"

"As much as the market will bear." She waited, as though she expected Doll to voice his disapproval. But Doll said nothing. "Money doesn't mean much to you, does it?" she finally asked.

"It means I can eat. Shopping gets to be a drag without it."

"You know what I mean. Be serious. It doesn't seem right to you that somebody ought to come out in the open and say up front they want to make a lot of money. You promised that you'd answer my questions. That's the first one. It's time to keep your word."

"Why does it matter what I think?" Doll didn't breathe his cognac, but he took a small swallow and savored the hotness as the liquid slid down his throat.

"I'm not saying it matters," Rachael persisted. "Only that I'm asking. Why are you afraid of the answer?"

The light was faint, but not so faint that Doll couldn't see the arch in her eyebrows. It didn't matter. He knew it was there. He resigned himself and answered.

"For me time is more important. You only get so much of that, and you can't buy any more. Money can get like quicksand. The size of 'a lot' can keep getting bigger. You start out saying that you want the money to buy things with, and you'll figure out later what you want to buy—instead of asking what you want to buy, and then how much you need to buy it."

"You find things to spend it on."

"I don't doubt you do. But do I want them more than the time?"

Rachael laughed. "So that's your worst case, is it? You make your fortune and die on the day you decide you're going to start spending it." The humor slipped from her face. "You were in Vietnam. I missed that part, didn't I, Doll? You were in 'Nam, and now life seems short, and you're determined to get your share while it's still there."

"Like everybody else," Doll said.

"That's glib and evasive," Rachael answered, but with more gentleness than Doll expected.

"Just rehashed social commentary." He smiled.

"Are you bitter?"

Doll shook his head. "If a person is bitter, it's because he thinks he did a thing that he should have got paid for and didn't. It's the vineyard story from the Bible. I think it's the only parable I ever understood."

"I don't know if I ever understood any, and certainly not that one," Rachael said. "I could understand how a person would be bitter if he'd been there . . . with everything that was happening at home."

"People do what they have to do," Doll answered, looking out to where he couldn't tell the black sky from the water. "I'm not so sure they really have that many choices."

"A philosopher, too?" Rachael shook her head. "I don't understand you, Doll. You're a mystery. Every time I think I do, I keep picking up different signals. You're hard; you're soft. You're a package of unresolved contradictions. I can't figure out who you are."

"That's because you're looking for consistency." Doll met her eyes. "Give it up. You'll drive yourself crazy trying to find it—in me or you or anybody else."

"Stop it, Doll. Just stop it." Rachael pouted and glared angrily out at the black bay. "Now you're patronizing me. Goddamn you! One minute I'm as much as saying I find you attractive. The next I don't know whether I oughtn't to hate you instead."

Doll walked with her around to the front of the inn to where she'd left the van parked. He opened the door and stood aside to let her get in. She stopped midway and looked up at him, and asked if this was how he planned to say goodnight. Doll nodded.

"Too much, too soon," he said, still holding the door.

She eyed him, tacitly challenging his masculinity, taunting him that any inadequacy had to be his and not her own. Finally, she winked to bid him goodnight and pulled closed the door of the van.

Doll stepped back and watched the taillights as she drove out the long, pebbled driveway toward the road.

He carried the snifters and teapot back into the bar. He was thinking about what he might yet be able to order up from the kitchen when he saw George Page coming toward him. Doll glanced around for the rest of Page's usual company, but tonight the captain seemed to be alone.

"Evenin', Mr. Doll," he said by way of salutation. "Be pleased to buy ya a beer, if ya want one." Then, for the first time, he seemed to notice the two glasses. Doll almost thought, for a moment, that Page winked.

"Course I'll understand an' step aside if ya got some better company," Page said slyly.

"None better," Doll answered. "I'll be glad to take the offer of the beer if you don't mind watching while I eat."

"Suits me. Suits me fine." Page turned toward the bar and held up two fingers. "You're a late eater, sure enough, but it's right an' proper that a man should put away his share a' good food."

They found a table. Page carried the beers. A waitress came around and took Doll's order.

"Meat an' potatas, that's a man's meal." Page grinned to reinforce his approval. Doll noticed that the length of Page's facial stubble seemed neither to have grown nor diminished since the first day. "Heard 'bout your talk with Farron, a' course," Page said. "Sorry t' hear, in a lot a' ways, you're not here 'bout the boat. Mainly for the Carrows, but I guess it's okay just so long as they all know an' understand."

Doll chose not to answer the several implied questions, and, after a moment, Page went on.

"Must say ya give a body food for thought, though, Mr. Doll. Thought, myself, that inquest they held on LeRoy back there would've done to settle the matter. Would've thought it, but maybe it ain't so."

"Did it settle it for you?" Doll asked.

"For me? Sure. Sure it did. But things like that, they go right by me. Maybe I'm just too easy t' satisfy. Course, it could've been somethin' else besides an accident. Went aboard LeRoy's boat this afternoon. Thought I owed it to myself to have a look."

Doll asked Page what he found.

"Well, a' course, I didn't have no look around like you did," Page demurred. "Just got myself on an old pair a' pants an' borrowed a swim mask one a' my nephews has got. Didn't do me no good. I never saw nothin'. But I felt, sure enough. I felt around back a' that stove with my hand. Guess you must've, too. Gotta admit you got a point. Hard t' see how LeRoy could've let it go that far."

Page waited, then smiled after a while.

"You ain't much of a talker t'night, are ya, Mr. Doll? Put ya right up there with ol' Ornan pretty soon. Sort a' hoped to get a little more for my beer than it seems like there is to get got."

Doll asked Page what it was he'd expected.

"Oh, shit, I dunno." Page looked down at the table as though he were suddenly embarrassed at having it all so out in the open. "Maybe at least to know if you thought ol' LeRoy was murdered or not. I mean, I can guess al'right from what I found an' from what you've been doin'. But I thought maybe that was somethin' ya wouldn't mind just comin' out an' lettin' a man know."

"I think he was murdered," Doll said. "Bad nose or not—maybe because his nose was bad—I think, from all I've heard, he was too good of a captain to have let that fitting work itself loose."

Page nodded. "Have to agree when it's put like that," he said. "LeRoy Carrow was a damn good captain. Ain't neither body 'round here gonna say a word against that."

"So tell me who wanted to kill him," Doll said.

"Well, now," Page replied through his broadest grin, "that there's the forty-dollar question, ain't it?" Page shook his head and took a swallow of his beer. "No, I wouldn't wanna guess myself into a corner on that."

"You and Ornan Atkins both. We've got a lot of closed-mouthed folks around here."

"Me an' Ornan. That's right." Page laughed. "By the way, since ya bring it up, ya remember t'other night 'bout ya comin' out with us sometime? Well, we's all goin' eelin' tomorrow. Me an' Jerry Lee, an' Ornan's goin' out with Joely Edwards. Come along, if ya like. The invite's still good. Means gettin' up early if ya wanna go an' a goodly drive t' where the eel boats is—up above the Ches'peake Bridge."

"Is there room?" Doll asked.

"Plenty. Wouldn't a' asked ya if there wasn't. An' me, or Ornan, if you like, we each could use a pair a' extra hands."

Doll remembered how close it had come to being a brawl that night in the tavern. It was easy to think how a man might get lost and disappear forever out on that bay.

"Okay, I'd like to go, Captain," he suddenly heard himself saying. "But the questions about Carrow won't stop for that. They'll still all be there tomorrow morning."

"Ain't gonna matter a bit to the eels." Page laughed again. "But I'll tell ya what we'll do, Mr. Doll. Ya start askin' questions on the boat, we'll agree ya git throwed over the side. How's that for fair? Short a' that, we give you free passage, some good fresh eel meat if ya want it, an', if we get lucky, maybe a couple a' bucks t' put in your pocket."

With no warning, Page's face turned serious. He wrapped his hand around the bottom of his beer bottle and, with his thumbnail, scored the center of the label top to bottom—all the while seeming to watch the operation with the intensity of a surgeon making an incision.

"Can I ask ya just one question, Mr. Doll? Ya ain't under no obligation to answer, an' the invite on the eelin's still good either way. It's 'bout that story 'bout ya comin' down here 'cause a' LeRoy's boat. Wasn't your story, was it, Mr. Doll? That story come from Ellis LeCates."

"If it did?"

"I know, I know. I understand what you're thinkin', believe me I do." Page closed his eyes for a second in what Doll took as an attempt to show how distasteful he found the topic at hand. "Ellis LeCates is a friend a' yours—an' ya took his idea, so, naturally, ya don't feel it's right t' throw the blame all back on him. Don't matter. Don't matter a damn whether I know or not. Only important thing that matters is that you do. LeCates brought ya here. Am I right 'bout that? Did he tell ya why he brought ya? I'm no damn gossip—may I drown tomorrow out on that goddamn bay if I am—but this ain't no ordinary situation we got ourselves here. Did he tell ya it all like he should've, Mr. Doll? Did he tell ya he'd got somethin' goin' on between hisself an' ol' LeRoy's wife who now's his widow?"

"It's not something I can talk about," Doll said, "eeling or no."

Page nodded and told Doll he could respect that. He left several minutes later with no more from Doll than the agreement to be outside by four o'clock the next morning.

Doll finished his beer as the waitress brought his dinner. He had her bring a second bottle. He might just as well not have bothered. He found himself back at his brooding again.

9

"Snakin's what it's called." Joely Edwards stared out over the tailgate from the back of Ornan Atkins' pickup. He didn't look at Doll as he spoke. The morning around them was anthracite black, without the smallest hint of the coming dawn. In the low places, they passed through thick patches of ground fog that made Doll feel as wet as though he'd been through a rain. "If Cap'n Page called it eelin'," Joely said, "it's just 'cause he thought that was all you'd understand."

He took a swallow from his beer can.

Doll had declined the beer, in part because of the time of day and in part because it was cold in the back of the truck—colder even than it had been the last time that he'd ridden there. So cold that the three men inside the cab kept the truck's rear window closed.

But, to the watermen, any time and any temperature seemed right. They drank their beer like tap water, choosing the times when they meant to get drunk, but, for the rest, being never drunk and never thoroughly sober.

"Snaking, then," Doll conceded. "Tell me how it's done."

"Crap damn!" Joely swore. Said sharply together, the two words sounded like the crack and ricochet of a rifle bullet. "Meanin' you ain't never been snakin' before? Cap'n Page, he know 'bout that? You're just costin' us money, man. You ain't gonna be worth your weight neither way."

"Something bothering you, Joely?" Doll waited until Joely Edwards turned his head and looked up from the opposite side of the pickup. "Because it seems like you've got some kind of burr up your ass, and I don't believe for one damn minute it's got anything to do with me not knowing a thing about snaking."

"You're so damn smart, go figure it out for yourself," Joely answered.

"All right. It's not so hard," Doll said. "You're like everybody else. You don't like being lied to."

"Goddamn right I don't," Edwards snapped back. "Cap'n Page, he had you right the other night when he was drinkin'. Would've kicked your ass into little pieces back then, if the Captain hadn't decided to make his peace. Can't figure why he had ya come out today. Had my way now, I'd pack your damn suitcase an' drag ya off a' that island behind some fast boat."

"You want an apology—for the lie?" Doll offered. "It was dumb, okay? A stupid idea. But I don't see how you got hurt by it, Joely. If you're gonna get your feathers up every time somebody tries to feed you a line of bull, you're gonna have yourself a pretty adventuresome life."

"And Farron? And his mother? What are they supposed to do with the boat? Did ya ever think what 'bout them?"

"Mind your own business, Joely," Doll said. "What goes on between me and them has nothing to do with what goes on between me and you."

"You say that, not me," Joely Edwards replied hotly.

He turned his face back toward the receding blackness of the highway and drank several more swallows of beer. If he'd shut his mind to what Doll had said, or if he was thinking it over, Doll had no way of knowing.

"Ya don't know shit," Joely Edwards said, turning back to face Doll. "Ya don't know shit 'bout even what you think you're doin'."

Doll knew that just Joely's saying it wasn't enough. Under the rules of masculine argument, a point like that had to be proved. So Doll only waited for Joely to push on and prove it.

"You go around sayin', now, ya think that LeRoy was murdered. Well, you're full a' shit, Doll. Ya know how I know? 'Cause ya can't kill a man in a blowup like that. I mean ya can, a' course. 'Cause it sure enough killed ol' Cap'n LeRoy. But ya can't count on it. That's what I mean. Nine times outta ten it wouldn't a' happened that way. A man that wants to knock somebody off don't settle for a way he's gonna miss every time he tries but one in ten."

"Okay, I'm full of shit," Doll said. The answer was a lot less condescending than it sounded on its face. Joely Edwards was right. Doll had seen the problem before.

"That's it?" Edwards asked incredulously.

"That's it," Doll replied. "You're right. I haven't got an answer to that now. I assume you don't want me to try to make one up to keep you satisfied."

"Could you?"

"I could offer a few maybes. None that would satisfy me," Doll said.

A long time and a long silence passed while the pickup truck bumped on through the predawn night. Joely finished the can of beer and stashed the empty in a plastic bag. More time went by before he dragged out a thermos and poured a portion of coffee into the top/cup. A second cup, which had been enclosed in the first, he filled and wordlessly passed across to Doll.

In the east, the stars got harder to see. Their number declined, though the sky had yet to show any evidence of gray.

Doll looked down at the luminous dial of his watch. They'd been on the road for more than an hour.

"Another forty minutes," Joely said, though Doll hadn't verbalized the question. "Goddamn long time t' bounce on your ass in the back of some damn truck. Trip's the worst part—'specially the mornin' run. Comin' back you're so dog damn tired, it don't seem half so bad."

To make conversation, Doll asked about the radio. Joely shook his head resignedly, then said that Carroll Messick had taken the boombox for the day.

"It's his box," Joely shrugged. "A man can't argue too much with a claim good as that. Ya asked 'bout the snakin' before. The money end of it? How that works? That what ya mean?"

"I don't know any of it," Doll said honestly.

Joely glanced up toward the cab. He seemed to be refreshing his memory on the head count.

"Today, there's seven shares. One apiece for each of us and one apiece for each a' the two boats. Between us all together, if the day's any good, we could bring in maybe a thousand's worth. That's what—a hundred an' forty, a hundred an' fifty bucks each share? My math ain't so sharp in my head, but it comes out t' somethin' like that."

"What's that in eels?"

"In eels? Oh, it's a damn right lot a' eels, sure enough. Five, maybe six hours a' steady work. Your pullin' muscles gonna know they've been pulled. You be all pulled out by the end a' this day."

The sun had been up for just over half an hour when Jerry Lee Godfrey untied the bow line of *Tarrier's Way*. He tossed it to the foredeck, where it made a slapping sound against the weathered marine plywood as it hit. He moved aft along the dock, undid and gathered up the stern line, and took a long, striding step down onto *Tarrier's* deck. Page, at the wheel, pushed the throttle forward. The boat nosed out from the half-collapsing wooden pier.

Ahead perhaps fifty yards, Ornan Atkins idled the engine of the *Jewel III* and waited for Page in the middle of the narrow creek. As *Tarrier* came astern, *Jewel* quickened her pace and followed the stream toward the bay.

The boats were small—smaller than Doll had expected. Page's was slightly the bigger of the two. Doll guessed its length at twenty-two or twenty-three feet. Both were white and very simple affairs, with an adapted automobile engine for power and hardly enough cabin under cover to give two men shelter from a vertical rain.

The engines burbled in the quiet water and reverberated back off the mud walls of the creek. The low, yellow sun turned the white of their wakes into vees of a silvery gold.

Doll waited to be told what to do. Jerry Lee had a bucket tied off to the rail with a rope. He dipped water from the creek, bucket after bucket, and set about filling a large rectangular tank that was kept on the sterndeck. Ahead on *Jewel*, Joely Edwards looked to be doing the same thing.

The mud sides of the creek fell away and leveled into marshgrass. The low chop of the bay began to loom up ahead. As the water opened, the breeze picked up. Doll felt it blow cool on his windward cheek.

"We got sandwiches an' beer an' two gallon thermos jugs a' coffee," Page said from the wheel. "Don't be afraid t' eat up your share, Mr. Doll. Ya get billed alike, whether ya eat up or not. Tell ya what, Jerry Lee, get me up a ham an' cheese an' I'll take a beer. Get yourself somethin', too, an' for Mr. Doll. Don't just bring. Make sure an' ask 'im what he wants."

Jerry Lee turned to Doll and stared at him expectantly. Doll asked what kind of sandwiches they had. Jerry Lee turned back toward Page.

"We got ham an' cheese," Page called over the noise of the engine, "an' roast beef, some kind a' bologna stuff, an' jus' plain cheese. Take your pick. If we got what we ordered, we got three of each. Usually, a hand takes one now, another when we break midmornin', then the other two for lunch."

Doll said that seemed like a lot of sandwiches.

Page laughed and said that Doll would still be hungry when those were gone.

"We gonna put ya t' work t'day, for sure," he said still laughing.

"Make it a cheese then—and a beer," Doll said.

"Hear that, Jerry Lee? That's a plain cheese an' a beer for Mr. Doll. Get it right now, an' don't forget yourself. You're gonna have t' open 'em up t' find out what from which."

"Yessir, Cap'n." Jerry Lee went forward and opened the red picnic hamper they'd brought on board from the pickup. He rummaged awhile, then tossed Doll back a can of beer. Page's he opened and took to the captain's station at the wheel. He brought the sandwiches around. Doll got the plain cheese that he'd asked for.

They were clearing the mouth of the creek by then. At the same moment, without a word of communication between them, the two captains throttled up. Their twin bows cut the bay chop, sending showers of spray astern at more or less regular intervals. Doll had to move several feet forward to avoid it. By then the sun was becoming warm. The bay breeze and wind from the forward motion of the boat made for a comfortable combination. On the right day—Doll took it as one of the central truths of his being—a boat on open water has no rival.

"Fifteen or so minutes now," Page said with his mouth partly full of ham and cheese sandwich. "Ya can see jus' in the crotch a' those two bars over there. Probably can't make the pot marks yet. Could if ya had glasses. Ornan'll go by those. His first set's a little short a' three hundred yards further on."

"What do I do?" Doll asked again.

"You?" Page laughed. "What do you do? Well, we'll have to see 'bout that, won't we now? You know either thing 'bout how t' cull snakes? You culled a whole lot a' snakes before?"

"Never a one." Doll was sure his answer didn't matter. He figured Page had it all thought out and was just going to take his own good time to get it said.

"No cullin', eh?" Page clicked his tongue a few times. "Well, I guess ya could steer. You've handled a boat before, I reckon. But then, you'd have to know how the pot lines run. Can't know that, an' I can't take the time as ya go t' tell ya. That'd just be a waste of a man. So's I reckon that don't leave a whole lot."

"I haul," Doll said.

"That's right, by God. You haul." Page finished the last of his sandwich and laughed even louder than before. "I steer. You haul. An' ol' Jerry Lee here culls. We all work our asses off, an' maybe we get us a good damn load a' snakes."

On almost exactly the fifteen minute mark, Page cut *Tarrier's* engines and the boat began to slow.

"See that marker there? See it?" he yelled. It was coming up at a walker's pace along the portside bow. "Hook it now. Jerry Lee, hook the first one for 'im. That-a-boy, lad. Hook it for 'im now. Show 'im the way it's supposed to be done."

Jerry Lee had the boat hook in his hands. He took a long step in front of Doll, snagged the line and lifted it high out of the water. At the same time, in the same motion, he flipped it onto a broad-channeled pulley.

"Now pull, Mr. Doll. Haul that sucker's ass off. Haul that line. Break your back. Bring on up all a' those squirmin' snakes."

Doll pulled. It began as easy work. He was hauling line with almost no weight and was aided by the boat's moving forward along it. Then the work grew, first by the weight of one pot and then by the weight of the five more that followed it. The first pot broke the surface of the water. The bottom end was full of a single, green, writhing tangle that looked to Doll like the incarnation of a faceless, green-haired Medusa.

At the moment the first pot reached the pulley, Jerry Lee snatched it away. In a series of moves so fast and so well executed that Doll couldn't follow them, much less have duplicated them, the mate released the thrashing mass into a cull box stretched across the rectangular tank. The pile exploded into a score of slithering, streaking individuals. Doll had no time to look at anything more. The second pot was visible just below the surface of the water.

They ran through the six pots, then six more lines of five or six pots each before the pace slackened. By then, Doll had the timing down to where he could pace himself to the system. Doll had the muscle job—no skill required except for snagging the line. All the rest was sweat and pull. Jerry Lee had the arty part. In the short time that the length of the line and the speed of the boat allowed the eel pot to stay on the deck, Jerry Lee had to open and empty it, restock it with cut-up horseshoe crab bait, and get it over the side again before the next pot appeared at the pulley. The rate at which things happened depended on how Page handled the boat, which he, in turn, had to measure according to the capabilities of his crew.

Doll found that Joely Edwards had been right about the pulling. In the first run of lines, it all happened so fast that Doll had no chance to notice the strain. After that, he fell into a rhythm, and it all seemed natural and very much easier. It wasn't until near the middle of the morning when his arm and back muscles began to feel the effects of the accumulated exertion. When the break for the second sandwich came, Doll felt like he needed both the food and the rest.

Jerry Lee sat forward, alone on the bow. Doll and Page sat aft.

"Well, Mr. Doll," Page said as he opened his can of beer. "For a while, you hauled pretty damn good for a man who ain't no regular snaker. Ya see all them damn snakes we got? Hate them damn suckers worse'n the devil, I do. But, oh, they make some beautiful money. Nice long green, just like them damn snakes. We do this good the rest a' this day, we gonna have ourselves one beautiful snake day."

"That mate of yours," Doll said, "has got the fastest hands I've ever seen."

Page half smiled. "He's good at cullin' arsters, too. He can take the helm when he has to. What he knows, he knows, an' he knows what he don't know. He's maybe not the one ya want t' sail ya up with them big boats in Bal'mer, but what he learns, he does real good. An' you're right 'bout what you said. He sure as the devil's in hell can handle them pots."

When they got back to the island, it was already late in the afternoon. Ornan Atkins stopped the truck and dropped Doll off at the driveway to the inn.

Doll went to his room. The first thing he did when he got there was to shed his watch and shoes and empty the pockets of his pants. He turned on the shower, regulating the water to as hot as he could stand it, and climbed into the tub clothes and all.

For a long, long while he did nothing but stand there. The nearly scalding water cascaded onto his head and sluiced down from his clothing in sheets. His shirt and pants clung to him. The fabric stank of a mixture of eels and sweat. White clouds of steam billowed up and rose around him, then boiled out through the open space between the top of the shower curtain and the ceiling.

Gradually, he peeled off the pants and shirt along with his socks and underwear and kicked the sodden laundry to the back of the tub. Then he stood in the rush of the water again. He still smelled of eels and sweat, but less so. His muscles were every bit as sore as Joely Edwards had promised.

By the time he was clean and dressed again, he was ready for his meeting with LeCates.

Ellis LeCates was at the back table, this time with a bottle of lemon soda. The store seemed to want for regular hours. It was open or closed—or sometimes at a state halfway between—depending upon LeCates' particular whim of the moment. He looked up and saw Doll, then looked him over closely.

"I see you got yourself some sun today," he said. "I heard that you'd been out on the water."

"Snaking, they tell me they call it," Doll answered.

"Filthy business from what I've heard." LeCates wrinkled up one side of his face. "Slimy bastards. I don't see how a man could stand to touch 'em, much less eat 'em. So you went out snaking. What did you get for all your trouble?"

"A hundred and fifty-eight dollars," Doll said. "From what they tell me, that counts for a pretty good day."

"Not what I meant. As you damn well know. What did you find out about Carrow?"

Doll took the opposite chair. "Nothing of any interest. Carrow's name barely even came up."

"Then what the hell did you go there for?" LeCates demanded. "I can't believe you get your kicks from feelin' up a bunch of filthy eels."

"Maybe I like the honest work. Maybe I needed the money." Doll had gauged the remark to draw a sneer, so he wasn't surprised when he got it. "We've got something we've got to talk about, Ellis. It's not going to get any easier if I keep on pushing it off."

"Then don't," LeCates said. His voice sounded indifferent.

"I'm going back to the day I got here. I asked you then, and you told me eye to eye that it wasn't you who killed LeRoy Carrow."

"So?" LeCates contained any evidence of excessive attention, but Doll noticed that he slid his newspaper aside.

"So you didn't say anything then about you being involved with Carrow's wife."

"Involved! What the hell do you mean by that, goddamn you, Doll? Elaine's a decent woman. Keep her the hell out of this."

"Can't be done," Doll said quietly.

LeCates pointed a stocky finger in Doll's face. "I don't doubt you can kick my ass these days. I know you were supposed to be some kind of hotshot in the service, so maybe you could've on the best day I ever had. But you keep that up and, goddamn you, Doll, I'm gonna have to make you try."

Doll slammed the table with his fist. The table was cardboard and lighter then he'd thought. It jumped about two inches into the air. LeCates' soda bottle toppled, spilling its hissing contents over the top.

"Don't bullshit me, Ellis. You're done pulling crap on me. And I'm done coddling your ass," Doll warned. "You're not so dumb that you don't know this island is one goddamn big public address system. You knew all along that, one of these days, somebody would hit me with that bit of news. As far as I can see, you're either a killer or a pathological liar or maybe both."

"I didn't kill Carrow," LeCates insisted. "And I never did anything immoral with his wife."

"You had an interest in her," Doll countered. "You're not denying that?"

"I never touched her, Doll."

"I asked you if you had an interest."

"I liked her. All right, more than liked." LeCates looked away. "I don't know what you'd call it. Love? Between a man and a woman how do you have that without there being anything physical? We never even talked about it. I never said a word to her. Maybe it's the first thing I ever did that I wasn't selfish about. So there it is. Whatever it was, nothing came out of it. So what can the blabberers make out of that?"

"Try motive," Doll suggested.

"Try what?" LeCates seemed not to understand.

"I mean whatever came from it, it gives you a tailor-fitted reason for wanting to see LeRoy Carrow dead. If this thing gets stirred up again, you're the first one that the cops are going to come to. You're not stupid, Ellis. You must have known that, too. So why would you use a stick to prod a hornets' nest when you're the one who's got the biggest chance of getting stung?"

"Because I didn't kill LeRoy Carrow," LeCates answered.

"But people have to believe that."

"I don't care about people, Doll. Haven't you figured that out by now? All I care about is what Elaine Carrow thinks. Her husband is dead. I didn't kill him, but that doesn't change that he's dead. That ought to clear the way for me, except that I still can't say what I feel."

"Because," Doll said, "you think that she thinks you killed him."

When LeCates spoke again, he spoke softly. "I told you, Doll. She's a very loyal woman. I don't think she believes that I killed LeRoy. I don't think she could even talk to me if she really thought that. At the same time, I know deep down that she can't be absolutely sure. She trusts because that's a part of her, but she can't know. You understand that, Doll?"

"But if I do my job, if I find whoever did kill LeRoy, then she has to know it wasn't you."

LeCates nodded. "No matter how much she might believe in me, as long as there's that doubt, I couldn't go to her the way I want to. There'd always be that between us. Something we couldn't set aside, couldn't ever even talk about. That's why I need you to clear me, Doll. I had to be cleared of Carrow's murder—even when it wasn't a murder. Even when I was never so much as accused."

"At whose expense, Ellis?" Doll asked.

"What d'you mean?" LeCates looked blank.

"You get off the hook, somebody else gets on it." Doll kept the explanation slow to let him read LeCates' reactions. So far, there was none that he could see. LeCates' face reflected only his continuing uncertainty. "LeRoy's nights up in Baltimore. A lot of tension in that house. Farron's reaction. Maybe even Elaine's? Suppose it came out that way, Ellis? That would be about a hundred and eighty degrees from what you want."

"You're crazy, Doll. That's not what happened. A man and his son had a fight. That's all!" LeCates answered. But the words were hushed and the skin of his face had gone to a shade that was nearly white.

"I'm not saying it is," Doll replied. "Only that it's something else that could've been. I told you when this started, Ellis. That's the problem with these things. The more you look, the more you find. Everybody's got skeletons. What you find when you look isn't always what you want."

"Suppose that was true, Doll—if it turned out to be Farron, let's say—what would you do?"

Doll frowned and replied the only way he could. "I don't

know," he said. "It's a bridge I haven't wanted to cross. Let's just hope it's a question I don't have to answer."

For a long moment, they both stood waiting, Doll waiting for LeCates to respond, LeCates apparently waiting for Doll to continue. Finally, both seemed to realize that there was nothing more for either man to say.

"I'll be taking another look at the land angle." Doll spoke, as much as anything else, to break the petrified silence. "I'll be at the county seat tomorrow. Maybe there's something to find in the property transactions. I don't believe it, Ellis, so don't hold out much hope. But it's one more place I ought to look."

LeCates nodded. Doll doubted he'd even heard what Doll had said.

10

"Mr. Doll."

The voice was as faint as a distant bird's call, so faint that Doll's conscious mind never heard it.

His thoughts were focused elsewhere. The day in the county clerk's office in Easton had yielded exactly the nothing he'd expected. He'd come away with a stronger sense for the historic local names and the dramatic impression that those names, year after year, formed a sharply decreasing percentage of the tax lists. The new names had different sounds. They might have been randomly drawn from a Washington or a Baltimore phone book. Several were corporate entities. Many more had their tax bills sent to other than local addresses.

No surprises in that. The records only confirmed what everybody already knew. That was what Andy Dowling had been telling him. That evening's meeting, Doll was sure, would say all the same things again.

He tried to put it all into perspective as he walked. But, as he approached the front of the school, the images of people began to intrude.

Most of the faces he saw were still anonymous. Many were people he knew by sight from the inn or who had passed him on the highway, faces vaguely familiar, but to which he couldn't put names.

Others he recognized. Wesley Mowen, Ardee Vaughn. Carroll Messick and George Page stood talking under one of the trees. Andy Dowling mixed with the crowd on the walkway. It was ten minutes before the meeting was to start, and the night was too warm to spend the extra time inside.

"Mr. Doll," the voice called again.

This time it rose just enough to be audible over the breeze. Doll turned in its direction and saw Elaine Carrow walking quickly toward him.

"Oh, thank God, Mr. Doll," she whispered when she was closer. "I called the inn because I didn't know where else to call. I didn't know where you might be. But Wesley Mowen said he'd heard by way of Andy Dowling that you might be coming here."

"What's wrong, Elaine?" Doll asked.

She hesitated, glancing first toward the highway, then down at the grass.

"Here, let's get ourselves out of the spotlight," Doll said. He led her north along the highway in the direction of the store. He felt the stares and wondered if Elaine felt them too. He glanced at her, and stopped wondering. She kept her eyes fixed on the ground and her hands knotted protectively across the pit of her stomach as she walked.

"The hell with them. Let them think whatever they want to think," Doll said.

She nodded. Bravely, he thought, under the circumstances. The people behind them were nothing to him. To Elaine Carrow, they were all the world she knew.

Dusk began to deepen into darkness. The time for the meeting to start came and passed. The crowd in front of the school dwindled and finally disappeared inside, leaving Doll and Elaine alone beside the road, beneath the shelter of a centenary oak.

At last she looked at him. Her voice still wasn't strong.

"What we talked about the last time. What you said you wouldn't tell. You haven't told anyone, have you, Mr. Doll?"

"I told you I'd have to talk with Ellis."

"But no one else."

Doll shook his head.

"Thank God. Oh, thank God." She breathed audibly. "Farron just called. He said things. . . . He sounded as though there was something he'd heard."

Doll touched her arms to try to reassure her. "I'm sorry. I wish I could tell you that's not possible," he said. "But you were right about the rumor. I'm sorry, but it's there."

She closed her eyes and breathed again, then stood in abject silence. "You said you spoke to Ellis?" she suddenly asked, as though she'd only then heard that part of what Doll had said. "What did he say?"

Doll tried a little smile. "The same thing you did. Plus that he wanted me to come here to clear his name. He didn't think he could say what he wanted to you any other way."

"He's so foolish sometimes." Elaine smiled for an instant, then turned her attention back to the dark, featureless ground.

Doll didn't try to reply. He heard the sound from out on the highway, the high-pitched drone of a two-stroke motor escalating rapidly into a scream. It could have been a lot of things. So how was it, Doll wondered, he knew before he ever looked up what it was?

Over Elaine's shoulder, he stared into the beam of light from the single, rushing headlamp. He heard the popping sound of the decelerating engine and the brief squeal of brakes before the tires of the cycle rolled off the pavement and onto the shoulder. This time, Farron dismounted the bike.

"I suppose I should have figured on the two of you together." He raised his voice, making his words clear over the chatter of the machine. "What's going on?" he asked his mother. "Or maybe I should ask you?" he said, spinning on Doll.

"What happened since yesterday morning, Farron?" Doll stepped into the middle of the fight, though there was nothing he could do aside from trying to draw off Farron's fire. "I thought we had things squared away for now."

"Yeah, all squared away. Seems 'squared away,' f' you, means all lies and more secrets, Mr. Doll. Seems like twice now I called ya out, and twice ya lied your way back into making me trust you. Well, I'm no three-time fool, so you just stay the hell out of what's none a' your business. This is all between my mother and me—us and your friend, that son of a bitch. It is LeCates, ain't it, Ma? I mean, maybe there were others, but that's the only story I hear going around."

Doll held himself physically in check. "If nobody here speaks another word or does another thing," he said rigidly, "you're going to regret those last words you said for the rest of your life."

"No, please, Mr. Doll. Stay out of this," Elaine said firmly. "Farron's right. This is something between me and him. It's our business. Family's. No one else's. So please, let it be like that if it's got to go any further."

Farron clapped his hands together in a slow, caustic round of applause. "Great idea. A little late," he lashed out. "You and LeCates. My father and every filthy, goddamn whore in Baltimore. I took your goddamn part, you know. How the hell dumb does that make me? I didn't know what everyone else knew. Hell! The whole damn island knows."

"Then they know about something that never happened," Elaine Carrow said.

"Sure. They all got the same filthy, rotten imaginations." Farron's eyes were hot and glazed.

Elaine shook her head, then seemed to make herself stare back at her son. "I never, ever was with any man except your father," she said quietly.

"Except LeCates."

"Not Ellis LeCates. Not anybody, ever," she repeated. "If you want me to swear that on the Bible, I will."

Whatever answer Farron intended died in a stutter of frustrated rage. His fists were white, his face blotched red despite his tan. His eyes clouded. The traces of tears began to form in the corner pockets near his nose. He swore an oath, half aloud and half under his breath—at his mother, his father, at Doll, at himself, at LeCates, at the world.

He swung onto the seat of the bike and kicked up the stand in one violent motion. The engine roared. The sand and pebbles flew, and the bike sped off north toward the drawbridge and out into the blanketing hollow of the night.

"Oh, God, what else can there be?" Elaine whispered. "I sensed it on the phone. I sensed it building today whenever I talked to him. I don't know when he first heard it. Last night, maybe. Maybe this morning. Why does that surprise me? I knew it had to come. Sooner or later, it had to."

"He'll come around. It may take awhile, but he will. Life can get to be a lot sometimes. You said it yourself. It's not a good age for perspective."

"He's so young. He hides things, keeps them to himself. I suppose that's why he has to be protective. He has to deny what he can't bring himself to understand."

Doll knew Elaine didn't expect any response. He offered a partial one anyway. "And when he can't deny it, he explodes," he said. "There isn't anything for you to blame yourself for." He held her by the arms again. "I want to apologize, too. I'm more sorry than I can tell you for anything I had to do with bringing that on."

"You? You're the one caught in the middle of this." Elaine sniffed back the heavy wetness that began to grow behind her eyes. "It all happened before you ever came here. All you've done is let it come out."

All true, Doll thought, for as far as it went. He didn't bother to explain that this wasn't the first time he'd made this kind of thing happen. He could tell himself, and even make himself believe a little, that the overall effect was salutary, but he also had to admit that it caused a lot of disproportionate pain along the way.

The room where the zoning meeting was held was one of those gym-cafeteria-auditorium combinations that have been the staple of American elementary school construction since more or less the middle nineteen-fifties. The folding chairs were easy to count. They were arranged in two precise rectangles, each ten chairs across and five rows deep. About a third of the seats were filled. Another handful of men eschewed the chairs, preferring, instead, to observe the proceedings from vantage points along the walls.

In front of the chairs were two double-length cafeteria tables. The five-member board, four men and a woman, sat behind them. A second woman, whom Doll took for the clerk, sat off to one side with a note pad, some oversized books, and a brace of sharpened pencils.

There were no microphones, no name plates for the members. The whole arrangement seemed very low key. One man in the front row of the audience wore a business suit. Andy Dowling had on a jacket and his flag pin but had pocketed his tie. Everyone else, the board included, kept to the simple, casual wear that, except for the most special occasions, was the commonly accepted standard for the island.

As Doll came in, the man in the suit was standing as he addressed the board.

". . . and, in that event," he continued, "could have gone ahead without seeking any variance whatsoever. What the petitioner is asking, Mr. Chairman, is only what he feels is in the obvious interest of the community as well as his own. If I may review . . ."

"Not necessary, not necessary, Mr. Clement."

The man who spoke sat in the center chair behind the bank of tables. He was short and pudgy, with a balding head and a cherubic face that seemed on the point of making a joke. He had a kind of whimsical charm, and vivid, rapidly moving eyes that announced he wasn't anybody's fool.

"I'll summarize the board's understandin' just t' make sure we're all in agreement on the facts an' what your client is askin':

"We're talkin' about the Hoxey parcel up toward the point along the highway. Three-point-six-six acres. Your client, Mr. Jarwaenahl, has held the land free and clear for—what is it?—eight years, Doris?"

The clerk checked her book and nodded.

"Taxes are paid through end a' June. Your client wants to subdivide. He's got enough width so he can do that in two lots with no variance. He wants to do four. But he can't because the back two won't have road frontage. He proposes to build a road at his own expense, meetin' our requirements and subject to approval and acceptance upon completion.

"His argument is that he makes more on the sale of the lots an' we make more on the taxes. Everybody benefits. That about the way he breaks it out?"

Clement stood again to answer. "Yes, sir. That's my client's proposal," he said and sat down.

"All right, then," the chairman said, leaning back from the table. "The floor is open to motions or discussion."

"Yeah. I got a question for the lawyer." The board member who spoke didn't wait for any further recognition from the chair. "That Hoxey land has always been half swamp. What the hell's he plan to do for septic?"

"Mr. Clement?" the chairman said.

"Thank you." The lawyer rose again and addressed himself to the member who had asked the question. "Thank you for reminding me on that point, Mr. Weller. If I can submit these. . . ." He handed a thin sheaf of papers to the chairman. "I believe there are copies enough for all the members. You can see there we've foreseen the problem and worked out the details with the land and water resources people. Approval of the variance will include the stipulation that all deeds for the lots include the provision that any septic system built on the land must conform to these approved specifications. That gives assurance in advance that any system installed will be more than adequate."

"That could mean four new families," another member said. "Four new families all out of our hands. You never know what you're going to get."

"I'll tell you this," a third member replied. "With the price that Jarwaenahl's gonna ask for those lots, they sure ain't gonna be on welfare."

A general titter ran through the audience. The chairman didn't call for order.

"You don't know that." The second member spoke again. "Price a' the lots isn't no guarantee. Suppose somebody buys a lot an' puts a summer place on it? Then they rent it out for the winter. Won't be good money in that. It's hard to rent down here for the winter. Owner's gonna have to take whatever folks he can get."

"Still a new house there," the third member persisted. "Owner's got to pay the tax on that. That's that much less has got t' be paid by you an' me."

"An' suppose whoever he rents it to comes out here with half a dozen kids? How much is that gonna cost up at the school? Suppose one of them kids needs special attention? Happened over on the western shore where it cost the school district twenty-four thousand for one year for one kid alone."

"I don't believe that," the third member said.

"Believe it or don't, it happened!"

The chairman turned to the lawyer. "Harvey," he asked, "I wouldn't ask ya t' speak against your client's interest, but can that story 'bout the twenty-four-thousand-dollar kid be true?"

"It's possible, but very unlikely," Clement said, standing again. "If the child had some condition that required placement at a specialized school. . . . But even on the remote chance that could happen here, it would be the county school district and not the island that would bear the cost."

The chairman recognized a man from the audience.

"But we'd all wind up payin' for it, I guess," the man said. "We ain't the western shore over here. Them folks come down with their city ways. They want all this an' that, what we all got along without for all these years. Then they come t' meetin's like this 'un an' say they want all nice streetlights an' sidewalks. Reckon that's so's their pedigree dogs won't have to crap in the dark an' get hit by the cars in the streets."

"Thank you, Henry. Thank you." The chairman ended the buzzing by wrapping a plastic pen on the formica surface of the table. "Anything else from the board?" he asked.

"Yes, I've got something else." The member who had asked about the septic fields spoke up again. "Now I've seen the lawyer's plat an' all, but I'd a' like t' have seen it before tonight. I can't say I got a real feel for how that land is gonna look. I can't see how I could vote tonight one way or t' other in any kind a' good conscience. I'd need to go down an' have myself a see."

"We can postpone our vote," the chairman said. "Before we do, if we're going to, I'd like to give Mr. Jarwaenahl's lawyer a chance to respond."

Clement stood to say he had no objection.

"I don't know if we need to postpone," the second member said. "I think we have what we need to know. I'd like to see us vote now."

The chairman's humor showed signs of beginning to fade.

Doll was aware of the humidity on his skin and the dampness of the perspiration along the spine of his shirt. The muscles in his back and arms still felt the effects of yesterday's work on Page's eel boat. Meanwhile, the wheels of parliamentary procedure ground on slowly. Interest throughout the audience waned.

Doll glanced around the room. Andy Dowling had found a prominent seat at the inside end of the aisle in the second row of chairs. George Page and Carroll Messick stood together against the opposite wall.

Doll found Rachael Teal. She sat alone on the outer edge of the right-hand block of chairs. Her clothes were muted, a loosely fitted pair of denim slacks and a white blouse with a modest neckline and equally modest princess sleeves. She sat with her arm stretched lazily along the back of the adjacent chair. She watched and listened. Her face showed attention, but no hint of any emotion. She reminded Doll of a seeded athlete, come to watch the performances of lesser players who, nevertheless, might one day turn out to be the competition.

People began to twist in their seats. Others filtered outside to where a breeze made the warm air seem cooler. Doll joined the ranks of the wanderers.

The night air outside the school was pleasant, or became so once Doll got beyond the pall of smoked tobacco which hung in the immediate vicinity of the door. He estimated a dozen people, then revised the count upward to include the few more that had followed him out. They divided themselves into couples and small groups. The talk was light, much of it sprinkled with laughter and not much at all concerned with the debate that continued to wear on inside.

Doll began to wonder how Elaine Carrow was getting through the evening. He considered the merits of stopping by the house. To do what? Add more to the scandal? What could he do that he hadn't done already? He'd said all the words there were to say. Say them again? Maybe just be there to listen—or just be there. Ellis LeCates should be there. Or maybe that was the worst idea of all.

Doll's peripheral vision picked up the shape of the man coming toward him. He was young, Doll's height or a little taller, with a medium-boned, muscular build. He wore a pair of peach-colored slacks, a shirt that looked like a pastel patchwork cloth, and gold-rimmed, amber-tinted sunglasses. Doll mentally added twenty years and forty or fifty pounds, and came up with a fair approximation of Ardee Vaughn.

"Doll, I wanna talk to you," the man said from a distance, loudly enough to make his voice carry. "I don' know what you think you're doin', but you're not gonna pull any crap that's gonna involve me."

He stood before Doll breathing deep but evenly. His face had a pinkish hue that Doll attributed to equal parts of vodka and adrenalin.

Doll held up his palms. "Easy, Gerry. You've got my attention—mine and everybody else's. Take it slow. Say what you've got to. I'm not going anywhere before you finish."

"You know me, eh? Well, good for you. Don't make me any promises, Doll. I already know you ain't goin' anywhere." His right hand snapped out and landed a solid push at Doll's left shoulder. Doll took it, using a backward step to absorb the blow.

"C'mon. Come back at me, you bastard," Gerry Vaughn

invited. "You're a pretty big man when it comes to shootin' off your mouth. Let's see how good you are with your hands."

"You keep this up, you're going to make a fool of yourself," Doll said.

Vaughn pushed at Doll again, but this time Doll evaded his hand.

"You think you can run from this? You can't," Vaughn threatened. "You've been bad-mouthin' me, Doll. You've been askin' questions and makin' suggestions—makin' a big goddamn thing about that fight I had with Carrow. You're a man who's got a lot to learn about mindin' his own business. And, if nobody else is gonna do the job like it ought to be done, I guess that's gonna leave it up to me t' teach you."

Vaughn shot a right uppercut aimed to catch Doll in the stomach. Doll sidestepped and watched Vaughn's surprise as his fist cleaved through nothing but empty air. Vaughn's face turned a deeper shade of pink. He put his hands on his knees, drew in a breath, and glared.

The small groups and couples, Doll noticed, had begun to congeal into a ringside crowd.

"You think you're gonna get fancy on me?" Vaughn's voice was low, almost inaudible. "No chance, buddy. No fuckin' chance. Let's see how good you get away from this."

He came at Doll like a well-trained lineman, legs driving, shoulders starting at the level of the knees, then moving in an arc upward toward the pelvis. The trouble was that the maneuver anticipated impact at a point. Beyond that point, the charging body got out of balance. Doll backed off a few steps, then pushed down on the midpoint between Vaughn's shoulders. Vaughn's equilibrium collapsed, and he slid on his chest across the moist earth.

He got up panting. The shirt and peach slacks were streaked with grass stain and dirt. His chin and forearms were streaked with abrasions. The amber-tinted glasses were gone.

"Goddamn fucking son of a bitch," Vaughn roared. He came at Doll flailing like a wild man, the way, Doll supposed, he must have come at LeRoy Carrow that night at the inn when it had taken three men to hold him back.

Doll did the only thing he could think of to do. He dropped in and under the blows, letting the worst of them pound on the flat of his back. At the same time, with measured accuracy, he slammed his fist precisely into the center of Gerry Vaughn's solar plexus.

Doll heard the huge outrush of air expelled from Vaughn's lungs as he ducked out from under.

With the support of Doll's crouching body removed, Vaughn slipped to his knees and tried to breathe, but, as of yet, his paralyzed diaphragm stubbornly declined to cooperate.

Doll waited as he watched Vaughn fighting to recover.

The crowd at ringside waited, too.

Breath returned, shallow and gasping. Vaughn struggled to his feet. He turned toward Doll. His jaw was set, and his stare fixed. Doll saw in his eyes the cold determination to set aside the pain.

It was strange, Doll thought, how, in another context, that same determination would be regarded as heroic. But here it was madness, anger risen to the level of insanity. He set himself, knowing that Gerry Vaughn was going to try him again. He tried to imagine what, short of knocking him senseless, it was going to take to stop Ardee Vaughn's son.

In the same moment, the man in the flat-brimmed hat came up on Vaughn from behind.

11

The handcuff snapped around Gerry Vaughn's left wrist before Vaughn even realized that anyone was near him. The trooper's baton was through the other cuff. He swung Vaughn like a man at the end of a short rope, keeping himself at the center and using the speed and the leverage until Vaughn's legs, unable to keep pace, collapsed and sent him sprawling forward on his knees.

"Easy, Gerry. Get up and I'll have to run you around the yard again," the trooper said matter-of-factly.

Vaughn glared at at him, breathing hard. He glared, but he made no effort to regain his feet.

The trooper let it stay that way, giving the tension and spontaneity of the moment the chance to subside. Doll watched him, studying the deliberate way he put it all together. The officer's height, his emphasized composure, the crispness of his uniform, all combined to assert his control. He wore a corporal's stripes on his sleeve. The tag over the flap of his pocket gave his name as Unruh.

"Are you done, Gerry?" Unruh asked.

Vaughn temporized, then did the only reasonable thing that he could do. He nodded.

"Good decision," Unruh said mirthlessly. "All right, then, get on your feet. Let's take a walk over to the cruiser."

"You're not gonna arrest me?" Vaughn asked sharply. He glared up again, and his muscles seemed to tense. Doll wondered if his hostility was enough to launch him on a second doomed offensive.

"Don't know yet," Unruh answered, seeming not even to notice the renewed signs of aggression. "Depends on how our talk comes out. You're not making conditions, are you, Gerry? 'Cause that might just make up my mind."

Vaughn shook his head once from side to side, like a lion trying to dispel the flavor of a piece of bad-tasting meat. His body quieted again.

Unruh glanced across the lawn to where Doll was standing. "You too," he said. "You're half a' this. You wanna come along this way, please."

With the highlights of the show over, the audience began to turn its attention back to where it had been before the performance had begun. By the time Doll, Unruh, and Vaughn had gotten to the police cruiser, the trio commanded only marginal attention and that from a much greater distance. Unruh put his baton away. He left the open handcuff dangling from Gerry Vaughn's wrist.

He took an unhurried moment to conduct a visual inspection of Doll, then directed his attention back at Gerry Vaughn.

"I tell you, Gerry," he said shaking his head, "how long you figure it's gonna be before you start to grow up?"

Vaughn's immediate reply was a sullen stare. He glanced belligerently in Doll's direction, then toward the trooper. "You don't know what he'd been sayin' about me," Vaughn answered. "I don't have to put up with shit like that from him or nobody else."

"So what did you figure to do?" Unruh asked stone-faced, "keep poundin' on him till you beat yourself into the ground?"

"I could've taken him," Vaughn objected. "I could've knocked the crap outta him if you hadn't come along and stopped me."

"Yeah, I saw how close you were getting to that." Unruh shook his head. "I figure if you'd gone at him one more time, you would've just about knocked yourself unconscious. You know what you make me think, Gerry? That maybe I didn't do you any favor tonight. Seems like you like to get a little buzz on, then go throw your weight around. Tonight you nearly threw yourself about two divisions out of your league."

"I could've taken him," Vaughn said again.

"Not from behind his back with a four-foot length of two by four. But hang on in there." The trooper grinned sarcastically. "One of these days you'll take somebody else. And, if you take him bad enough, you'll wind up in the lockup with a Neanderthal cellmate who likes shovin' his dong up your ass. Did you ever stop to think these days about all the great diseases you wind up with from somethin' like that?"

"You gonna arrest me, or you just gonna talk me to death?" Vaughn grumbled angrily.

"Suit yourself," Unruh answered indifferently "Far as arresting you goes?" The trooper glanced toward Doll. "For right now that depends on him. Without him cooperating, I haven't got the grounds. If he wants to press changes, well, that's something else again. So what do you say, mister, what do you want me to do?"

"We had a difference of opinion. Nothing to lock a man up for," Doll said.

"Then you get lucky this time, Gerry," Unruh told Vaughn. He reached into his pocket for the key to unlock the handcuffs. "But I'll warn you one last time. You got a temper that's real close to getting you into trouble you can't handle. It can only come out two ways, you know. You either beat on somebody, or somebody beats on you. And either way you wind up on the sharp side of the stick."

Unruh unlocked the cuff. Gerry Vaughn massaged his wrist.

"Go on. Get out of here," the trooper said.

Still rubbing his wrist, Vaughn moved backward away from the cruiser. From a dozen feet away he stared menacingly at Doll.

"It ain't over," he warned, "so don't think it is. I'm gonna have your ass on my wall before I'm through." With that he turned and strode off defiantly into the night.

Unruh shook his head again.

"There are some guys you can't tell anything to," he said in a voice that affected discouragement, but which, Doll guessed, reflected a core of cynicism only lightly disguised. He turned toward Doll.

"But don't take away from that the idea that I'm on your side any more than I'm on his. I've been hearing your name a lot lately, Mr. Doll. To put it on the line, I figure you got your nose a long way in where it doesn't belong, and I'm not gonna spend a lot of time worrying about how somebody might come along and decide to take a piece of it off."

"Then you know I've been asking about LeRoy Carrow," Doll said. "What about him, Corporal? What's the unofficial line on how he got killed?"

"You got more balls than a pawnbroker." Unruh laughed for himself or for Doll. There was no one else around to see his apparent enjoyment. "No unofficial line, Doll. Accident is all it was. Coroner's inquest had all the facts, and it said so."

"But what do *you* think happened?" Doll prodded.

"I think," Unruh answered, "that part of what I get paid for is knowing where my business starts and where it ends."

"Must be handy," Doll said, "being able to turn yourself on and off like a spigot."

"Handy, but not easy." Unruh grinned in mocking indulgence. "There are times, like before with Vaughn and now with you, I get the unprofessional impulse to give people advice. All the official paperwork, for example, says the state police response time to the island is something like fifteen to eighteen minutes. That's bullshit, Doll, between you and me—but it keeps the governor and the legislature happy. You see what I'm telling you, don't you now? You get yourself in trouble here—and you're already way ahead on that score—don't plan on the cavalry coming in the nick a' time to get you out."

"What about Covey Wallace's place?" Doll asked. "What's the official line on who salted it?" Obviously, the question was funny, because the only thing that Unruh did was laugh.

"Christ, Doll," he managed to get out as the intensity of his amusement wore off. "You're one fabulous piece a' work. Somebody's gonna hand you your ass on a plate sure as shit."

After piling all the reasons on top of one another, Doll gave up sorting them out and ignored them. Instead, he chose to follow his instinct and assure himself that the Carrow house was at least more or less in order.

The porch light was on, burning in a carnival yellow color. White-winged moths and a horde of lesser insects swarmed around it. Farron's cycle was nowhere in sight.

Elaine answered his knock and let him in. The two girls, she said, were already in bed. She had been sitting alone in the kitchen—just sitting, and listening to some music on the radio. She managed a vague smile for Doll, if only, perhaps, to show him her composure. He saw the puffiness around her eyes, but noticed the redness had had sufficient time to fade nearly to the point of having vanished.

"Thanks for coming," she said. "You didn't have to. I've gotten myself back together again. I'm sorry about how I was out there before. I'm sure you must hate sharing other people's scenes. I know that I do."

"I'll go," Doll said. "I just wanted to be sure you were all right."

"No, don't go, please. At least not yet, if you don't mind." She went to the stove and took off the kettle and started to fill it with fresh water. "I was going to make coffee for myself. Now I'll make some for the both of us. This time I won't have no for an answer. It's funny, the relief that comes when the worst finally happens. No matter how much I knew what was coming, I couldn't have gotten ready for that."

Doll gave in to the coffee without an argument. "Farron'll be back. You said it yourself before. He'll work it out, and it'll be okay."

"Oh, I know." She kept herself busy putting out cups and saucers, spoons, sugar, and milk. "Life is always like that. A thing falls apart, then old things come together in new ways. And when it settles again, we always think of the new way things are as being permanent. But it never is, and then it happens all over again.

"When I was in high school, the teacher made us read that 'Stopping by a Woods' poem. Everyone knows it. You know the one I mean? Anyway, the teacher said it was about the poet's death wish. I thought that was stupid. I wasn't able to imagine anyone who'd ever want to die."

"You're not saying you do?" The words came out as blunt and clumsily as that because Doll couldn't think of any tactful way to say them.

"No, I don't mean anything like that." Elaine smiled at him

again. She seemed almost about to laugh because he'd taken her remembrance so literally. "What I was saying is that I can see now how all the changes start to wear you after a while. You get to where you say that enough is enough. That you'd just as soon not be around to see any more. The Bible talks about Eternity. Eternity never changes. I suppose that living makes people ready for that."

The water on the stove had started to boil. The steam that came from the spout reminded Doll of a speech balloon emerging from the mouth of a comic-strip character. The character became Andy Dowling, who had said something very close to those same words.

Elaine got a jar of coffee and spooned a portion into each of the cups. She added the water, then returned the kettle to the stove top.

"I wonder about LeRoy sometimes," she said as she came back to the table. "I don't think he ever believed in Eternity. I've always thought that a lot of men don't. I'm sorry, Mr. Doll." She looked up at him suddenly. "That's a very personal question. I was just making talk. I didn't mean it for you to answer."

Doll fairly jumped at the opportunity not to. He could only have hedged for her anyway, he told himself. He could have said no to Heaven and Hell. He could have told her that no person on earth was competent enough to commit acts deserving of infinite reward or censure. A just God made Heaven and Hell impossible. But Eternity, or what that might mean? Doll shrugged mentally at a concept he found incomprehensible—but knowing that no less a leap of faith was needed to say that the empirical world was all there was.

"I don't think what a man believes makes a whole lot of difference," he said.

"He was a good man." Elaine stirred some milk and sugar into her coffee. "He was good to me. He never laid a hand on me in anger. He was good with Farron and the girls. He was a simple man. He fished and got drunk up to Bal'mer with the other men. Men'll do that now and again. Wives don't necessarily let on, but they know, if they know their men at all, it don't mean nothing. All he ever wanted was just to keep on livin' like he did. He got into fights like any other man. But he never had an enemy. Not till he saw what was happening to the island and started out to try to stop it."

"That's what they all say about him," Doll answered, "that he couldn't handle the change."

"Even when," Elaine said, "it was hardly there to see. Lord, Mr. Doll, I'm not usually like this. I'm ashamed of myself to be such a talker tonight. In some ways—I was thinking before—I say thank God that LeRoy's dead. I think of what it would be like the other way around. And I say thank God that it's me who had to go through this rather than him."

"By 'this,' you mean Farron?" Doll asked uncertainly.

"Farron. Everything. I don't know." Elaine Carrow answered in a whisper. "You don't understand, Mr. Doll, how everything's changed. Two months ago I was a waterman's wife. I had a husband, a home, a family. A community I knew, that I was a part of, and that I was at peace to have around me. That was my life. I knew things out there somewhere were changing, but the change was slow and far enough away so I could look someplace else and not have to see it. Then a trapdoor opens. Suddenly, I have no husband. My family's pulling itself apart. There's no money coming in, and my name in the place where I live is a subject for every common gossip."

She put her head in her hands and rocked and spoke to the half-empty cup on the table.

"Dear God, forgive me! I don't believe I'm doing this. Between the lines, I hear myself saying 'why me?' and I know that's wrong because 'me' is anyone else. Just my turn this time.

That's all it is." She raised her head and raked her fingers through her hair.

"Thank you." She exhaled and smiled. "I think maybe that's done it. It had to come out—like the ooze from an infection. Somehow I know you understood that. You have a gift for being easy to talk to, Mr. Doll."

"It's getting late, and I'd better get going." Doll stood. "If you need me for anything, you can always reach me back at the inn."

Elaine stood too and observed that he hadn't touched his coffee. Doll smiled the oversight away.

"You live alone. Ellis told me," she said. "You were married once, but something happened. You have no children. For a man like you, I think that's very sad."

"My own fault," Doll replied uncomfortably. "I guess I'm just too hard for anyone to stay with." He took a backward step to get himself closer to the door.

She shook her head. "But if you ever want to tell me," she said, "maybe something you need to get off your chest. If you need the favor returned, Mr. Doll, I can sometimes be a good listener, too."

Doll's head turned sharply in reply to the knock at the door. Elaine Carrow went past him to open it and let Ellis LeCates into the kitchen.

His face was angry despite what must have been a nearly supreme effort not to let the anger show. Doll heard the puffy, bull-like snorts that replaced LeCates' normal breathing.

"What the hell are you doing here?" he said, confronting Doll.

"He came to make sure that I was all right," Elaine cut in.

"Well, are you?" LeCates' whole demeanor softened when he spoke to Elaine. His eyes became quiet. The rate of his respiration slowed.

"I'm fine, Ellis . . . Mr. LeCates. Well, it might as well be Ellis," Elaine conceded. "I told Mr. Doll I was all right too. He was kind enough to listen. He doesn't care for my coffee much, though, I'm afraid."

"I heard about Farron." LeCates halved the distance between himself and Elaine, leaving Doll cut off to the side and out of the line of conversation. "He stopped at the bar across the bridge and got to talking to someone who got back to me. I'm sorry, Elaine. It's Doll's fault, and it's my fault, too. It isn't yours."

"It's nobody's fault and it's everybody's fault." Elaine ran the tips of her fingers along the back of one of the chairs. "I can't even blame myself anymore. Was Farron all right? Was he drunk? Too drunk to drive? I hate it when he drinks and rides that bike."

"I don't know," LeCates answered. "I didn't ask, and the person who told me didn't say. Do you want me to go after him? I got a lift here, so my car's back at the store. But Doll's is just up the road at the inn. I could take him along for insurance."

Elaine gave the offer no more than a moment's thought.

"No. No, I don't think that's a good idea," she said. "I may worry, and yes, maybe there's the chance that he'll kill himself. But in the mood he's in now? You and Mr. Doll especially. I don't know what he might do. Or how you'd get him home. Or how I'd keep him home, even if you got him here."

"Do you want to talk to Ornan Atkins or Jerry Lee or someone else you think he trusts?"

"I think, Ellis," Elaine replied, "that I've got to let him find his own way this time. I think he will. I really believe that. And I think that, once he does, he'll be all right—that everything will."

"If that's what you want." LeCates nodded in a way that did more than concede. He seemed to tell Elaine Carrow with that motion of his head that anything she wanted was hers if he had it to give.

Ellis LeCates dared to touch her hand, and Elaine dared to let him hold it, and Doll, feeling every inch like the third sleeve on a hand-knitted sweater, looked on.

He thought about a muffled cough to remind them he was there. Instead, he told them as quickly as he could he had to go.

"No, wait." Elaine Carrow stopped him again. "Not yet. I'm sorry." She withdrew her hand from LeCates'. "This is getting a little heady for me. Everything's so fast, so upside down. I can't be here alone with you, Ellis. I'm sorry. Even if we both know each other's secrets, I'm still, for now at least, LeRoy's widow."

She turned to Doll.

"But I don't want to be by myself. Not yet, anyway. Not with Farron out there. So there's no other solution, Mr. Doll. For a little while at least, you and Ellis will both have to stay."

"Three-handed canasta?" LeCates proposed sardonically.

"I'm sorry, Ellis." Elaine smiled at him sympathetically.

"All right," said Doll, "but you two talk." He glanced toward the darkened living room. "There's a basketball game somewhere on the television. . . ."

The reception wasn't any better, maybe not as good, as Doll could have gotten on the set in his room at the inn. It took him nearly fifteen minutes before he finally figured out the two teams that were playing. But perhaps that was less the picture's fault than it was Doll's halfhearted attention. The distraction was considerable. For the first time he met LeRoy Carrow face to face.

The man in the photograph was hard to see in the dim light of the single lamp that Doll had lit. The five-by-eight color print in its gray cardboard frame depicted a family group: the man who had to be LeRoy Carrow flanked by Elaine on his right and Farron to his left, with his two daughters kneeling in front.

The shot was the work of an amateur with no talent for the subtleties of photography. The framing was bad, the focus less than perfect, and the depth of field haphazardly set to do nothing to draw the family out against the cluttered background. They were at an event, a picnic or something like one. Carrow's arms were draped around his wife and son. The hand that extended over Farron's shoulder held an open can of beer.

To Doll's mild surprise, Carrow was shorter than either Elaine or Farron. His hair, in contrast to theirs, was as black as charcoal and, for a moment, until he looked closer, Doll almost thought that he sported a Lincolnesque beard. But it wasn't that, nor that Carrow kept a careless stubble on his face in a manner reminiscent of George Page. Instead, the hair was so dark and thick that, even clean-shaven, his cheeks gave the impression of being in shadow. Doll couldn't see very much of his eyes. They seemed half closed against, Doll guessed, the combination of beer and sun.

The shirt he had on was featureless and open to the waist. He wore jeans and shoes that looked like brogues with a slash of white sock intruding between. His cap was cocked back on his head at an angle too steep for Doll to read the advertisement on the patch above the brim.

He was wrong for the part of an outraged man. That was Doll's single, strongest impression. He remembered Elaine's description from earlier—a man who did hard and dangerous work, who liked his family and the good times, who liked his beer and his nights with the boys, and, now and again, maybe a little bit of whoring it up around the bars in Baltimore. That was the man that Doll saw in the photograph, and that, of course, was exactly the life that LeRoy Carrow had died trying to protect.

12

Doll bent the truth in what he told LeCates. Not in saying he was tired. That part was true enough. But in telling him he was going straight to his room and to bed.

LeCates had badly wanted to interrogate him. No sooner had Elaine let them out and closed the door, than the first assault had begun. He'd wanted to hear every word she'd said—the generalities, the details, all the inferences Doll had drawn from each. Ellis LeCates was forty-five years old, Doll had thought, a middle-aged man, in love and jealous and a child.

It had been all that Doll could do to keep LeCates' questions at arm's length during the brief walk from the Carrow house to the roadside end of the driveway to the inn, with LeCates insisting all the while that he had to know more.

By "more," he'd meant a lot more. Doll had foreseen the inquisitor's examination, which LeCates had tried to disguise with the offer to close out the night with a final round of drinks. Perhaps he should simply have faced the issue and told LeCates that he had no intention of allowing himself to be pumped. Instead, he'd chosen the easier path and lied. It was, he decided, his just reward, that now, as he sat with his ale at the bar, the hefty figure of Ardee Vaughn approached him.

The sides of Vaughn's neck were a murrey color, as though the skin had been rubbed with a blue-tinted rouge. A cigarette dangled from between the thumb and index finger of his left hand. His right held a glass that was mostly drained of its whiskey.

"I think we've got some talking to do," he said to Doll in a voice that implied close restraint. "Maybe we'd be better to do it at one of the tables."

Doll took his ale and followed after Vaughn, who picked a corner as far as he could away from the bar's other patrons.

"I hear you manhandled my kid tonight," he said accusingly. "You're going around saying, now, you think Carrow was murdered. You're saying it was maybe my boy who killed him. Just who in the goddamn hell do you think you are?"

The temperature wasn't hot in the room, but Doll noticed the beads of perspiration that speckled Vaughn's forehead. His face was flushed with the rosiness that a sufficiency of whiskey can bring.

"What do you want to do?" Doll asked. "Do you want to listen to what happened, or do you just want to let off that head of steam you're working up? 'Cause I'll tell you something for nothing, Ardee. It's been a damn long day already. And if it's gonna start getting nasty again, I'd just as soon say goodnight and end it right now."

"Now you just hang on there a minute, Doll. You can't go around bad-mouthin' people and expect nobody's gonna take notice." Vaughn pushed the argument forward, but he seemed to Doll to speak his part without conviction. What pretended on its face to be anger came out sounding much more like a plea. Behind the words, the message came across that the Vaughn name had been badly used, that Doll had been one who had misused it and now the expectations of others required that Vaughn do something in its defense.

"No offense intended," Doll said. He knew the words fell short of an apology and meant them to. "If it helps anything, I tried to explain that to Gerry. I couldn't find a good way to get him to listen. Maybe there's a special way to do that I don't know."

"He came home looking like you dragged him through a horse barn," Vaughn complained.

"All I did," Doll said, "was keep myself out of his way."

"You also went around saying that he killed a man, goddamn it!"

"I think you know better than that," Doll answered. "I haven't made it a secret that I think LeRoy Carrow was murdered. I didn't invent the fight he had with your son. You don't need a whole lot of imagination to ask yourself if maybe it didn't go further. If Gerry doesn't like getting splashed, then he ought to learn to stay further away from the water."

"But to say he murdered somebody, Doll. . . ."

"I'm telling you again, Ardee: I asked a few people if they thought it could have happened that way. I never said to anybody that it did."

"But you sure made clear that he could have done it, damn you. Do you really believe that, Doll? Do you really think my son killed LeRoy Carrow?" Vaughn asked.

The Olympian answer came not from Doll or Ardee Vaughn, but from the crash of the door across the room. Framed in the doorway, Vaughn's son stood, his clothes still stained with earth and grass, his jaw tight, and his eyes fired with a roaring intensity that suggested something very close to maniacal rage. His right hand held a pump-action shotgun. His grip on the weapon was loose, his finger curved around the trigger. He kept the barrel pointed at a forty-five-degree angle toward the ceiling.

"Jesus Christ, no," his father swore in a whisper.

A few gasps and inchoate screams sounded and instantly died. The room locked into a stunned and terrible silence.

Gerry Vaughn walked slowly through it to where Doll and his father sat. The soft soles of his boat shoes made no sound against the floor. The barrel of the shotgun lowered. It pointed now at a section of wall a foot or so over Doll's head.

"Don't, Gerry. Stop," someone called from the bar.

Vaughn's son struck the voice silent with the smallest redirection of the shotgun.

"Gerry, for the love a' God, don't be a fool!" Ardee Vaughn stood, trying to fill the space between Doll and his son.

Gerry Vaughn altered his position to the side, reclearing his line of fire at Doll. The elder Vaughn began to move again, but Doll touched a hand to his sleeve.

"Yeah, that's right. It's between the two of us," Vaughn's son growled. "You're gonna die, Doll." The bore of the shotgun lowered. "You see that hole there lookin' down your throat? It's gonna close that mouth a' yours for good." He let Doll stare down the black, open muzzle of the gun. Then Gerry Vaughn's left hand reached out for the slide handle and started to snap it backward toward the stock.

In the same instant, Doll's right hand caught the barrel, driving the gun's muzzle upward toward the ceiling. His left wrapped around the receiver just forward of the small of the stock.

Gerry Vaughn resisted instinctively, his arms twisting back against Doll's force to prevent the gun from being wrested from his hands. Doll continued to twist, until, suddenly, he reversed momentum, throwing all his power into conjunction with Vaughn's. The shotgun spun in the opposite direction, the barrel toward the floor, the butt end toward the ceiling. The flat of the stock caught Gerry Vaughn squarely along the side of the head. It made a dull and ugly sound.

The impact was more than enough to leave Vaughn stunned. His eyes were uncoordinated and swimming. As Doll yanked the shotgun free from his hand, he sank to his knees and settled groggily, half kneeling, half sitting on the floor. This time the fight was gone from him. He stayed where he dropped with his head lolling, holding his hands to his skull against the pain.

Doll took in a breath and stood a moment, then handed the shotgun over to the father.

For what seemed a long time, Ardee Vaughn only contemplated the weapon he was holding. Finally, he slipped the safety on and passed the gun to another man standing nearby.

"Get rid of it," he mumbled. "Sell it, put it up for auction, or throw the goddamn thing in the bay. I don't give a good goddamn what the hell you do with it. I never want to see the son-of-a-bitchin' thing again for as long as I live."

Ardee Vaughn slumped down exhaustedly into his chair.

The intensity ebbed by degrees, the same way that a scene in a theater fades when the stage lights gradually darken, then dissolves into a memory as the houselights come up and the audience readapts itself to the plotless vicissitudes that mark out the pathways of day-to-day life. The silence gave way to low, murmured voices, then to louder, and finally, almost compulsive, talk.

Only the corner where Doll stood spurned the revival. No words passed between Vaughn and his son. Both stayed silent and still where they had been, accepting the fiction that accorded them their invisibility.

The man who had taken the shotgun returned from somewhere without it. He made the offer to drive Gerry home. When Ardee Vaughn gave his sullen agreement, his son went along without complaint.

Ten minutes later, Vaughn was near the end of his second whiskey since the trouble. During the first, he'd said nothing at all. He'd only stared down at the table, seeming to contemplate the mystery of the steadily falling level of the liquor in the glass.

His hands were cupped about the drink, so that, had it been removed, he might have looked as though he were praying.

"I suppose you figure I ought to thank you," he said, finally gazing up at Doll. "Well, there's no 'suppose' about it. I should. Can't even make myself think about what could have happened. You let him off earlier, too, with the cops. I didn't say it before. Had to stand up for him. You understand.

"God!" Vaughn shook his ponderous head. "A man's only got one real job in life. One real job, and I screwed up really good."

Crises brought on confessions. Doll had served as the priest a great too many times before.

"Spoiled him. Spoiled him rotten," Vaughn was saying, and signaling for a fresh whiskey at the same time. He used the intermission as well to light a cigarette. "Taught him everything. The business. How to hunt. How to fish. Be a buddy to him. That's what they say you should do. Well, I did all that and still screwed it up. The only thing I could never teach that boy was any kind of self-control. I'm ashamed of him, Doll. I'm ashamed of me. That doesn't come as an easy thing for me to say."

"Then don't say it," Doll answered. "Change it, if you have to do something. There isn't any positive value in guilt."

"Gotta say it." Vaughn shook his head again. "Stupid bastard. Mark my words, he'll get himself killed before it's through. He didn't kill Carrow, Doll. You won't believe me, but, I'm telling you, I know he didn't. So he pulls some damn-fool stunt like he pulls tonight, and what does he do? He makes himself look guilty as hell!" Vaughn's fist hit the table, not loudly, as though he were still afraid of drawing attention. "You know it. I know it. Everybody figures he must've done it. 'Hey, look there, he had that fight with Carrow. Hey, look—we were all there and saw it—he would've killed that guy Doll if he hadn't lost the chance.' Stupid son of a bitch. Mark my words. I'm tellin' you.

He'll get himself tried and put away for something that never even happened maybe—something he never even did."

The barkeeper brought Vaughn's third whiskey. Doll declined the offer of a fresh bottle of ale.

Doll's first choice would have gotten him out of there, out of the bar and away from Ardee Vaughn. But the questions he had would have to be asked sometime and, Doll reasoned, he wasn't likely to find Vaughn equally communicative anytime soon. In the end, he decided that the "sometime" might as well be now.

"It happened. Carrow was murdered," Doll said. "Somebody loosened the fitting on the back of his propane stove. He couldn't smell—"

"Spare me. I heard the theory," Vaughn interrupted. He ground out the last of his cigarette with a vehemence that implied he was grinding Doll's conclusions into the ashtray beneath it. "That's all goddamn guesswork, Doll. That's all the hell it is. Coroner's report still says it was an accident. I'd just as soon—maybe sooner—believe them as you."

"But say, just for a minute, it was a murder. There's no way for you—unless you did it yourself—to know that Gerry, or anyone else you'd care to mention, wasn't involved."

"You don't think so?" Vaughn answered and smiled. "You like to think you're a smart guy, Doll. Well, you're right, leastways relatively speaking. You're probably a whole lot smarter than me. But I know my kids. Good and bad sides alike. And I'm tellin' you for the last goddamn time that my Gerry didn't murder LeRoy Carrow."

"Then you're telling me that you know who did," Doll replied.

"Maybe I do. Maybe I do—know who did." Vaughn took a swallow from his glass, smiled once, as though he were pleased with himself, then went back to staring fixedly across the width of the table at Doll. "Maybe you do, too. Except, maybe, you've got some reason for not wanting to find the answer that's maybe right under your nose."

Doll leaned back in his chair and poured the remaining ale from his bottle. "You sound like a man who's got a piece to say. So why don't you just say it, without all the built-up suspense. You talk. I'll keep quiet and listen. That way neither of us wastes the other's time."

Vaughn frowned and seemed to pout for a moment, then nodded as though he accepted the point and began. "Rachael Teal," he said. "You ever think about her? She got plenty a' reason, no matter what she says. She's never kept it a secret from anybody that she'll do whatever she's got to do to get herself rich."

"Like a lot of other people."

"Not like her, Doll. Not like her," Vaughn said with something that sounded like total conviction.

"You figure she rigged Carrow's boat?"

"Wouldn't put the job past her. Women these days know a lot more than you think. But even, let's say, she didn't rig it herself, it's not hard to see her hiring out a man who did."

"Like who?" Doll asked.

"How do I know?" Vaughn fumbled through his pocket chasing down his package of cigarettes again. "All you gotta do is look around the room here. Hell, there's got to be a half dozen just in here tonight who would've done it for her if she only asked 'em right."

Doll shook his head. "That's all talk, Ardee. And all that about having the job done: throw some money in instead and it could apply as easily to you or Gerry, or anybody else, as to her."

"Then what about what happened to the Wallace place?" Vaughn asked. "That was our deal. My business's profit, Gerry's commission, Doll. You figure we also cut our own throats by salting his land?"

"What are you getting at?" Doll asked. "My impression was that Carrow got the credit for that. I'm only putting things together, but to judge from the fight that your son picked with LeRoy, I'd say he was pretty convinced on the point."

"Oh, Carrow sure enough got the credit," Vaughn admitted, "if talk across the back fences counts. And you see for yourself how Gerry jumps at whatever happens to be handy. But nothing about it ever got proved, and old LeRoy, he denied the saltin' every chance he got."

"So Rachael, because she didn't get the contract?"

"You got trouble with that?" Vaughn shrugged. "Course you do. I figure just about most any man would. So what if it's not her? Then what about those people she works for? Those Washington boys are big fish, Doll. I don't mean they're tarpon or mackerel either. They're sharks. So, maybe they don't always work through her. She thinks they leave her alone out here. Maybe she's wrong."

"What makes you say that?"

"Nothin'." Vaughn shrugged. "Except that you can't tell me it's not true."

"So the field's not closed. Okay," Doll acknowledged, "if that's the point you're making, I agree. But the other side is also true, Ardee. None of what you've said tonight gets your boy off the hook either."

"Goddamn you. You're some kind of vicious bastard, aren't you, Doll? You feel like you gotta have my boy for breakfast. Son of a bitch! If Gerry had done it, if he really had, do you think he could keep his goddamn mouth shut about it? Bullshit, he could, Doll. You know it yourself. He hasn't got the stones. If my son had killed LeRoy Carrow, the fool would've bragged on it all over half the damn town before the friggin' sun was down on the next day.

"There now." Vaughn shook his head and rested its massive weight in the palms of his hands. "I've said it and I'm done. I'm supposed to be happy because I raised a son who I just said hasn't got the balls or the brains that make him fit to be a murderer. How does anybody ever get through this life? Can you tell me that, Doll? You can't even tell the times you win from when you lose. How in the hell does anybody get through it?"

With his palms pressed against the side of his head, his cigarette stood out from his fingers like a crooked chimney poking up through the roof of a house. Its thin trail of gray-white smoke drifted up only to dissipate into an indistinct haze in the atmosphere above.

Doll left Ardee Vaughn in the bar. It was time and past it, he decided, that he got himself upstairs and to bed. He closed the door to the public room behind him and started across the enclosed porch toward the door. He'd gone less than a dozen feet before he heard the voice of Wesley Mowen calling his name out from the office.

"Had yourself quite some night as I hear it," Mowen said when Doll had reached his office door. " 'Fore I forget, I want t' say thank you. Would've been a frightful, terrible thing for the both of us if you'd managed t' get your head blowed off in there."

"Would've marked up the wall and been hell to clean up," Doll answered. "I can see why you'd be glad it didn't happen."

"Took that ol' shotgun away right neat they tell me. Cool as a dead flounder, that's what they say you were. Looked like you'd been doin' that kind a' thing for the best part a' your natural life."

Doll smiled at Mowen, not a very big smile. If Mowen wanted to fish, Doll decided he'd oblige him to a point. "A man really wants to kill you," he answered, "comes at you with the shotgun loaded. He doesn't waste the time it takes to snap a round into the chamber."

Mowen matched Doll's smile and then went on to exceed it. "Don't figure, myself, it would a' made a difference either way. But a man wants t' keep his light under a barrel, I guess I figure he's got his right. Ya' know it's all around 'bout what you think happened t' LeRoy. No secrets around these parts. But, like ya said when we talked before, ya found out all 'bout how word travels for yourself."

"I don't," Doll replied still smiling, "even take my thoughts as private anymore."

"Ya learn fast, too." Mowen laughed, seeming to enjoy himself. "Ya know enough now so I reckon ya see how that can be."

"How what can be? How the news travels? It's a small place with not a lot of people—and all of them have telephones."

"Telephones! Yeah, I guess they got 'em. Don't know that they use 'em though. Maybe you don't learn so fast. Maybe you was just spoofin' me a'fore. These folks and their kin a'fore 'em been together through a lot, Mr. Doll. Wouldn't surprise me one little bit if more than a few of 'em really did read one another's mind. Tell ya somethin' about it, if ya got the time t' listen. A' course, whether ya do or not is up t' you."

"All the time in the world," Doll said, and, to his astonishment, found that he meant it. He felt surprised at how much less tired he was after having gotten Ardee Vaughn behind him.

"Blood's what ya got t' remember. Blood's a whole lot thicker 'an water," Wesley Mowen began. "Three kinds a' blood we got on this island. Bet that's something' ya didn't know. Starts out early on with the old blood. That goes a way back 'bout as far as ya can go."

"Before Independence," Doll recalled aloud. "It says that on the road sign just before you cross the bridge. Says the island got settled first in sixteen hundred something."

"Middle sixteen hundreds." Mowen nodded. "Folks think 'bout those colony days, all they think is Massachusetts and Virginia. Maryland got started up just four years after Boston. That's a fact. Old country all the way around here. There's that sign t' tell ya, but you're probably the first that's ever read it. Old blood 'round this island can go back that far."

"Who's that?" Doll asked. "What families would that be?"

"Edwardses, Atkinses, Millses, mostly. Others got lost somewheres on the way. Family named Farron, but the last a' them died off back 'round 1953. Farron Carrow's name comes from them. I reckon ya probably guessed that. LeRoy's mother was Farron, but, a' course, she wound up a Carrow. Was her brother, the last a' the Farrons, that died childless back in fifty-three. Always gives me a pang when I think a' that, the last twig in the branch of a family dies off. Like somethin's lost that can never be got back.

"Then there's the Mowens, too." Mowen grinned, not trying too hard, Doll thought, to deflate the boast. "Though, if I'm honest with ya, that gets a trifle cloudy. We got here later than some a' those others, but not so late as the new bloods, who come on later still."

"Ellis told me the island had a lot of history," Doll said. "I can see where people get used to one another when they've been together in a town for that kind of time."

"Well, now. . . ." Mowen smiled again. "Don't let people put you on too much with that. People get t' braggin', but t' say the ol' place was a town on the books is one thing. T' say that it acted much like one is something else. What you got t' remember 'bout all those early times is that t' think on it right ya got t' think small. All the men, women, and children on the island at one time, ya could count, for the most part, without ever takin' the trouble t' take off your socks. Be more like it t' think a' the place 'tween here and Easton as the town, with the island sort a' bein' the westernmost end. That's the proper way t' see it for most a' the time that the old bloods was here by themselves. Still like that a little, if ya stop t' look around. Ya saw it a bit yourself t'other night when ya went up the road for some drinks with a few a' the boys."

"When did it all start to change?" Doll asked.

"When the new blood come," Mowen said sagely, "but that didn't start till some years after the Civil War was done. Just about a hundred years ago, now. New folks came in. Those'd be like the Carrows, Messicks, and Pages. Donalds, they're not around anymore. Family called Ryan was here for a while, but pulled out back around the Great Depression. But that gets away from what I'm mostly sayin'. Got our own churches when the new blood came in. That's when the island began t' come together. What ya see here now grew up mostly all outta that time."

"You said there were three kinds of blood," Doll prompted.

Mowen laughed and nodded his head. "That's a fact. An' the third kind is no blood," he answered. "Like ol' Ardee Vaughn back in there in his cups or your particular friend, Ellis LeCates. They're no part a' this place. I don't mean that unkindly. But the fact is that they never will be, Mr. Doll. It's time and it's ancestry. There's no way a' denyin' that's a powerful part of it. But there's the water, too. They never worked it. Their families never did. They're not tied to it. They don't know it, don't feel it. Never could the way the old and new bloods can't help but do.

"So why do I tell you all this?" Wesley Mowen shook his head. "Returning the favor for stoppin' a ruckus? Well, there's probably somethin' in that. Respect, because twice tonight ya went out a' your way not t' hand Vaughn's kid his ass, which ya could've and which he surely richly deserved? But how 'bout 'cause I knew LeRoy Carrow boy to man, Mr. Doll, and if what you're sayin' happened was what did, it was wrong. People'll tell you—hell, I know what they say—that LeRoy was holdin' on too tight t' the past. Well, maybe he was, and maybe he wasn't. But I figure after all you've heard, you ought t' hear what it used to be—and t' know that it was somethin' a' value. It's not like some folks'd have ya think, that all he was hangin' on to was sand."

13

Half an hour past midnight, Doll left Wesley Mowen in the office and began the short walk through the night toward the stairs to the second-floor annex and his room. The warmth of the earlier evening was gone. A cold damp had replaced it. Doll hunched up his shoulders against it and quickened his pace as he covered the length of the parking lot. The number of cars had dwindled to six besides his own aging VW bug. One was a van. Its headlamps winked at him as he passed it. He went to the driver's side and found Rachael Teal.

She rolled down the window. "You kept me waiting forever," she said.

"Sorry," Doll answered. "It's been that kind of night. Maybe it wouldn't have been so long if I'd had some way of knowing you were out here."

Her face was turned partially toward him, but Doll saw none of its features. All he saw was her oblique profile in shadow against a background of black.

"Ardee's still in there, I gather? Tossing down enough courage to make himself go home?" The questions were either unimportant or rhetorical. She went on without waiting for Doll to answer. "There's a story his kid went in there with a shotgun tonight—came out a little later with no gun, a keeper, and his tail between his legs."

"It got a little tense for a while," Doll acknowledged.

"Not for you, the way the story's going around. The locals say you were about as slick as goosegrease. That's more or less a quote. I've never seen goosegrease, so I've no idea how slick that is. But I gather from the way they said it that, on the scale of slickness, it's at or somewhere near the upper end."

Doll took his own turn at silence.

"I also heard that that was the second round," Rachael continued. "There was another one without the gun earlier over at the school. I only wish I'd known ahead they were coming. I'm sorry to say I missed them both."

"You didn't miss much. Gerry's the reactive type. He doesn't plan out what he does. That makes him only semidangerous."

"Not to everybody. To someone who's been through Navy special forces school—well, maybe that isn't exactly what it's called. You see? I have to keep figuring you out in parts. You have to admit that you're not especially forthcoming."

"Why go through the bother?" Doll said. "There's no profit in me. All you'll find is that I'm a waste of your tenacity."

"*My* tenacity!" Rachael laughed aloud. "Don't talk to me about tenacity, Doll. You're there. You're real, at least. For me, figuring out what you are comes under the heading of recreation. You, on the other hand, go around chasing after some specter of a killer who you think murdered LeRoy Carrow—after something you don't even know for sure is there, and you do it to a point that nearly succeeds in getting you killed!"

"You're overdramatizing," Doll replied. A night breeze moved, and in that moment, he thought—or imagined—his nose caught the slightest scent of her. Not perfume—or, if it was, very moderately used—but powder, or something, or nothing, and then it was gone.

"What I want to know is why you do it," Rachael went on. "LeCates got you to come here, so it's got something to do with him. I have a theory. I could put it to you. But even if I had the right one and you knew it, you wouldn't tell me."

"You said it yourself. I'm not always as forthcoming as I might be," Doll answered.

"That's exactly what I thought I'd get." Rachael turned her head more fully toward him. Doll guessed that her face held a smile of self-satisfaction, but in the deep shadow there wasn't any way that he could tell.

"It's late," Doll said and pushed his body away from the side of the van. "It's late and, as we said, it's been an exciting evening. I'm sure we'll get a chance to talk like this another time."

"Don't bet on it. You can never be sure." She let the meaning of the words hang cryptically. Her voice, on the one hand seemed to tease, but on another level it didn't. "You know, you're really a hard case, Doll. You're a man. You're single. Not gay, by all accounts I've heard. I'm a woman. I thought you might have noticed that. There are times I find myself wondering where your head's at."

"Is there someplace that it ought to be?" Doll asked uncomfortably. What he found himself reading into Rachael's lines caught him off guard and confused him.

"It's the middle of the night," Rachael said, spelling it out. "We're here in the middle of an empty parking lot, and I, for one, am freezing. You've got a room up there, about a hundred feet away. Can't you think of any other place where we might be better off to be?"

Doll heard the sharp, metallic snap of the latch, then the scrape of rollers as she slid the van's door open. As she did, the dome light came on, first glaringly brilliant, then fading, as Doll's eyes adjusted, to what seemed a meager fraction of its initial strength.

In its white glow, her face seemed pale, the way it had the other night beneath the flood of the halogen lamps. The red bow of her mouth stood out as Doll remembered. She climbed down from the van's high seat with a fluidity of movement that she managed to make elegant and stood before him.

She seemed smaller now than Doll's mind recalled her. He noticed that her shoes were flats, that she was still in the modest blouse and jeans she'd worn that evening at the meeting in the gym.

She was softness again. Doll credited her powers of illusion, admitting to himself that he couldn't resolve which aspect—or aspects—of the woman before him were real. The calculating coolness she'd let him see seemed melted away like the morning ice from a springtime pond. The caustic wit, which she'd used only a moment before, seemed suddenly misplaced in the context of her character. What Doll found instead was something nearly like an adolescent sensuality—as though the qualities that pass for contemporary innocence had managed to survive in her, but beneath a protective, pragmatic shell. Doll didn't know in that moment what was authentic and what was subterfuge. What he did know was that her invitation inundated his awareness.

He took time, though the time began to seem forever. He remembered the half-accusations that Ardee Vaughn had made. He fought against himself to resist being drawn, and, when he'd decided he could resist, he abandoned the fight and gave in, wondering, at the same instant, about something he had said before—if any man was ever really master of his soul.

Their first time lasted for more than an hour. It was, in turns, languid and lustful, sometimes tender, sometimes playful, shared, and blindly compulsive in its ending. Doll lay on his back in the small double bed drawing long, deep lungfuls of air. Beside him, Rachael rested her head in the notch of his shoulder, her knee across his leg, and her breath minutely trembling the wispy airs on his chest. They stayed like that a long time, drowsing, not exactly sleeping, not needing to talk to offer lies or cover up recriminations.

"Doll? Are you awake?" Rachael whispered.

"I am now," Doll replied.

"You weren't asleep. You're teasing me again." She moved, minutely, adjusting her position, reminding Doll of the nearness of her body and leaving him to decide if the reminder he'd been given was intentional.

"Strange, the way I thought I was sleeping," Doll mumbled.

"You were thinking. Tell me what you were thinking about. No, don't tell me. I can guess. You've got a one-track mind once you get it focused. All you've thought about all these last few days is LeRoy Carrow."

"Not all."

"No, not all." She laughed softly and kissed him on the shoulder. "But almost all. Why do you do it, Doll? What do you owe to Ellis LeCates?"

"Nothing," Doll answered for the record. And that was true, he thought, as far as it went.

"You knew him back when you were married?"

"How did you hear about that?" The flesh of his arm felt her shrug.

"Secondhand. Or third, or fourth. Ultimately," she said—as Doll had already guessed for himself—"it came from LeCates. Have you really been alone by yourself for all the time since then?"

"You have a way," Doll replied, "of making all your questions sound like part of an interrogation."

"Are you in love?" she asked.

"Am I what?" Doll struggled to regain his mental footing.

"Don't gasp like that." Rachael made a fainthearted effort at suppressing her amusement. Doll didn't know if he'd gasped or not, but the possibility was a close enough thing that he didn't take on the risk of an outright denial.

"I wasn't asking if you were in love with me," she said. "You'd have to be an emotional invalid—and you're not—to rush into anything close to that because of what happened tonight. What I meant was do you have anyone that's—well, what you'd call somebody regular or special? You don't seem like the kind who'd be happy with an endless list of one-night stands."

"Somebody regular back home, while I'm here like this with you? That wouldn't say much for any level of fidelity, but I'm probably out of date about that." And maybe that was true, Doll thought. The hardest person for him to set in perspective was always himself.

"You *are* antiquated." Rachael sighed. "Maybe that's part of what makes you so interesting. Half of you, Doll, is like unwrapping an enigma. The other half is what you knew without thinking had to be there all along. I want to know more about you. Where you were born. How you grew up. How a man with as many parts as you ever wound up with the shock troops over in 'Nam. How come you haven't got a neck that's thirteen inches wide?"

She pressed the length of her body against him and brought her mouth to within a shallow breath's distance of his.

The next time Doll woke, his watch showed the time as just after four in the morning. He sensed Rachael's movement beside him, then the slight heave of the mattress as she transferred her weight from it to the floor. He waited and listened until he heard the whispering rustle of fabric. Then he spoke.

"You're getting dressed?" The inference was obvious, but it seemed a somehow necessary question.

"Like a good girl, darling," she answered softly. She came over to the bed and kissed him, chastely this time, on the mouth. "Have to guard what's left of my reputation. Besides, I need my sleep if I'm going to do any kind of a decent day's work today. And it's getting pretty clear I'm not going to get it as long as I'm there in bed with you."

"It's going to be cold as an Antarctic winter out there."

"It already is. Tell me something I don't know," Rachael answered. "My teeth are starting to chatter. But the van, bless its heart, has got a good little heater. Not so nice as some other ways of warming up, maybe." She wiggled her hips into her pants and buttoned and zipped the front. "But, for now I'm afraid, it'll have to do."

She came and sat on the side of the bed. Bending down to him, she kissed him again, this time more strongly than before.

"Thank you for a lovely evening," she said. "I really had a very good time."

"The pleasure was mine," Doll replied.

"Doll . . . ?" Rachael hesitated. "You understand all this, don't you, Doll? You understand it's been very nice—and that, on a scale of anything else, it means nothing."

"Meaning no trade secrets."

"That." Rachael laughed softly. "And that tonight was nothing more than it's already been."

"You think I'll have trouble handling that?"

"I don't know. Will you?" she said. "Your trouble is that you're sort of caught on a cusp. I understand that. My time came later, when all the old rules had already changed. I answered all the sexuality questions for myself a long, long time ago. I'm happy with who I am, Doll. I left the guilt and the hangups behind, and I'm happy with the freedom of me."

"Good for you," Doll said. He thought about it and decided he meant it sincerely.

"Good for me. Good for you. Good for everybody, if they'd let it be. Good night, Doll. If I stay much longer, I'll find myself driving into the sun."

"How about a question before you go?" Doll asked.

"What question?" Rachael asked guardedly.

"Business," Doll answered. "Nothing confidential. I promise."

"Oh, c'mon, don't spoil it all, please, Doll. We had a great night. Can't you leave it at that? We've been all through the exploiter scene. You said you saw both sides and that you weren't taking anybody's part."

"And I'm not," Doll replied, "as long as it's clean. I'm talking about Covey Wallace."

"What about him?" Doll found a new and unmistakable edge in Rachael Teal's voice.

"What kind of a deal did your Washington people have you offer him?"

"You said nothing confidential, Doll. I never said an offer was made. I'm not saying now if there was or not. Either way, it isn't any of your business."

"What about what happened to his land?"

"You mean that it was salted?"

"By who?"

"By your friend, LeRoy Carrow. Is that what you mean?" She let her anger show. "I'm leaving, Doll. I don't know what you're getting at. I only know you're managing to turn what had been a very pleasant night into a bore."

"Do you know it was Carrow who salted that land?"

"And just who else would it be?" Rachael demanded.

"Who else might be an interested party?"

"Me?" she exclaimed. "Is that what you're implying? You son-of-a-bitching bastard, Doll."

"I look for motive, Rachael," Doll said quietly. "If Wallace sells out through Gerry Vaughn, you're out of it. If that falls through, you're a player again. Why do you care if the land's salted now? By the time your people are ready to do anything with it, the damage will pretty much all have leached out."

"And you think I'd do that. You perfect bastard," Rachael swore under her breath.

"I didn't say that I thought that you would or did," Doll said as she reached for the door.

"Then why bring it up?" Rachael spun around to face him. Doll sensed the movement, though all he saw was blackness in the opposite corner of the room.

"I'm asking about the people you work for," Doll replied. "You said they sent you out here to work on your own, that no one was looking over your shoulder. What I'm asking you to do is to think about that. Ask yourself who salted Wallace's land. Just take as a supposition for a minute that it wasn't LeRoy Carrow. You know already it wasn't you. If it wasn't you and it wasn't Carrow, then who else stood to benefit?"

"Where'd you get all this, Doll?" Rachael's voice moved closer toward him as it came from out of the darkness. Conversely, it sounded quieter, as though a part of the anger in it had been, for some unaccountable reason, left behind. "Those aren't your questions, are they?" she said. "They sound to me a lot more like they come from Ardee Vaughn."

"If you like," Doll conceded. "I don't see that it makes a lot of difference where they come from."

"It makes all the difference." She sat on the edge of the bed and kissed him again. "You're really too gullible, Doll. You shouldn't try to play at being a real-life detective. Ardee is jealous. Can't you see that, darling? He's protecting his business as well as his son. You take in all the stories you hear as though they were equals. You've got to learn to do a better job of sorting out the nonsense that gets added in along the way."

She kissed him for a final time and stroked his hair before she left him. Smiling at him from the yellow light of the hall, she closed the door to the room behind her.

She left a vacuum in her absence. Doll tasted the taste of her lips when he breathed. The smell of her lingered in the sheets and on the pillows. The memory of her touch and of the texture of her skin beneath his own stubbornly remained in his head despite his irresolute efforts to expunge them.

And for all that, he admitted, he still didn't know her.

Finally, in an act of the will, he drove the specter of her from his mind. The night swam emptily around him. His freed thoughts drifted without his direction back once again to the island and LeRoy Carrow.

He saw into the future as Ardee Vaughn had offered it—an island of neat, generous lots with cropped green grass, with shrubs and tended shade trees—picture-perfect houses equipped with the latest accouterments of comfort, curving driveways and double-wide garages built to shelter expensive and highly polished cars.

The future that Carrow had both feared and hated.

Along the docks, the workboats were gone. In their place, twin-engined sports fishermen and sleek-lined sailboats packed the crowded recreational marinas. At the north end of the island, where now an abandoned gas station stood, Doll saw a store sided in cedar with broad bow windows displaying books that told how the island once had been and overpriced nautical odds and ends and other local memorabilia.

It all came to Doll as an ugly vision set against the history that Wesley Mowen had told. And yet, Doll told himself again, there was nothing that he or Mowen or anyone else could do. If there was value in the pictures he dreamed, it came not from the chance to change the future, but from understanding a little better something of the desperateness with which LeRoy Carrow had tried to keep the present from turning into the past.

He thought of Elaine and wondered if Farron had managed to get himself home. For a moment, Doll thought he might walk there—put off sleep that little bit longer, at least to see if Farron's motorbike was in the driveway. But then he gave up the idea when he remembered how close it was to morning.

Farron, who had grown up too late and too respectful, who had had no foothold left to support him at the final moment when he'd learned that adult idols have feet that are even less solid than clay.

Unlike Gerry Vaughn, who hadn't, as of yet at least, had the courage to grow up at all.

His last thoughts were disorganized and seemed to repeat themselves in slowly orbiting circles. They came to him again in pictures. Ornan Atkins' storm-gray eyes. Eyes from nowhere, out of nothing, without the context of a surrounding face. Replaced through no conscious connection by George Page's cactus stubble and grinding mouth—grinding tobacco, grinding up mouthfuls of ham and cheese sandwich, grinding out words between swallows of beer. Jerry Lee, there on the stern of Page's eel boat, his ox jaw set, culling the eels, trapload after trapload, with never a break in his concentration. Carroll Messick and Joely Edwards hurling half-full cans of beer at the retreating back of Covey Wallace's car.

The pictures came and went and came again until, at last, they dissolved into nothing as, finally, Doll slept.

Doll's morning came three and a half hours later. The sky was pale, the sun orange and already well up. Through his window he could see in the distance two men in a small open boat out a hundred or so yards on the bay. He blinked and tried to bring them into focus, but couldn't. Too little sleep, he thought to himself. His eyes weren't working as of yet. They burned and contended against the light.

He turned away from the window and saw the bed, the crumbled sheets and oddly angled blankets, the physical evidence left behind to revive again the memory of Rachael Teal. Doll questioned if the night had been a mistake and decided almost at once that the question was both unanswerable and pointless. He threw it away and wandered mechanically into the bathroom.

From the mirror, he looked back at himself. He had no clear agenda, it was true, but already he had a powerful sense of being late at getting it started.

Doll needed an hour to get himself out. Half of it he used to replace his usual run with a thirty-minute aerobic program of push-ups, stretches, and bends. After that, he showered the sweat off, shaved, and dressed. Coffee, black, and a double large juice in the bar took him ten minutes longer.

14

Elaine Carrow had the first slot on Doll's unwritten list.

She opened the door almost as he knocked, from which Doll guessed that she'd probably been close by in the kitchen. Her dark, blond hair was combed back. Her eyes were clear. Her skin was pale as it usually was. The emotional flush of the previous night was gone from her face. Her lips were able to manage a small, only slightly wilted smile.

It didn't matter, Doll thought, that what he saw was mostly a façade. He glanced deliberately toward the empty driveway.

"He still hasn't come home?"

"Not yet." Elaine shook her head and brushed her hair back with her fingers. "Come in, Mr. Doll. You can't stand out there." She opened the door to its full width to admit him.

"But he will," she said once Doll was inside. "He's alive, anyway. He got through the night. The police haven't called. There's always the bright side, isn't there? If the worst means it's time he goes off on his own, then that's what has to be."

"And you?" Doll asked.

"I've thought a lot about that." She fiddled away her nervousness by dusting the handle of a cabinet with a cloth she discovered on a counter. "I have the two girls. I had to remember. How could I almost have forgotten that? They have to be raised.

That's what I have to do. With LeRoy gone now, and maybe Farron, too, I'm going to have to figure out some way to do it."

She affected another smile. "Don't look so solemn, please, Mr. Doll. I have this house. I could sell it, the way things are, for very good money. I could buy a mobile near Cambridge or Easton and still have plenty left over."

"And do what?" Doll asked.

"Work." Elaine made the answer seem obvious. "I can check in a supermarket. I've done that before. I can pack fish, if there's any caught to be packed. Women—even older than I am—have had to make out on their own before."

"If none ever had before," Doll said, "somehow I'm sure you'd be the first."

Elaine looked away, toward the kitchen window that overlooked the bay.

"I'd offer you coffee," she said, turning back to him, "but you won't drink it when I make it. I have milk, cocoa, beer, and soda. I could make you eggs, or something else if you wanted." She paused and twisted at the fabric of her sleeve. "Ellis called before. He'll be by shortly. I'll offer him something. Maybe you want to wait for him."

"Maybe you'd rather I didn't," Doll suggested.

"No. No, I wouldn't," Elaine answered quickly, as though she'd already thought the matter through. "Ellis is one of the parts of all this. Life doesn't let us have everything, Mr. Doll. There are ways in which I wanted Ellis and ways in which I wanted my marriage to LeRoy. Now it looks as though I may wind up without either. If that's the way it works out, what can I do but put it down to a regret?"

"Does Ellis know what you're thinking?" Doll asked.

Elaine closed her eyes, drew in a breath, and shook her head. "Not yet," she whispered. She opened her eyes again. "I'll tell him. I'll make him see that it isn't his fault. Nothing that he did. Maybe when things settle out again. . . ." She left the thought unfinished. "I only hope he'll understand."

"He'll have to."

"No one has to, and Ellis is a schoolboy." She tossed her head back as if, with the gesture, she could shake the problem of Ellis LeCates from her mind. "You never answered me about some breakfast," she said, redirecting her attention to Doll.

"Coffee," Doll answered. "And I'll drink it. This time I promise."

"And you will." Elaine laughed. "You'll make yourself drink it, I know. You'd drink it if I made it from bay mud not to hurt my feelings. You don't have to worry. I'm not that tender."

She turned to the stove to put on the water.

"You know, it's time," she said, "you were married again."

Doll looked up, too sharply.

"Not me! I didn't mean that." Elaine Carrow's cheeks colored to scarlet. "To the right woman, someone young enough so you'd still have time for children. I told you you'd be good with children. So many people who have them and aren't good. It almost becomes an obligation if you would be."

"I wouldn't be that good." Doll found himself drawn to the window that Elaine so liked for looking out at nothing on the bay.

"I think you would," Elaine persisted.

Doll felt skewered, and all the more infuriated because the position in which he found himself, he knew, was of his own making.

His own arguments ridiculed him. When you made it your business to put a magnifying glass to people's lives, a level of more than casual intimacy developed. The deeper you looked, the more you saw. It began to bring on delusions of godhood—until suddenly, when you expected it least, something happened to let you know that the lens worked from both directions—that the life you were so intently gaping at was equally capable of gaping back.

"I'm not good at long-term commitments," he answered. But then he recalled what Rachael Teal had said about his feelings toward one-night stands and decided that he wasn't all that good at short-term commitments either.

"All right, Mr. Doll. I'll let you alone," Elaine said, as though she'd been reading his mind. She got a mug from the cabinet and set it out before him. "I only mean that it's not fair to you—not fair that you should give people help, then not allow yourself to take it in turn."

Doll welcomed the respite of silence as Elaine meted out a spoonful of coffee and topped off the mug with boiling water.

Doll not only drank the coffee, he wound up by being grateful for it. It gave his hands and his mouth something to do. He wanted to go. At the same time, he wanted to be there when LeCates came. But then, "wanted" was the wrong word. He felt the obligation to be there—for Elaine, for LeCates, and for himself and the role he'd had in what had happened since he'd come there to the island.

What made the waiting all the worse was that he couldn't keep up his end of the talking anymore. Whatever he tried to say came out, to his ear, sounding like some new, convoluted offer of help—and so reopened the threatening prospect of Elaine trying to help him in turn.

Had Doll's sense of humor been intact, he might have found his predicament comic. His efforts at making conversation with Elaine became like a complex machine, the single function of which was to shut itself off.

"We could always try the weather," Elaine suggested.

"You're right. I hear myself and I sound like an idiot," Doll said. "My father was from back-country Virginia. That says more than it sounds. If you know what people are like back there, you'd understand why I've always had trouble talking to others about myself."

It was half the truth, Doll told himself, as much as he'd ever let anyone know.

"I think people talk more around water," Elaine answered. "Something about water—I don't know what it is—seems to make people open up more. I don't know why that should be so."

Doll heard the noise first. Elaine, by her face, heard it only a second later. The whir of the engine, low pitched and steady, then the burbling sound as the clutch was disengaged and the machine coasted smoothly into the driveway.

Elaine reached across the table and put her hand over Doll's, then, just as quickly, took it back and looked sheepishly away.

"Do you want me to go?" Doll asked.

"No." Elaine shook her head emphatically. "It doesn't mean he's come to stay. It doesn't mean anything. No more lies, Mr. Doll. Not to protect him or me or anybody. He's got to see things like they are and do whatever he's got to do about them. That's the only way it can be."

They waited. Elaine said nothing. After a moment Doll even doubted she knew he was there. She divided her attention between the tabletop and the window, not even able to look at the door.

Only when it opened did she finally turn toward it.

Farron pulled it closed behind him and stood silent just inside. His face was streaked with dirt and his eyes half closed. His shirt and pants were damp. They clung to his skin in this place or that and puckered in others. His muddy blond hair was tangled and matted. He tried, with notably poor results, wiping his hands on the legs of his pants.

"Help me, Ma, please," he said. "I'm sorry, and I don't know what to say."

They held one another for a good part of forever, each of them heaving and snorting together and by turns. Elaine found a wad of tissues in her pocket. She wiped Farron's face and shared the rest with him until the short supply was gone.

"There, now. . . ." Elaine pushed herself back and smiled.

Farron began to speak, but she silenced him with a finger to his lips.

"It's over. All behind us," she whispered. "There's not another word that ever needs to be said."

"Mr. Doll . . ." Farron glanced beyond Elaine.

"Welcome home," Doll said, and Farron nodded.

Elaine poured a third mug of coffee and beckoned Farron to the table.

"I know what I look like," he said mostly to Doll because Doll was already sitting there. "I'm sorry."

"You look like you slept with the cat," Doll said, grinning, "and you smell like you fell in its dinner."

"Guess I do," Farron answered and laughed. "I slept in the cabin on Uncle Ornan's boat. Night cools off the air, and all the water drops out. An' I was sweatin' pretty good. Guess that all added some to the problem."

"You could've frozen out there," Elaine said as she brought the mug of coffee.

"Naw. I was under all the rain gear." Farron sipped at the coffee and grimaced. "No offense," he said, "but it don't go down too good this mornin'. Guess my stomach's a little weak. Guess I'm not all settled out."

"You're home," Elaine said. "The stomach's nothing to care about."

"Well, you're gonna hear from Uncle Ornan." Farron tried another swallow of coffee and seemed to make out a little better than he had on the first. "It was him that found me this mornin'. Called me some right nasty names an' said he'd take a tarred rope to my hide. Made me feel right stupid, Ma. Told me to go home an' clean myself up or else he'd throw me over the side an' start on the job for himself."

"I never knew," Doll said, "that your uncle was that much of a talker."

"Uncle Ornan?" Farron sounded surprised at that. "Sometimes he's got a lot a' things to say."

"Farron . . ." Elaine reached to the pocket where she'd had the tissues, but seemed to give up on needing them when she found they weren't there. "I've been telling Mr. Doll that I've had to do some thinking lately. Some of it's about you. Some of it's about other things. But what you have to know first is that nobody has a private right on being wrong. I was wrong when there were things I didn't tell you. That isn't going to happen anymore. Tell him, Mr. Doll. He's old enough to have the right to know about what might have happened to his father."

It was a topic Doll had reason to want to avoid. At the same time, he resigned himself, there was no way of avoiding it forever.

"You asked me once," he said to Farron, "if I thought that your father was murdered. I'm telling you now that I think he was. You told me he was careful. Everybody else I talked to said the same thing. If he didn't let the stove fastening come loose, then somebody deliberately loosened it. Up to there it's easy. After that the questions are hard."

"You mean who did it? Gerry Vaughn?" Farron said.

"Why him?" Doll asked.

"The fight. The one at the inn."

"He's not," Doll said, "the only person that your father had a fight with."

"Who else?" Farron's face looked blank.

"No, Mr. Doll!" Elaine's voice exploded with outrage. "I won't let you do this. I thought you were our friend. Now you turn on us like this. I won't have it. Do you hear me? I won't."

"I don't understand. What's he sayin'?" Farron pleaded, staring at Elaine.

"That you and your father had a difference of opinion," Doll replied. "From stories I've heard, that also wound up in a fight."

"Because a' him goin' up t' Bal'mer?" Farron's mouth contorted into a broad, ironic smirk. "Yeah, some fight. We went 'round the barn a little, as you might say. He whipped my ass, Mr. Doll. I never threw a solid punch. You ever know how hard it is to swing on your father?"

"That's enough. Stop it!" Elaine demanded. "Farron, you don't have to say anything more. I told you, Mr. Doll, you're no friend of ours if you keep this up. Couldn't you see that he'd put it all so far from his mind that he didn't even understand what you were talking about?"

"I told you about the skeletons," Doll said quietly, reminding Elaine. "You faced up to your own, and you beat them. Whatever happened to LeRoy, Farron's got to do the same."

"I didn't do it. I swear, Mr. Doll," Farron insisted. "I didn't loosen the fitting. I didn't kill my father. Any more than I could make myself hit him, I couldn't have made myself do it."

"There. That's enough. I won't have you asking him any more questions." Elaine looked toward the window. "God," she whispered. She blinked and rubbed her eyes with her fists, then ran her hands back through her hair. "Maybe I'm the one who's been wrong all along. I shouldn't have let this ever get started."

"It would be a bad time to stop it," Doll said.

Elaine returned her attention to the room. She stared hotly at Doll. "Why, Mr. Doll? Why?" she asked. "Why would it be a bad time now?"

"Because we've stirred the pot." Doll gave that much the time to sink in before he tried to explain further. "In a place this size, you couldn't do anything else. Somebody loosened that fitting. Whoever did knows we've been looking. That makes him—or her—nervous, and nervous people sometimes can be dangerous. I'm not saying we can't back away, if that's what you really think you want to do. I am saying, for a couple reasons, I think it would be a mistake not to see it to the end."

"Not if Farron's going to be hurt by it," Elaine answered vehemently.

Doll glanced at Farron, then turned away. He knew too much of his objectivity was eroded. It was too easy to see what he wanted to see in Farron's face.

"There's only one way that Farron can get hurt," Doll said to Elaine. "Do you remember how Ellis wanted to go ahead with this? Do you understand why he wanted that?"

"Because he wanted his name cleared," Elaine recalled.

"That's right," Doll acknowledged. "And there are others, Elaine. People who had open differences with LeRoy, and whose names keep coming up whenever there's talk about what happened. Farron, just now, mentions Gerry Vaughn. Somebody else brings up Farron. Somebody else says Ellis or Ardee Vaughn or Covey Wallace. What I'm saying is that all but one—maybe even all—of those people aren't guilty. For all of them, the record deserves to be cleared. All of them, Farron included."

Elaine made no immediate answer. Her eyes moved from Doll to Farron and on into some middle distance, where they seemed to focus on nothing. Doll let her think. He'd made the commitment that first day he'd seen her to let her make the decisions. With hindsight, if he'd known then . . . . But now it was done, and there was no taking it back.

"Mr. Doll," Elaine said, turning toward him. "If you don't mind, I think that Farron and I need some time alone to talk."

"I'll leave, then," Doll said, standing.

"No. Please don't." Elaine rose with him. "We can use another room. It won't take long. And what I have to say when we're done will give you the answer you need."

Alone in the kitchen, Doll went to the window and gazed out at the bright sunlight on the water of the bay. A long way out a slow-moving workboat plied the water. It might, he thought, on another day, have been *Tarrier* or *Jewel*, crabbing or tonging. Watermen had to be adaptable workers. They harvested what the bay chose to offer in the best way that they could.

Doll let his eyes drift—and waited.

A moment passed, and something about the trees near the house caught his attention. The leaves were new, pale green miniatures of what they would be in another month. For a dozen decades or more, those same trees had watched over the slow, seasonal pace of the island. Doll wondered, two decades from now, what they'd look down on. Two decades was nothing, he thought, in the lives of trees.

"Mr. Doll." Elaine and Farron stood in the doorway to the kitchen, side by side as they had in the photograph, except, of course, that, in the literal sense, LeRoy Carrow wasn't between them. "We've had our talk. You can guess, I'm sure, what it was about. Farron says he had nothing to do with what happened to LeRoy. I believe him, though I realize I can't expect you to take that as a fact. The point is, I suppose, that we want you to go ahead with what you're doing. If there's someone responsible for what happened, we both want to know who it is."

Doll nodded to say that he understood. "You know there are implications in that," he said just to be sure.

"You mean about Farron," Elaine said evenly, "about me

not being able to take this decision back. You don't have to be afraid of that, Mr. Doll. You must know that from all I said before. It seems to be my time for burning bridges."

"Good morning," LeCates called in through the door that he'd already partially opened.

"Ellis, good morning. Come in," Elaine said, turning toward him.

LeCates came into the kitchen, looking between Doll and Farron and doing his unsuccessful best not to look disapproving in the process. Finally, he settled his attention on Doll.

"Morning." He smiled thinly. "Seems like you get up pretty early these days." When Doll offered no reply, he shifted to Farron. "What about you? I'd say that you're up early, too. Especially considering. You have yourself a good time last night? From the look of you, you must have had a doozer."

"It's done, Ellis. It's over. We settled all that," Elaine said.

"It's not over." LeCates seemed almost to surprise himself as he heard himself contradict her. "He's got no right to do what he did to you. Look at him there. He looks like something skid row passed over. What gives him the right to be anybody's conscience?"

"What gives you the right to be his—or mine?" Elaine asked. If she'd smashed LeCates with the frying pan, probably she would have done less damage. "I'm sorry," she apologized almost at once. "I only meant . . . I know that you're trying to help me. Only, let it be over, Ellis. Just let all of last night be over."

LeCates didn't look up from the floor.

"I was wrong last night," Farron said to LeCates. "I'm not blaming anybody for anything anymore. I learned me that lesson at least."

"Then something good came of it, anyway," LeCates muttered, still not taking his eyes from the floor.

"More than just that." Elaine crossed the kitchen and sat in one of the chairs at the table. "There's more that has to be said—not about the past, about the things that were, but about how some things have to be. I'd say them to you alone, but it's also important that Farron hear them. Mr. Doll doesn't have to, but he knows them already, so there isn't any point in telling him to leave."

"What things, Elaine?" LeCates asked.

His manner was quiet. Doll thought that he'd never seen him so humbled. He waited to hear what Elaine had to tell him. He seemed, at that moment, neither to care or even notice that Doll and Farron were also in the room.

"I've had to think things out," Elaine said. "If Farron didn't come back—or even if he did. He's a man, Ellis. Look at him. He's got a life to live. I haven't got the right to hold him here. Then there's the girls. I've got to take care of them. It doesn't mean there's any change in the way I feel about you. But it means there are other things that have to come before that."

"I don't understand," LeCates said grimly shaking his head. "I understand the words. I understand about the girls. The rest? I don't know what it means."

Doll watched Elaine dry her hands in the folds of her skirt.

"Don't ask me," she answered. "I don't know what it means. Not if you're talking about anything that's concrete. But I know there have to be things that come first. I know it has to be the girls. I know somehow I have to put that together, whatever it takes. After that—after that's done—I don't know what happens, Ellis. I can't promise anything. I can't promise that there's going to be anything left for you and me."

"You don't sound like you hold out much hope," LeCates said.

Elaine let her skirt fall back into her lap.

"Don't ask me to do the impossible, Ellis," she whispered. "I don't know right now. I just don't know."

15

Excluding the screened porch which ran across the width of the front, the house where Covey Wallace lived was roughly square. As houses go, it was small. Doll estimated thirty feet to the side. All the rooms were confined to the single floor.

The low-pitched roof was covered with black asphalt shingles, except for where it had been mended. In those places, the choice of color had apparently been made on the grounds of price and availability. Some patches were white and others brick red, and others still an off-shade of brown. The sides of the house that Doll could see were, likewise, randomly patterned. Mostly the outside walls were clad in rigid, white asbestos shingles of the kind that had been in vogue in the early nineteen-forties. In places, though, the original cover was broken or gone. No one had bothered fitting replacements, and the under-coating of tarpaper was left to show through.

All around the house, the grass and bushes were brittle and brown. The plant life of the neighboring houses, contrastingly, showed the signs of early greening.

As Doll started up the walk, almost at once, the dog began barking. Doll took a second to locate the source inside the screen-enclosed porch. The animal, as best he could see, was a mixed-breed, black and white, not unlike the house, and about the size of a collie. Its fur was matted and badly in need of washing, but the teeth that it showed looked to Doll very healthy indeed. The barking and the dog's excitement grew apace as Doll approached. Each time the dog hurled its weight against the screen, Doll found himself assessing the chances that the warped and rusting wire mesh was going to hold.

The door from the house onto the porch opened about half its distance.

"Wha'cha want here?" a voice called out from the semidarkness inside.

"Mr. Wallace? My name's Doll. I'd like to talk to you," Doll called back to the man whom he still couldn't see.

"Know who ya are. Got nothin' t' say. Ya hightail back where ya come from, or I lets out the dog."

"I really wish you wouldn't do that," Doll called.

"Then move off. Ya picked yer side. Ya chose t' hang with them sumbitchin' drudgers. You an' me ain't got nothin' t' say."

"Thought you might feel like that." Doll reached inside his jacket and brought out a brown, oblong bag. He held it up at arm's length for the man in the half-opened doorway to examine.

At first there was no response, then, "Wha'cha got there?" the voice shouted back.

"Bourbon. Bonded. It's a bribe if you're Wallace," Doll answered across the yard.

"Oh, I'm Wallace, a'right." The small man stepped out from the door onto the porch. Doll remembered him from the car, the thin face barely visible over the steering wheel. Now Doll could see that his whole frame was slight. His face was hairy, not stubble like Page's, not bearded, either, because the concept of beard implied some discernible shape.

"Bribe, eh," Wallace repeated appraisingly. "What I gotta do t' get it?"

"I've got some questions," Doll said. "You've got to give a fair try at giving me the answers."

"Bourbon. Bonded." Wallace rolled the words around like a memory. "Okay, Doll. I figure yer bribe's 'bout good fer what yer askin'. Get y'self up here. Ol' Millie girl won't hurt ya none. Go, bitch, go!" he shouted. Obediently, the dog went in past Wallace, and Wallace closed the door behind her. He opened the screened door to the porch for Doll. "Leastways," he said, "she won't while she's inside."

The floor of the porch was littered with what Doll decided might have been the unsellable refuse from a yard sale. There were dusty jars, parts of unidentifiable machinery, and broken furniture, all interspersed with little piles of offerings that Millie, over months or maybe years, had from time to time left behind. There were two rattan chairs that seemed partially sound and two cement blocks that served as a table between them.

Wallace sat in one of the chairs and pointed for Doll to take the other. Doll put the bottle on the blocks in between. It stayed there for less than a second before Wallace picked it up and examined it.

"Good fer yer word so far anyways," Wallace said and nodded.

"That's quite a fight you've got going with the drudgers," Doll replied. "One of those beer cans nearly took off my head the other night."

"Yer own fault." Wallace shrugged indifferently. He fumbled with his shirt pocket, brought out a pack of cigarettes, and lit one. He puffed at it, then swished away the smoke with his hand as though he hated to inhale the stuff himself. "Ya ought'a be more careful 'bout who ya take yer drink with."

"You figure they've been using their boats to drudge your beds?"

"Boats! Christ's balls, Doll, you don't know half a' what yer talkin' 'bout. Where was ya back winter?—Four months back when the bay got frozed over? They put a goddamn car out on the ice. You kin believe that. They put out a goddamn car an' drudged the tongin' beds with that."

"Is that true?" Doll asked.

"Course it's true. Ask 'em. They tell ya themselves if ya feed 'em enough hooch. They're thievin' bastards, all of 'em drudgers. That's how ya know if a man's a drudger. If ya feel his hand while he's pickin' yer pocket, ya got a better 'an nine in ten chance."

"LeRoy Carrow?"

Covey Wallace constructed a compound curse built from seven of the filthiest words that he knew.

"Do you know that for sure? It's important," Doll said. "Do you know for sure that Carrow's the one who salted your land?"

"Ya takin' his part?" Wallace pulled his weight forward on the chair. " 'Cause if ya are, ya son of a bitch, I'll break yer bottle, bonded or no, across the top a' yer head."

"Can we take it a little slower, before you put your neck in a noose?" Doll suggested.

Wallace's eyes narrowed, and his forehead dropped. He seemed to consider the point for a moment, then eased back in his chair and sucked at his cigarette.

"You know who I am," Doll said. "By now the whole island, including you, knows that I think that Carrow was murdered. If the betting on who did it was handicapped, you've got to know that you and Gerry Vaughn would be the odds-on favorites. Did you ever step back and think for a minute if that's a race you really want to win?"

A long and very silent plume of smoke issued upward from Wallace's mouth.

"Ya really figure Gerry killed 'im?" he finally asked.

"I don't know who killed him. It could've been Gerry. And don't fool yourself into thinking I've given up on you." Doll looked hard at Wallace, who raised an eyebrow, but showed no more reaction than that. "But what I'm asking now," Doll went on, "is who else is there. Who else is there who you can think of who wanted to see LeRoy Carrow dead?"

"Ya mean the Teal chippie?"

"I don't know. Is she who I mean? Did she want Carrow out of her way?"

Wallace shrugged. "She was a buyer."

"Your place? She talked to you about it? Before or after the salting?" Doll asked.

"Both. Don't make either difference," Covey Wallace answered.

"You didn't take it either time?" Doll pressed.

"Wasn't enough. Either time," Wallace replied. "First time I thought it was a lot too low. Figured I'd make out better with the Vaughns, an' I would've. Second time, after I got salted, I still figured the place was worth more 'an she was offerin'. Figured t' wait 'er out. Leastways get a little stubborn. She ain't come back at me yet. Course, that's only so far."

"She offered you one of her option contracts?"

Wallace nodded.

Doll asked how it worked.

"Hanged if I know." Wallace took in a mouthful of smoke and spat it out without inhaling. "Never got close enough on price so's I took the trouble to read it. Not that that would've done no good. Who the hell can read all that legal mumbo jumbo?"

"Do you still have a copy?"

"Course I got one. A blank one," Wallace answered as though the fact that he'd retain a copy ought to have been obvious to anyone. "Ya even think 'bout signin' somethin' like that, it ain't the kind a' thing ya throw away."

* * *

Doll took the blank contract on loan from Covey Wallace, knowing he'd need more time to read it than he wanted to spend on Wallace's porch.

Back at his room at the inn, he scanned its four pages before settling down to read them closely. On that much alone, the typeface was small enough by itself to be threatening. Sentences ran on for the lengths of paragraphs. Here and there he came up against Latin phrases. For the rest, the legal jargon was thick enough that Doll felt discomfort at trusting its meaning to any layman's interpretation, including his own.

After the additional hour that it took him to read the contract carefully, Doll's first impression hadn't changed.

The sign that said "Vaughn Realty" was painted in blue letters shadowed in red against a background of white. In the upper right-hand corner an outlined ship that might have been a skipjack sailed on a waterless sea. Below the more prominent name of the firm, were the smaller words "Residential-Commercial," below that a phone number, and finally, discreetly, the name of "R. D. Vaughn, Licensed Realtor."

The office was a neatly painted house along the main road. In front was a shell-paved parking area, which, at that moment, held two cars. The first Doll recognized from the lot at the inn and decided it must belong to Vaughn. The other was a very familiar van.

A small chorus of fairy bells tinkled as Doll opened the door to the office. The tiny noise caused a trim, blond receptionist to look up from her desk. Doll recalled the appraisal of Ellis LeCates on Ardee Vaughn and hips. But the receptionist never got past her initial smile. At the moment she began to speak, Rachael Teal emerged from a door that opened on one of the interior offices.

She looked at Doll and seemed to let her face show surprise.

"Good morning," she said, then glanced at her watch. "Or should I say that? It's nearly noon. Are you just getting up? What makes you such a late sleeper?"

"I tend toward laziness," Doll answered back. "But not you, I see. You're getting in a good day's work as always."

"As always." Rachael smiled widely.

"Oh, Doll." Ardee Vaughn came to the office door and stood behind and to the side of her. "You're about the last person I ever expected to see here. Especially today."

"Why, Richard?" Rachael asked too expansively. "Can't you guess that Mr. Doll has been seduced by our local properties market? You have—I'm sure it's true—haven't you, Mr. Doll? Or perhaps it's something personal. I think maybe I should let the two of you alone."

"I could use a few minutes, if you've got them, Ardee," Doll said.

"Why not?" Vaughn scratched at his collar. "It's hard to see what else you could do to my life."

"Then I'll let you both alone." Rachael began to walk to the door, but then turned back. "But, on second thought, no," she said, looking at Doll. "It's almost noon. You told Richard 'a few minutes,' so I gather that your business won't take long. I'm proposing lunch, Mr. Doll, if you're up to it. I was in something of a rush this morning and didn't take the time I usually do for breakfast."

Her invitation wasn't what Doll would have preferred. At the same time, especially after seeing Vaughn, he knew there was more that he'd have to ask her. He nodded his head to agree.

"Fine." Rachael smiled. "Then I'll meet you outside at my van. Don't feel you have to hurry in here on my account. There's plenty of work I can do out there in the meantime.

"Good-bye for now, Richard. Our paths will cross again, I'm fairly sure." She waved coyly at Vaughn as she turned and left.

"Ballsy broad." Vaughn shook his head as he closed the door to his private office and pointed Doll toward a chair. "You want some coffee? I'll have Charlene put on some fresh water."

Doll declined the offer. "How's your boy this morning?" he asked.

"Well, I don't figure he'll be in to work today," Vaughn answered dourly. "His eye's all red. The whole side of his face is black and blue. He could've had a concussion, you know."

"Not with a skull that thick," Doll said.

Vaughn looked up. He seemed unsure of how he ought to react. "Humph. Yeah," was all he finally said. "What do you want, Doll? Why did you come here? Somehow I get the feeling it wasn't to ask after my boy."

Reaching into his pocket, Doll brought out the contract. Without offering an explanation, he handed it across the desk to Vaughn.

Vaughn skimmed through the pages quickly, glanced at Doll, then looked them over again.

"Hers?" he said, poking an end of the contract in the general direction of the office parking area.

Doll nodded. "I take it you haven't seen one before?"

Vaughn shook his head and asked where Doll had gotten it. "You went to see Covey?" he said when Doll had answered. "And you got him to let you take this? You got as big a set of balls as she does, except you haven't got a set of knockers to match."

"And now that you've seen it," Doll went on, "I figure that means you owe me a favor. I've read it through. I think I know most of it, but I want to go over with you what it all means."

Vaughn's fingers ran over the papers. "Like what? What do you want to know?" he asked.

"They're options, like she said they were," Doll began. He waited for Vaughn to nod his affirmative answer. "Tell me in everyday language how they work."

"Well, there are two sides, two avenues, to the purchase of the property," Vaughn answered now with a practiced professional caution. "But even that starts us off too far ahead. Begin with the idea that you own a piece of property that you're free to sell anytime you want for the highest price that you're able to get. Now let's say I think I might want to buy that property, not now, but at some time in the future. I want to protect my opportunity to buy, so I pay you something now for the sole consideration that you limit your right to sell."

"How much do you pay me?" Doll asked.

Vaughn waved a hand indifferently into the air. "It's negotiable. It isn't stated in the contract. If I were guessing—if I were doing it—I'd go to somewhere between three and five percent of current market value."

"And what do I as the owner give up?"

"Well, then we get back to the two avenues," Vaughn explained. "Let's take the easier one first. This contract gives the company that Rachael represents a very basic right of first refusal. What does it mean? Let's say at some future time you decide to sell your property. You're free to put it on the market pretty much as you usually would and get the best offer that you can. But—and it may not be that big a 'but' to you—before you can accept that offer you've got to first give Rachael's company the opportunity to purchase the property at the offered price. If they exercise their right, you have to sell to them. If not, you're free to accept the offer from the second party. In either case the price paid to you is the same."

"And the second avenue?"

"A little more unusual," Vaughn said. "It's less of a restriction than it is an inducement to accept a fair market value offer from the company at an unspecified later date. Again, the company gives you now some negotiated dollar figure. The understanding is that at some future point they'll make you a fair market value offer on your property. You're protected," Vaughn included as an aside, "in that the fair market value is adjudicable. Anyway, the assumption is that, at that future time, you'll accept the company's fair offer. You have no obligation to accept, but, if you don't, you have to return to the company its original payment to you plus a specified rate of interest."

"But why go through the trouble," Doll asked, "when the company could make an offer anytime without putting any inducement up front?"

"It's simply psychology." Vaughn smiled. "By that time, you've decided that the money they gave you for the option is permanently yours. The odds, in fact, are that you've probably spent it. The bottom line is that you're far more likely to simply accept their offer and sell."

"But either way," Doll said, "the present owner comes to see his property as less of a place that he thinks of as home—with all those connotations—and more as an investment with a profit to be reaped."

"Yes, I suppose that's true," Vaughn agreed. "It's funny in a way, because it's almost the opposite of what I do. I make the better part of my living selling people dreams."

He reached down into his desk drawer and took out a pack of cigarettes. He started to pop one out, then threw the pack back.

"God," he said. "My goddamn son. I think my head felt worse than his this morning. Every time I try to light one of those up, I feel like I'm gonna be sick."

* * *

Rachael picked the place for their lunch. Doll found himself back in the same tavern where he'd spent the evening only nights before swapping drinks and occasional threats with George Page and the others. This time, though, they sat on the opposite side, at a table in the restaurant instead of the bar.

"What did you really want with Richard?" she asked when they'd gotten themselves into place.

A waitress came by, and both of them ordered a beer from the bar.

"A lot of things," Doll answered vaguely.

A framed drawing of a pair of waterfowl captured his attention, or was it only, Doll thought, procrastination? The artist had caught the detail of the birds, portraying them more in the manner of a naturalist than a painter. There was fine, gray lettering along the bottom of the print, too far away for Doll to read, but presumably reporting the species of bird that the picture represented.

"You asked him about his son?" She went on without waiting for an answer, as though that topic held no interest for her. "That and what else?"

Doll considered the question for a moment, then reached into his pocket and handed her the copy of the contract.

She glanced at it, turning it over in her hand and, without any comment or evident emotion, handed it back.

"That's it?" Doll asked. "That's the end of your reaction?"

Rachael exhaled as though she were tired and bored. "What did you expect? Indignation? That's a technique, not a reaction. Where'd you get it from? Covey Wallace, I assume. Never mind. It doesn't matter. That's what you went to see Vaughn about? Why?"

"So I was sure I knew what it said," Doll replied.

"Why not come to me?"

The waitress arrived with their beers and took their orders. The fun seemed to have evaporated from Rachael's mood.

"You would have told me to stay out of your business," Doll said. "I couldn't accept that. I needed more for an answer."

"So now you know how the options work. Was it worth it, Doll? Was it worth all the effort? How does it help you with LeRoy Carrow? Does it get you anything more than you already had before?"

"New ways of seeing things." Doll tasted his beer. "The way that a man sees his house. Maybe that's all it comes down to."

"Do I take it you're being mysterious?" Rachael asked.

"These option contracts—how many was it you said you had? I take it they're not in the public domain. Is there any reason that you can't tell me who they're with?"

Rachael lifted her beer toward Doll and saluted him with the rim of her glass mug. She smiled. "Why don't you just go to hell," was all that she said by way of an answer.

Doll met her toast and touched the rim of his glass to hers. After that they both sat saying nothing until a merciful waitress brought them their food.

Rachael picked at hers with a more than evident lack of enthusiasm. "What did you mean before about the way that a man sees his house?" she finally asked.

"It's hard to explain." Doll shook his head. "You're not tied to things. You live on the road. In rented rooms. Half out of a van."

"You don't mean a house. You mean a home. I told you once before: Don't patronize me, Doll. Don't close me in like some stereotyped Shylock. I won't take it. And you'd be wrong."

"I'm sorry. I didn't mean to patronize," Doll apologized.

"I know the kind of home you mean. If it's any of your

business—which it isn't—I once even had one. Or I didn't, so much as my parents did. Nothing grand, you understand. Just an averaged-sized house on an average-sized lot in a middle-income town in middle Pennsylvania. But a place that's real, with all kinds of ancient relics in the attic, and where it seems like the memories run back to forever."

"It's what I had in mind," Doll said.

"I know damn well what you had in mind. Damn you." She sat there angrily, her scarcely touched soup getting cold on the table before her. "Well, all the rooms and those relics and memories cost money to keep. Or maybe you never had to learn that. It was fine while my father was with us. But then that changed. Do you have any idea what it's like, Doll? Have you ever seen your accumulated lifetime sold off at a yard sale to strangers?"

Doll shook his head. He hadn't, but he knew it as a fact of life. He'd been in 'Nam when his widowed father had died. His sister had done the closing out. The thought struck him only belatedly now that he hadn't even thought of the burden that that must have caused her at the time.

"I told you I wanted money, Doll. It's never going to happen—I'm never going to watch my life being sold off again. I may live out of a van right now. I won't be living out of one forever."

They were nearly total opposites, Doll thought. Opposites at almost every place you looked. Doll, by choice, was a seminomad, an impecunious derelict who, only now and then, took up his profession and who, ironically, since he'd come to the island, found himself caught up in a sudden experience of place. And Rachael, who wanted the trappings of security, became a wanderer by default, darkly compelled to earn her own sanctuary by striking out at the very thing she sought.

"Did you ever think that maybe you're in the wrong business?" Doll asked her.

"And you?" she replied. "Is that your contribution? It's a world of lesser evils out there, Doll. That doesn't always say a lot for the positive values of choice."

16

By the time Doll got back to his car, the blue morning sky had clouded over. The air was heavy and promised rain.

In the early light of the morning, the prospect of Elaine, Vaughn, and Covey Wallace had seemed enough to fill the day. But now, with the day half done, he'd seen them all and, for what he'd found, felt very little closer to knowing LeRoy Carrow's murderer.

His mind played at cause and effect. Had the now sullen day brought on his mood, or did it simply reflect it? Whichever was true, he had the unmistakable feeling of losing momentum.

It all seemed like climbing a steep hill of sand, where the secret, Doll knew, was not to stop climbing. That was how the hill could beat you. Even little steps meant progress. Even when it began to seem like the progress was very near to nothing at all.

There was no one on board the *Winston Mills*. Doll asked around and easily found Ornan Atkins' house from word of mouth. It was one of the few times that the smallness of the island had worked to his advantage.

The house was on the eastern side and overlooked the inlet pond that separated the eastern and western claws. Atkins' colorless pickup was parked in the driveway beside the house. Doll found Atkins half beneath it, on his back, poking a caged electric light up into the bracing behind the right wheel. A small collection of tools lay on an oiled rag near his side.

"Afternoon," Doll called, taking in what he could see of Atkins' legs and feet. Atkins made no move to get out from under, although he could hardly have failed to see Doll's car stop as well as his on-foot approach.

"Some way I kin help ya?" Atkins answered, prodding some part with the fingers of his free hand.

"I hoped we could talk," Doll said.

Atkins made no immediate answer, but continued his inspection of the wheel. "Free country," he acknowledged after he seemed to feel that sufficient time had passed. "Say what ya got to. Won't interfere none with my work here. Ya mind passin' over that long, thin screwdriver—that one that's right there next t' your foot?"

Doll squatted down and passed the tool. "I wanted to talk about who might've wanted to murder LeRoy Carrow."

"So?"

"So, what?"

"So, talk," Atkins answered from the obscurity beneath the truck. "I don't see where anybody's stoppin' ya."

"All right," Doll replied, determined to make the best that he could of a palpably doomed situation. "Let's start with the fact that we both know what happened wasn't an accident. I'm not asking you to say yes or no. You already gave that answer without saying it. If it wasn't an accident, somebody did it. I take it we're in agreement at least up to there."

Atkins kept up his work on the wheel.

"There are a lot of candidates," Doll went on alone. His head conjured up the image of a running back hitting at the year's all-pro defensive line. "There's Gerry Vaughn. Covey Wallace. But the more you look, the more the list gets longer."

"That a fact." Atkins put the screwdriver back on the rag and substituted a pair of pliers.

"Your nephew's another possibility," Doll said.

"Killed 'is own father? Don't ya say so!" The words implied a mild and dispassionate level of interest, when, in fact, as Doll was fully aware, they were a sardonic joke made at Doll's expense.

"Don't you care about any of this?" Doll said, and at once regretted having allowed himself to be baited.

"Well, now, I do and I don't, Mr. Doll." Atkins moved, but only enough to adjust his angle with respect to the truck wheel. "I care for Elaine, and I care for Farron. I care for my neighbors around here, too."

"But not LeRoy Carrow."

Atkins tugged at something with the pliers and grunted. "LeRoy's dead, Mr. Doll," he said matter-of-factly. "Don't know that I see what good I could do for 'im."

He drew up his knees and hauled the top half of his body out from under the pickup. He looked up at Doll with his storm-gray eyes and half stood, brushing the dirt on his hands off on his pants.

Doll stood with him, stretching the stiffness out of his legs.

"Then there's the rest of it. That'd be you," Atkins said, standing up the rest of the way and meeting Doll eye to eye. "It was all well an' good before with the inquest. The matter was done, an' life was gettin' 'bout goin' on. Then along you come. Nobody from the island asked ya, 'cept maybe your buddy from up the store, an' he don't count. Ya got all that talk ya give t' Elaine 'bout what ya call justice, but I'm not all that sure ya know y'self what justice is 'bout."

"I never pushed it," Doll said in his own defense. "Elaine

knew all along that all she had to do, anytime she wanted, was tell me to go home."

"I know that, too," Atkins answered, "an' I'm just not sure that it makes so much difference. Elaine's confused 'bout a lot a' things. Hell, she's got every right t' be just now. Maybe you're part a' that confusion. That's maybe somethin' else that's wrong with ya, too."

"And the rest?"

"Nothin' I ain't told ya before. I don't take much to liars, an' you came here lyin', boy. Ya stuck your nose in deep where it don't belong. Ya got a friend who don't seem t' know you're expected t' leave a married woman alone."

"Okay, Captain." Doll held up his open hands to concede that the cause was lost. "Thanks for the time and the evaluation. It's been a long time since I had such a thorough critique."

He nodded and began his walk back toward the car.

"Now where ya off t' now, Mr. Doll? Don't suppose it'd hurt ya none t' take another minute 'fore ya go."

Doll stopped and turned back toward Atkins. The interruption was the last thing he'd expected.

"Farron," Atkins said. "He said ya was there when he cut out last night. And again when he came back this mornin'. Also he told me a' what you'd accused 'im."

"I told him what I told you," Doll replied, "that he was on the list of people that had to get looked at."

"An' he an' Elaine went an' talked, an' then they told ya t' go ahead with what ya was doing."

"That's right," Doll said. "You got the kitchen tape recorded?"

"An' ya stood up t' him, t' Farron, for Elaine last night."

"I told him he was out of line," Doll answered. "He was in a pretty ugly mood."

"Hell, I know that." Atkins frowned. "You remember it was me who sent him home this mornin'."

"Well?" Doll said when he got tired of waiting for Atkins to string together this newest accumulation of transgressions.

"Well . . . ya made some fans." Atkins folded his arms across his narrow chest. "I don't know why, but those two trust ya. Don't change my mind, but, well . . . I guess it's gotta go down as a mark in your favor."

"Thanks for that anyway," Doll said. He waited an interval for something more. When it didn't come, he started again toward the car.

"One more thing," Atkins called from behind him.

For yet another time, Doll turned.

"Lord knows, ya give my mind a powerful lot a' trouble," Atkins muttered, vaguely shaking his head. "I make no promises, Mr. Doll. None at all, so don't come back on me whenever tellin' me I did. But I'll say this much. Ya come back t' see me at some future time. 'Tween now an' then, I'll think some on what ya been sayin'."

Doll went to the water, as he almost always did when he needed to think a thing through. On the island, that gave him several good choices. There was water a few hundred yards in virtually any direction he went. Without very much thinking about it, he found himself back at the skipjacks' wharf again.

The time was late afternoon and, as he'd expected with the deteriorating weather, the area was still deserted. The clouds had lowered throughout the day, and now a thin, misty drizzle was falling. He put up the collar of his jacket against it as he walked—and thought about what Ornan Atkins had meant when he'd talked about justice.

That first day, when Elaine had asked him, Doll remembered he'd talked about justice as an abstract social value. No specific good for any particular person, he'd said. Some harm to one, certainly, if Doll was able to find him. He hadn't said that. Maybe he should have. He thought, at the time, it had been understood, but now he had doubts whether even he himself had understood it.

The people on the island hadn't been people to him then. That was maybe what Ornan Atkins was saying. They'd been people to Atkins all along, people he knew. That's what justice meant in a certain sense, an exchange to even out scores between people. But no exchange would bring LeRoy Carrow back. So what became the point of a social abstraction? Were judgments more subtle when smallness allowed it—when even the islanders that Mowen called the new bloods had been there for something on the order of a hundred close-lived years?

Doll walked slowly, looking at nothing, hearing the foghorn and not hearing it, not conscious of the droplets of water that clung to his face. The scene was like a wash painting, all in mute tones of white and blue-gray and gray—except that his eye caught a small splash of color.

Farron Carrow also seemed oblivious of the rain. He sat on the side of the wharf with his feet hanging over the water just astern of his father's sunken boat. Doll wandered up and sat beside him. Farron looked incuriously over.

"Afternoon, Mr. Doll," he said.

Doll said hello. "What are you, like me?" he asked. "Too damn dumb to come in out of the rain."

Farron laughed a little. "Guess ya could say so," he replied.

The drizzle that fell made tiny ripples on the surface of the water that filled the skipjack's cabin. The school of shiny fish, it seemed, had taken up residence elsewhere for the day.

"What'cha doing here?" Doll asked.

"Don't rightly know." Farron shrugged. "Feel a little funny 'bout it, havin' t' tell someone else, if ya wanna know the truth.

Since ya ask me though, I guess ya could say I was kind a' sayin' good-bye."

"To?"

"Well, everything." Farron stared out way across the water, and, for a while, he just looked. "My father. The boat. The island. They're all gone, Mr. Doll. Dead or awfully fast dyin'."

He rolled his head back on his shoulders and, gazing straight up, let the thin rain fall directly on his face.

"Ya know how it is how some minutes stand out? Ya forget almost all a' it, but somehow this or that particular minute happens to stick in your mind. It's like once I remember my father fixin' an outboard, runnin' it in an oil drum. No special thing. He did it all the time. But this time, it was the old Evinrude. Twistin' this an' turnin' that. Cursing at the thing like he always did. Tell me why it's that particular thing I remember."

Doll offered no explanation. He didn't have one.

"Truth is," Farron rambled, "I was kind a' tryin' to make this one a' those times. Don't know if ya can do it just when ya want t', but I had t' try."

"Your mother's still talking about leaving?" Doll said.

"She's thinkin' on it. Too early t' tell how it's gonna come out. Best thing I can do for her an' for me is give her the room an' get outta her way. Besides, it's what I was goin' to do, come when the job at the station run out. Get started a little early. That's all it means. High time I guess I broke the chain."

"Have you talked about this?"

"Oh, yeah. We had a good talk." Farron smiled and nodded. "After you an' Mr. LeCates left, we sat down an' just talked for most of an hour. God, it was funny. Ya never saw two people, each backin' over hisself, tryin' t' help out the other one more."

Doll smiled too. He could imagine the scene—poignant

almost, but the kind you have to back off and laugh at before things start to get sloppy.

"I talked to your Uncle Ornan this afternoon," Doll said, changing the subject. "I could use his help. Let me say it right out. I'd appreciate anything you could say that might persuade him to help me."

"Uncle Ornan? You'll be okay. He likes you, Dr. Doll. I only talked to him this mornin'."

"Your uncle said that he likes me?" Doll's voice was that of a man who had just heard a message he found more than somewhat hard to believe.

Farron frowned at the question, but only a little. "Well, no. He didn't say it," he answered. "Uncle Ornan don't come out an' say things like that. Maybe it's more that ya gotta know 'im before ya can get a sense a' what he's thinkin'."

"Yeah, I figured it had to be something like that." Doll brushed some of the accumulating water from his face. He had the impression it had started to rain harder.

"One more thing," he said, "then I'm going to get myself out of this weather. It's not something I want to ask, Farron, but I have to. I'm not after anybody except for who I said. And I'm certainly not trying to throw any dirt on your memories of your father."

Farron angled his head toward Doll. "No," he said. "I've made my peace. My father's beyond any harm that anyone on earth can do 'im. An' I still want t' see whoever killed him caught. You go ahead an' ask your question, Mr. Doll. If ya say it'll help, I'll answer if I can."

"Covey Wallace's place. Did your father salt it?" Doll asked.

Taking in an exaggerated breath, Farron looked out over the sea again. "Yessir, he did," he admitted to the water. "He wasn't gonna tell me. I sort a' had t' catch him at it. Was a rainy night. Dark. Rainin' harder 'an this. I saw 'im loadin' some sacks from the shed t' the truck. Said I'd help 'im, but he sent me away. Didn't figure."

"You knew it was salt in the sacks?"

"Didn't then." Farron shook his head. "Only I took special notice when, later, he came back without 'em. 'Is clothes were wet, too. Wetter than they would've been if all he'd had to do was just unload what he'd loaded. Had t' take time t' spread it around, ya see. Didn't know that that night either. Not till the next day after when the word began to get round 'bout the saltin'."

Farron stared at Doll as though he were waiting for something. Finally Doll realized that what he was asking was if the admission about his father had helped.

For Farron's sake, Doll said that it had. The more truthful answer would have been that, at that moment, he just didn't know.

Doll hadn't planned to stop at LeCates' store, but the logic of the day—if there was such a thing—ultimately carried him in that direction. In what must have been a record-breaking rush of business, the store had a trio of customers. But all three, as it turned out, were single-item buyers, and the purchasing frenzy quickly ended.

LeCates retreated from his post at the cash register, wiping his hands on the front of his apron. At the table at the back of the aisle, he gazed out the window at the rain and tasted what remained of his tepid, half-finished coffee.

"Maybe it's time to put a stop to it," he said as he put down his cup and turned to Doll. "I'm going to talk to Elaine about it. Maybe I should never have called you, Doll. Maybe I shouldn't have ever let it get started."

"Maybe you shouldn't have," Doll acknowledged, "but you

did. And now—say whatever you want—Elaine understands that it's gotten too late to back out."

"You sound like you're pretty damn sure of yourself."

"It's not me, Ellis. I gave them their choice. They could have ended it all this morning. The problem is Farron. He's in the same place as you were yourself. Him and Covey Wallace and everybody else. Nobody gets cleared until whoever is guilty gets caught."

"That's a neat lawyers' trick, Doll, but it's phony as hell. The fact is that, if Farron's being accused, it comes down to you who's doing the accusing."

"And you, Ellis? You don't care about being accused anymore?"

"That's right, Doll. I don't care anymore." LeCates glared out the window at the shadowy dusk, past his own reflection in the glass.

"You've thought it all through?"

"That's right. I have."

"And that's what you decided? All right, you go ahead. Do whatever you want," Doll said. "You want to crawl into a grave and pull the ground in after you, that's fine. Just don't expect the rest of the world to crawl in with you."

"What? What are you talking about?" LeCates turned angrily back from the window.

"You," Doll answered sharply. "I didn't see it up till now. I didn't realize just how much that last dive took out of you."

"Dive? What the hell are you talking about?" LeCates demanded more loudly.

"You learned something, didn't you, Ellis? You learned how to quit." Doll gave the first words time to sink in. "You quit on diving. Then, later on, you quit on you. Then you have your who-knows-what-you-call-it with Elaine, and up comes trouble and you quit on that. Gets easier and easier, doesn't it, Ellis? Pretty soon it gets so it's all that you know how to do."

"That's none of your business!" LeCates shouted.

"No. You're right. It isn't," Doll agreed. "What business is it of mine if you want to run away every time you hit a problem? Like this store. It doesn't need you. It does everything but run by itself. And that's about as much of life as you can handle."

"You got no right to talk to me like that," LeCates answered. His manner had turned mercurially from hot to brooding.

"No. You're right again. I don't," Doll said. "What else did Elaine tell you this morning? Did she say she's thinking of getting off of the island?"

LeCates nodded and looked to the rain again. "She said it after you left." His voice was tired and beaten. "She talked about maybe Easton or Cambridge. Selling the house and working so she could take care of the girls."

"Is that what you want to happen?" Doll asked.

"You know it isn't," LeCates grumbled. "She's got her mind set. What can I do?"

"Offer her an alternative. Give her a choice."

"Like what? Don't you think I'd do that if I knew what to offer? What's the angle? What do I say to her, Doll? For godsake, don't keep it a mystery if you know."

"Try taking it step by step—and slowly," Doll suggested. "She needs time, Ellis. Time to put LeRoy away and time to get her life back under control. You try to rush her through either of those things, and you're going to lose her."

"How long?" LeCates asked.

Doll shook his head. "There's no answer, Ellis. As long as it takes."

"And in the meantime, while she moves to Easton or Cambridge?" LeCates said, frowning.

"If it were me," Doll replied, "I guess I'd try to give her as many reasons as I could why that shouldn't happen. Real reasons. Make things happen. Start by hiring Farron to work in the store."

"Here? In the store? Christ, Doll!" LeCates thundered. "The place only just about supports me. Besides that, the kid hates me. You're crazy, Doll. None of this is any good."

"All right, then, it isn't," Doll said. One of the few things worse than giving advice, he thought, was giving it when it wasn't really wanted in the first place.

"No, wait. I'm sorry," LeCates said, speaking softly now. "What's the rest? I hire Farron. There has to be more."

"You loan him the money to haul his father's boat. Set it up in a yard. Outside storage isn't that expensive. Let him rebuild it as he comes up with the money and the time. Go partners with him, if you want to."

"Elaine . . ." LeCates asked, almost anxiously, "have you said anything about all this to her?"

"No," Doll replied. "I haven't because it isn't my place. And I won't, even if you ask me to, Ellis. It's something you've got to decide and follow through on for yourself."

LeCates looked up, meeting Doll's eyes from across the table. "It's hard for me," he said quietly. "I didn't realize it before. I've never been married, Doll. It was easy to want it when it couldn't be. Now that it almost seems like it could, I think maybe I'm afraid."

"She's a good woman," Doll answered. "Better than either of us deserves." Aside from that, there was nothing he could say. If the prospect had offered itself to Doll, he knew that he, too, would have been afraid.

17

By the next morning the rain was gone. The temperature had dropped throughout the night. On the wharf, beside Ornan Atkins' skipjack, Doll watched the clouds of his breath condense before him. Atkins' truck was parked nearby. It was early still. Just after seven. No other cars were in sight.

In one of the most honored of nautical traditions, Doll called out for permission to board. The stern hatch to the cabin opened, and Ornan Atkins stuck his head out.

"Oh, it's you, Mr. Doll," he said.

Atkins liked Doll. It was good, Doll thought, that Farron had confided that. Because, without having been told, from the captain's voice and manner, Doll would never have guessed it.

"I was wondering," Doll called back over the bluster of a sudden gust of wind, "if you'd had the chance to think overnight about what you were saying yesterday."

"Ya mean 'bout people not bein' able t' trust ya?"

"I mean about what happened to LeRoy Carrow," Doll said.

"Humph," Atkins snorted. He cocked his head and studied Doll at his leisure. "Maybe ya know," he said, "that Farron came t' see me last night. Spoke a few words in your behalf. When I pushed 'im, he said that ya'd asked 'im t' do that. I get nervous when folks start a peckin' at me, Mr. Doll. When I get that way, I got a real likelihood t' lose what little memory God's left me."

"Call it another mistake," Doll said. "I've made enough so I gave up counting. I'm still asking for your help, Captain Atkins. I'm sorry if you think I tried to get it the wrong way."

"Yeah, well. . . ." Atkins glanced around at the sky and the water. "Nice day," he said approvingly. "Once it settles down, should be a steady breeze. Guess we all make our share now an' again. Why don't ya get off the land, Mr. Doll. Climb on up, an' come aboard."

By the time Doll got down into the cabin, Atkins already had a cup of coffee poured for him. The cabin, like the one on LeRoy Carrow's boat, was a small, enclosed space, but for two men, at wharfside anyway, it was comfortable and surprisingly warm. Atkins sat atop a seat locker on one side. Doll took up a similar position more or less across.

He took a swallow of the black coffee and felt the heat of it slide all the way from his throat to his stomach.

"That stuff'll rot your guts out," Atkins warned. "Pot gets cold, we don't throw it away. We use whatever's left for tarrin' ropes."

Doll took another small swallow. "Coffee never tastes anywhere else like it does on a boat."

"Ain't that true for certain," Atkins replied. "Kind a' gives us a point a' beginnin'."

"How's that?" Doll asked.

Atkins shook his head impassively. "Got a story t' tell ya. Got t' start it somewhere. Don't know for sure that it's what ya need. I'll say right off I don't like tellin' it. In the first place, it smacks too much a' gossipin'. Second, it breaks what ya might call a kind of a confidence, an' I ain't one t' hold a whole lot with that."

"If it helps, I'll promise that it won't go any further," Doll offered.

"You'll promise!" Atkins' scowl seemed to Doll to imply an irony. "That's what I promised too," Atkins said. "An' now I'm gonna break my word. You'll forgive me if I put even less faith in you."

"You make your point," Doll answered.

"When I speak my mind," Atkins said, "I usually do."

Some seconds of silence followed, during which Atkins gave every appearance of a man postponing a chore he didn't like.

"Well, then, I reckon it's time I got to it," he said finally, seeming to have resigned himself to what had to be. "T' start, I need t' go back a few years. 'Bout six or so, as I count it now. I was here on the boat doin' somethin' or other, when this man comes up alongside an' asks if he can see me."

"You asked him what he wanted," Doll ventured.

"Course I did." Atkins nodded. "Him all dressed up in his Sunday suit an' tie. Well, he takes out this thing, looks 'bout like a wallet but don't hold no money, an' shows me this card which says he's a legal officer with the Army on the adjutant general's staff. I asked him if all that meant he was an Army lawyer, an' he said that, as a matter a' fact, that's just what he was."

"An Army lawyer. What did he want with you?"

"Hang on, boy. That's where I'm headin'," Atkins answered. "Just as soon you'd let me get there by m'self."

Doll apologized with a silent toast from his coffee, and Atkins went on.

"I asked 'im the same thing m'self, naturally—which is when he started talkin' 'bout this 'confidential matter.' Well, I told him what I'd tell anybody else, includin' you. I don't talk t' nobody 'less I know what I'm talkin' 'bout. 'Bout then he sees that he's gotta break the ice somehow, so he starts out t' tell me this story. This is what ya got t' keep t' y'self, Mr. Doll."

"I promised you that, Captain Atkins," Doll said.

Atkins took a swallow of his own coffee and nodded. "It was Jerry Lee Godfrey that he come 'bout," Atkins said. "Might've guessed, if I'd put my mind t' it. Jerry Lee was in the Army then. They sent 'im t' someplace in Germany. Anyway, from the way the lawyer told it, Jerry Lee had got himself into some trouble. He got mixed up with some German girl, an' the girl, she had at least another boyfriend. Well, Jerry, I guess, couldn't handle that. Turns out the other boyfriend also had a boat he kept on one a' those lakes they got over there. So one night Jerry Lee gets the idea an' wires the boat."

"Wired it how?" Doll asked.

"Old trick." Atkins shrugged. "He put a can a' gas on the engine block where it'd tip when the engine's cranked. Then he snapped a plug wire off an' stuck it close enough to the block so's it'd arc. Enclosed space, gas fumes, spark! Blew the son of a bitch and the girl t' hell an' clear outta Germany. That was the problem the Army had on its hands."

"The Army didn't charge him?"

"They did and they didn't. That was part a' what the lawyer was there t' help the Army work out. He wanted t' know what I thought 'bout Jerry Lee. They were doin' some kind a' psychology somethin'. Don't know what it was, an' I don't hold t' much with that stuff. But, you see, the Army had nothin' personal against 'im. He'd made a right good soldier for 'em up t' that."

"So they let him go."

"Not exactly." Atkins slapped his hands on his thighs, giving Doll the impression he was near to the end of the story. "But I guess ya could say that it comes t' that. They gave 'im 'bout a year in the stockade an' then let 'im out on some kind a' mental paper. Whatever they called it, I dunno."

"Then, when Jerry got out, he came back to the island."

"There again, no. I don't know why he didn't. Could've been, I suppose, he was ashamed. God knows where he went. I don't. I don't know if anybody does. All I know is that a few months later—that is, after he got out—George Page found him up in Bal'mer. Stumbled on 'im, actually did, while Jerry Lee was sittin' on one a' them streets. It was damn near Christmas when it happened, I recall. George brought him home an' gave him a job on his boat. Ya could do that then when times were better. For a while, he took Jerry Lee into his house, till Jerry got back on his feet enough so he could rent himself his trailer."

"Page just did that? Why?" Doll asked. "What's the link between the two of them? And where was Jerry Lee's family?"

"Godfreys are gone." Atkins shrugged. "Never was a lot of 'em. Jerry Lee's mother was dyin' when he went into the Army. She knew she was an' made 'im go. She knew that someone'd have to look after 'im. Page an' him? I dunno what there was. Folks'll take in stray cats an' dogs. Why is it always such a surprise the few times they take in one another?"

"So you think from all that it was Jerry Lee who loosened the fitting in Carrow's boat?"

"You remember what ya told me once, Mr. Doll, 'bout me not wantin' t' see some things? Well, I was thinkin' 'bout that amongst other things last night, an' I decided that maybe ya just might be right. What I told ya is Jerry Lee killed two people once an' that there ain't a lot a' difference 'tween the way he did it an' the way that LeRoy died. But I don't know that he did LeRoy's boat, an' I got no idea why he would've. So I'm not makin' accusations. If they're gonna be made, it's gonna have t' be by you."

"Jerry Lee Godfrey?" LeCates looked doubtfully at Doll. He stepped down on the axle of the handtruck and pulled back on the handles until the load of milk cases balanced on the wheels.

He gave the appearance of deliberating his answer as he rolled his modest cargo across the store to the case.

"Jerry Lee," he repeated again as he began to pack out the cartons. "What makes you bring up him?"

Doll worked at keeping his promise to Atkins and asked LeCates if there was any reason not to bring up Godfrey's name.

"No," LeCates answered after taking a second to consider the point. "He's just not anybody who gets talked about a lot. He doesn't say much. Keeps mostly to himself. Just like he's something out there in the background."

"What about Page? He talks to Page."

"Well, he works for him. Why shouldn't he?"

"No more than that?"

"Well, yeah, there's more," LeCates admitted. "It's a strange kind of thing. I don't know exactly how to describe it. You've got to start off with that . . . well, that all of Jerry Lee just isn't there."

"Page looks after him?"

"I guess you'd say that. Has for as long as I've been here." LeCates finished packing out the milk and paused to dry his hands on the bottom of his apron. "You'll see Jerry Lee alone sometimes. You say hello, all you'll get is a nod. Anytime he's got to mix with people, he mostly always goes with Page."

"He lives alone?"

"He's got a trailer." LeCates pointed at the wall of the store in the general direction of where the trailer was. "Kinda run down, like you might expect. Not too far from here, across the road on the western side of the neck. I don't figure he owns it himself. My guess is that somehow Page does, and that he rents it out to Jerry Lee on some kind of arrangement they've got between them."

"Anybody else besides Page that he's close to?" Doll asked.

"Well, close? I don't know. Some ways that he's close to Farron maybe. At least he used to be. Found that out the hard way. You know how I am. I'd been here a year or two, when Farron came in for something. I made some wisecrack about Jerry Lee—about him looking like a moose, but not being as smart. I figured that was pretty mild stuff, till Farron came at me. I thought, for a while, he was going to take off my head."

"What's the link?"

LeCates shrugged. "Don't ask me. The kid didn't say."

"What about LeRoy?"

"Meaning what? Was LeRoy any special friend of his or was there something bad between them? Doesn't matter either way. I don't know."

"Could he have murdered LeRoy?"

"You mean loosened the fitting? Sure," LeCates answered. "It's funny, but he's not dumb in all ways like you might think. From what I hear, he's not bad around engines and boats. You ask if he had the know-how to do it, I've got to say he did. If you ask if I know any reason why he would, I don't."

"What about for someone else, if they paid him somehow—maybe money, maybe sex, maybe something no bigger than a favor for a friend?"

LeCates took time to think about that before he answered. "Could be," he said finally and nodded. "I could see him getting talked into the thing. I knew a guy in Florida after your time. He had a big, dumb sheep dog. The guy would stand by the side of his pool and hold out a stick, and that big, damn dog would come running and jump—then next thing you know, it'd be paddling around trying to figure out how it got in the water. Time after time, that dog'd jump. Every time I see Jerry Lee, I wind up remembering that dog."

"Gullible," Doll suggested.

"Yeah, that's the word I was trying to find." LeCates ran his hand through his hair and tried a thin smile. "Somebody who knew the right buttons to push could probably talk Jerry Lee into just about anything."

"Okay, Ellis," Doll replied mechanically. In his head, he felt the hill of sand turning rapidly into a roller coaster. The slow climb up was finished. The eternal pause at the top had passed. He had a sense of the building speed that would grow into the roaring descent—and then it would be over.

"I'll need some better directions on where Jerry Lee's trailer is," Doll said.

"I can do a map." LeCates went to the cash register counter and began to draw on the back of a receipt tape. Lines and little squares appeared. He began to label them as he spoke, keeping his eyes away from Doll's.

"I want you to know, about Elaine . . ." he said, "that I've been thinking about what you said. I don't know, Doll. I woke up in the middle of the night last night. By this morning, my head was more messed up than ever. You remember I used to laugh at all those fortune readers they had around Tampa? It's a funny world. You get crazy enough, I guess, so you reach out for anything."

"Doll." Rachael looked up at him from the door of the motel room. "How did you find me? Don't tell me. It had to be Ardee Vaughn. I didn't expect to be seeing you again. I wasn't even sure if we were speaking."

Her dark hair shimmered. She wore a straight, gray skirt and white, ruffled blouse. A contoured maroon blazer lay carefully folded across the made-up bed.

"I was getting ready to go out," she said. "As usual, you have an awful sense of time."

"Can you give me ten minutes?" Doll asked. "Set a timer, if you want to. Throw me out then if I'm finished or not."

"Ten minutes." She offered him a wry little smile and stepped back from the door to let him in. "I suppose after all we've meant to each other, I ought to be able to spare you that."

Doll glanced around and found that the large room had a homier ambience than he'd expected. It wasn't just a place to sleep, but rather a modest efficiency apartment, complete with a half-sized refrigerator, cooktop, and sink.

A cereal box stood out on a small countertop, and a washed bowl, spoon, and cup were set out to dry themselves during the course of the day. There were clothes on hangers and a suitcase on a folding, aluminum stand—enough to give the room the transitory imprint of its occupant, but too little for any hint of her to remain there once she'd gone.

She closed the door and turned to face him.

"I'll come to the point," Doll said. "It's about LeRoy Carrow. I'm sure you guessed that much. But, as long as I'm here, I also want to say I'm sorry about yesterday."

"What for?" Rachael asked. Her voice made yesterday into nothing.

"For making things uncomfortable," Doll answered. "You said I had a one-track mind. I guess what I mostly did was prove that you were right. More than that, I backed you into a corner. I didn't mean to, but I made you show me a part of yourself that I was too shortsighted to understand might have been there all along."

"And I was short-fused enough to let you get to me." Rachael sat on the edge of the bed and crossed one knee primly over the other. "I was hurt and angry because you beat me by getting your hands on that contract. So I reverted to feeling sorry for myself. It was a maudlin little confession, Doll. I hated myself all afternoon for having made it."

"You're generous."

Rachael shook her head. "I'm practical. Isn't that what I've told you all along? That's the sad thing about us, Doll. We aren't synchronized. Chance gives us a moment to meet, and in that moment we're mismatched."

"Mismatched?"

"I care about business and dollars. You're the romantic, come to the aid of the underdog and looking for something you'd probably call truth. That's a neat little package, isn't it? All folded into a box and tied with a tight ribbon. It isn't the way things are, of course. We all bring our baggage along, all full of complexities and contradictions. But who's got time or even the patience to go that deep? So we keep it simple because it's easier that way. You've got too much sympathy for the loser, and I want too much to win. Opposites, you see. Mismatched. That's what I mean."

She pinched at the bridge of her nose with her fingers. "I'm sorry. I can't cry," she said. "I'll run my mascara." She blinked her eyes, took in a large breath, and then exhaled it. "You said that you came about LeRoy Carrow. What do you want?"

"I think I know what happened to him," Doll replied. "I think I know who, or at least a part of who, was responsible. I think I may even know why."

"All right, then. Good for you." Rachael watched him impatiently. "I assume you didn't come here just to play this for suspense."

"Your option contracts," Doll said. "They give the seller a virtually guaranteed instant buyer anytime he wants one. As soon as the price goes up enough to suit him, he's in a position to take the cash and get out."

"You know that's true. You've seen the contract," Rachael admitted grudgingly.

"So your seller has a reason to want the price driven up. Maybe he's not interested in the long-term future. Maybe he wants his bread to be buttered right now."

"And you're making that into the motive. You're going to make it out one of my clients who killed Carrow. Who, Doll? You said you knew who. How can you know when you don't even know who my clients are?"

"Now you know why I'm here," Doll said quietly.

"Then you've just wasted your ten minutes and mine." From her seat on the edge of the bed, she glared up at him hotly. "Why, in God's name, would I tell you that, Doll?"

Rachael shook her head incredulously. "If you're right," she said, "all that can do is bring me bad press. The least it will do is slow down everything. It may even stop it altogether—make useless all I've done this far. And then there are the confidences involved. Whatever made you even think I would help you?"

"I didn't really think that you would." Doll smiled. "That isn't any kind of accusation, Rachael. You've got priorities and your own reasons for them. You gave me fair warning the first time we met, and you never gave me a reason to think the rules had changed."

"Then why come at all?" Rachael demanded.

"Because you never know if there might not be a small chance. But that's not really true." Doll ran his hand back through his hair and tried to find the words that he wanted. "Because I think it's going to come out. Because I think, before it does, you deserve the chance to shore up your position. Because I think you had the right to hear it from me face to face."

For a moment, she stared at him, then stood and smoothed the sides of her skirt with her hands.

"You would think all that," she said, smiling at him.

"And," Doll added, "because I thought it was important to say good-bye."

"Why can't I hate you, Doll?" Rachael Teal closed her eyes and slowly opened them again. "You're going to cost me—I don't know how much—money. I'm probably going to have to start somewhere else all over again. So why is it I hear myself saying that, all together, this isn't something that I'm going to regret. Mismatched, Doll. That's what we are, and that's too bad. In other ways, though, we were great."

She came to him and kissed him, until, finally, she released him and backed away. She opened the door and held it for him, leaving that alone to say her own good-bye.

18

By the time Doll got back to the island it was early afternoon. At the wharf, the skipjacks were tied off and empty. No member of their crews was anywhere in sight. Ornan Atkins' pickup was gone from his driveway, and, though Doll was by no means surprised when he tried, no one answered his knock at the door of Jerry Lee's trailer. Doll could find no special meaning in their absence, but the watermen seemed to have abandoned the island for the day.

The vacant afternoon, Doll filled with running, doubling his normal distance, telling himself he was making up for the days and miles he'd missed. After that, he tried the magazines that the inn supplied on the bottom shelf of the bedside table—all back issues, read by their subscribers first, then donated to the general cause—*Outdoor Life*, *Sports Afield*, and, as things began getting desperate, particularly selected articles from *Family Circle*. It was easier being active, doing anything. Waiting, by itself, was the hardest thing to do.

Finally darkness came. Doll let the afternoon turn into night. His watch showed a few minutes after eight o'clock the second time that he visited Jerry Lee's trailer.

On this occasion, the door opened. Jerry Lee looked out, standing in silhouette with the incandescent light at his back. His face was in shadow, his expression hard to see. His lower jaw stuck out like the bulbous, underwater prow of a modern-day Persian Gulf tanker.

"Who's that?" he said, squinting out at Doll. His breath was rich with beer. Doll watched for the telltale signs in the fluidity of Jerry Lee's movements and speech, but the patterns were sufficiently erratic in their normal state that Doll wasn't able to estimate how many Jerry Lee had already had.

"Mista Doll? What'd ya want wif me?" he asked when Doll had answered.

"To come in for a minute or two, if I could," Doll said.

"Com' in? Com' in what for?"

"To talk. Just to ask you a question or two." It was no fair match, not in any sense. Doll remembered the irony of Rachael Teal talking about winners and losers and him protecting the underdog. He laughed darkly at himself and thought about how absurdly foolish people came to look in their pretenses.

"I dunno. I dunno if I'm supposed t'," Jerry Lee said.

"Why not?" Doll asked, finally abandoning one set of scruples to another. There were different rules for different times, the Navy had taught him. To get a thing done, you sometimes had to choose. Now and then, when he had the time for it, Doll wondered if that was true.

"I dunno," Jerry Lee replied.

"I stopped off at the wharf down where the boats are. Nobody was there this afternoon. I figured you must have gone snaking again."

"Crabbin' t'day," Jerry Lee said. "Heard this mornin' they was runnin' good over Trippe an' Brannoch Bay. Maybe go snakin' t'morrow."

"Have a good day?"

"Fair t' middlin'." Jerry Lee shrugged and stepped back from the door. "Guess it's a'right for ya t' come in."

Inside the trailer, the air smelled rank. The beer was the most predominant odor, but beneath it Doll's nose caught a more general melange of sweat and cooked food and mildew, as though the place hadn't been aired in months, if not, perhaps, years.

The space all about the room was cluttered with objects tossed about by a tornado's logic. The walls were decorated with photographic art work clipped from the pages of the less culturally pretentious men's magazines.

"Chair's over there if ya want it. Jus' throw that blanket off." Jerry Lee, meanwhile, sat in a hand-me-down chair at the end of a formica table, where he'd stationed his bottle of beer. A game show host leered from a small-screen television on one of the counters in the open kitchen.

Doll settled into the chair. "Hard life these days, isn't it?" he said. "You enjoy working out there on the bay?"

"Take it or leave it." Jerry Lee shrugged and swallowed some beer. It seemed never to occur to him that he might have offered a bottle to Doll. "Don't like it when it gets t' freezin'. Seen men slip an' die out there when it gets t' be like that."

"Off the skipjacks?"

Jerry Lee nodded. "Water freezes right on the damn decks. Yer boots get all icy. Goddamn lousy bay when it's cold."

"You ever think of tongin' instead?"

"Ya be out there all alone, then." Jerry Lee shook his head.

"Better with other people you can talk to—Joely and Carroll, Captain Atkins and Captain Page. What about the captains, Jerry Lee? They hard to work for? A man gets to hear all kinds of stories. Some of them drink, others beat you like slaves. What's it really like with them when you're out?"

"Cap'n Page is nice." Jerry Lee shrugged again. "Cap'n Atkins, he don't say too much."

Not to me either, Doll thought to himself. Then he remembered what he was there to do, and instantly the moment lost its humor.

"How's Captain Page nice to you?" Doll asked.

"Well, you know. . . ." Jerry Lee took a swallow from his beer and looked away. "He helps me out. Sometimes I don't look after myself good as I should."

"How does he help you?" Doll pressed.

"Wha'cha mean?" Jerry Lee looked back at him, not disingenuous enough to hide his deepening frown.

Doll tried to make the question into nothing. "You said that he helps you. I only asked how."

"Maybe how ain't none a' yer business. Maybe you ought t' get outta here."

"I didn't mean to touch on anything personal. I'll back off." Doll held up the palms of his hands in mock surrender. "Like you say, it's none of my business. I'll change the subject. How about Captain Carrow? You talk very much to him?"

"Cap'n's dead," Jerry Lee said sullenly.

"But before?"

"Get outta here, Mr. Doll." Jerry Lee began to get up from the table. "I ain't got no more t' say t' you."

"Sit down, Jerry Lee," Doll said evenly without moving from the chair. For a moment Jerry Lee stared at him, then slowly, subordinately, sank back into his seat.

Doll waited before he began. "Do you know what happened to Captain Carrow?" he asked. "He was murdered. Did you know that, Jerry Lee?" Jerry Lee said nothing. There was nothing in his eyes. It was as though, Doll thought, he'd somehow backed into some corner of himself and left behind for the world to see only a barely animated mountain of bone and flesh.

"It was all made to look like an accident," Doll continued for the benefit of whatever audience he had. "But LeRoy was too good a captain to have an accident like that. No, Jerry Lee. Somebody else deliberately loosened that fitting and counted on the fact that Captain LeRoy couldn't smell the gas.

"There's another way to do it, you know. Maybe even easier. All you do is tug loose a spark plug wire and let enough gasoline get loose in the bilge. Only skipjacks don't have engines on board, so that wouldn't work, would it, Jerry Lee? You had to come up with something else, and you thought of the propane."

The accusation produced in Jerry Lee no reaction whatsoever. He sat as he had been, staring vacantly, not moving, hardly breathing, just waiting like a machine set to stand-by. He seemed to have the power to turn the outside off.

Doll spoke again, though, by now, he had no idea how much of what he said was getting through.

"I don't think you had your own reasons, Jerry Lee. I think you did it for someone else. You don't have to be afraid. I'm not going to ask you for who. All I want is this: I want you to go and tell that person I was here. I want you to tell them everything I said, everything I said, and one thing more. I want that person to meet me, Jerry Lee." Doll glanced at his watch. "At nine-thirty, exactly an hour from now. I'll wait on the wharf next to Captain Carrow's skipjack. Exactly an hour. Do you understand what I just said?"

There wasn't an answer, only the blank that had been there before. Doll got up from the chair and moved toward the table. As to the effect on Jerry Lee, he mightn't have moved at all.

Doll went to the door of the trailer and let himself out into the night. The last that he saw as he closed the door behind him, Jerry Lee remained at the table, his beer sitting untouched before him, sitting just exactly as he was.

If the message he'd left would even get delivered, Doll had no idea. He felt certain from Jerry Lee's reaction that he'd found a very large part of the truth. And, in a sense, that meant he'd won. So much, he decided, for the rewards and satisfactions of victory. Doll knew that he'd never count that last bit of work as being among his finer hours.

He waited in the seemingly endless blackness. No more than thirty minutes had passed since he left Jerry Lee in the trailer. He sat on a crab trap and stared out at the sea and allowed the night to grow around him.

It was something Doll had learned about the night.

As the day is rich, the night is poor. The day has colors in a thousand brilliant hues and sounds so plentiful that sometimes even the trained ear isn't able to select among them. In the night, so much less is offered for the mind to absorb that each individual part becomes more.

He heard the quiet water rise to pat at the sides of the boats at the wharfside, then fall back with a gentle splash upon itself. Crickets chirped, slowly because the night was cool. A silent breeze now and then gave itself away, rustling the new leaves that shuddered on the very highest branches of the trees. Sound carried farther than Doll could see. Somewhere on the water he heard the low, regular drone of an engine. He strained his eyes to no avail to find the navigation lights betrayed by the hum of the motor.

From the land, the sound carried too. Doors slammed abruptly, here, then there. Cars started and passed. The whir of their tires passed and dopplered away. Now and then there were snatches of distant conversations along with occasional bursts of music. The night was still very young. Its myriad enticements were only starting to get themselves underway.

Headlights rose and fell away again. The lights in rooms in the houses winked on and after a time winked off again. Some windows glowed with yellow light and others with the shiny white fluorescence of reflected television screens.

All that and still there was mind-space left for imagination, which, after all, Doll thought, was perhaps the greatest magic of the night.

A car pulled into the parking area on the opposite side of the wharf from Doll. There was nothing Doll was able to see of it beside its headlamps. It slowed to a stop at the outer edge of the lot, more or less across from Page's and Atkins' skipjacks. The headlights went off. The soft strains of music from its radio drifted over the water, interrupted by the snap of a can top and high-pitched laughter. A flame breathed two cigarettes to life. More laughter. The memories that the laughter stirred in Doll were bittersweet.

He turned back to the water as though to deny his presence as a voyeur. The white lights of the land shimmered on the blackness of the bay. Navigation marks blinked their distinctive patterns in colors of white, red, and green, guiding and warning the mariners who took the trouble to learn their voiceless language.

Behind him, against the darker shadows of the trees, a woman made her way through the backyards of the houses. Carrying what looked like bags of groceries, she came from the direction of LeCates' store.

For the instant that she held Doll's attention, she almost caused him to miss the closer by noise.

It came, this time, from Doll's side of the wharf—a crunch more than anything else, the kind of sound that a shoe would make on a surface of cracked shell and gravel.

Doll waited. It didn't repeat, which told Doll a great deal more than if it had.

The wharf didn't offer much for cover, unless someone who wished to stay out of sight was willing to climb on board the boats to do it. At the far end, toward the road, was a streetlight. Halfway between the light and Doll was a collection of oil drums and other marine cast-offs. The source of the footfall, Doll reasoned, had to have come from there.

He checked his watch. Forty-five minutes since he'd left the trailer. His visitor had apparently decided to be early. Doll let himself look toward the drums.

"All right, Captain. The hunting is over. We might as well make the party official," Doll called softly.

The rounded shape of George Page's stomach emerged from behind the cover of the oil drums. He walked slowly, seemingly cautious, but Doll guessed that he wanted the time to think. Finally he reached the place where Doll sat and stood before him.

"So ya knew," he said. "I thought, when ya didn't tell Jerry Lee, that ya still might be runnin' a bluff."

Doll shook his head and looked up at Page. "Not the way it came together. I'm sorry, Captain. It had to be you."

"Then ya took on y'self one hell of a chance. We're talkin' here 'bout a murder, Mr. Doll. What the hell would ever make ya think I wouldn't go on t' another an' kill you? Seems like ya almost went outta ya way t' give me the chance."

"I wanted to see if you'd try," Doll acknowledged. "I think I understand most of it now. There are still some parts I need to have explained."

Page smiled faintly, giving a short respite to his jaw and the tobacco. "More than ya know," he said, squatting down before Doll. He picked up a pebble from the ground, flipped it out toward the water, and listened for the sound of the splash. "I'll tell ya that, 'cause there's no point in lyin' now. But first ya tell me how ya come t' settle on me."

"You told me, partly." Doll leaned forward, resting his elbows on his knees. "You remember what you and everybody else said all along about the island being as small a place as it is?

I heard about Jerry Lee's trouble after a while. You know the place better than I do. You should've realized that I'd have to hear it sometime. After that, it all began to sort itself out."

"How so?" Page looked up.

"Once I turned up Jerry Lee, you're an obvious choice. But why, in the end, the only one?" Doll replied. "Who else? Not Gerry Vaughn. He talks too much, and he gets too much fun out of doing his own work. I also had a hard time, especially, seeing him going to any waterman for help. That last part's also just as true for Rachael Teal. And true for Covey Wallace, in his own way. No matter how mad he got, I couldn't see him throwin' his lot in with any drudger. Farron? He might have gone to Jerry Lee, but he had the chance to call me off and didn't do it."

"Could've been somebody else."

"It could have," Doll agreed. "Truth is, there were too many possibilities all along. But then, once Jerry Lee figured in, I remembered that your boat was up for sale. And then, I found myself coming back to Rachael Teal and her contracts."

"So you went t' her an' got her t' tell ya," Page anticipated.

"She wouldn't," Doll answered, "but, then, you just did."

"Nothin' I wasn't gonna tell ya anyway." Page ran a hand across the stubble on his face and spat. "You've done a whole lot a' damage, Mr. Doll. I can only hope, when it's all said an' done, that you're sure in the end it was worth it."

Justice and picking among sets of rules again. Doll remembered Ardee Vaughn: You can't even tell when you win.

"Ya take Jerry Lee," Page was saying. "Reckon ya know ya shook him up some t'night. He's run off t' somewhere. I couldn't hold him." Page hunched up his shoulders. "Don't hardly matter, I guess. Once this breaks, they'll catch him 'fore long. Don't know what they'll do t' him. Reckon either way he gets locked away. Ya don't know how that afflicts me, Mr. Doll.

'Cause, like ya say, he killed ol' LeRoy Carrow for me. Not that I wanted that. That's the part ya don't know. God knows I never wanted that at all."

"If you didn't want it, how did it happen?" Doll asked.

"Well, now ya finally asked the right question." Page smiled with no trace of humor. "Do ya ever think 'bout gettin' old, Mr. Doll? I'm fifty-nine, an' I busted my tail all my whole damn life out on that bay—March gales an' stinkin' hot summers, an' winters where the ice hangs so hard on your face that it closes your eyes. I'm old, Doll. I wanted somethin' from whatever time the Lord gives me left. That, since ya had t' drug it out, is my terrible crime."

"You wanted to get out the hard cash money you've got tied up in your house."

"Course I did. Ya know damn well what my boat is worth. I needed the price on the house to go up. The higher the better, so I could buy myself a little Florida time. Man's got a right t' that, don't ya think? An', all the time, ol' LeRoy kept up his damn-fool hollerin'. Until one day I cursed him. I did that, Mr. Doll. I screamed at him when I knew he couldn't hear me, 'LeRoy Carrow,' I shouted, 'You're a sumbitchin' bastard, an' I wish on all that's holy you were dead!' An' then he was. I mean, don't ya call it a miracle, Mr. Doll? A downright miracle, the way that God'll sometime answer prayer?"

Doll didn't know what to call it. He looked at Page, shook his head, and then stared out across the hulk of LeRoy Carrow's boat at the water beyond.

"Like a cat," Page said, his voice seeming to marvel at the analogy. "Ya take in a stray an' ya feed it, an' then, one day, it comes t' where you're sittin' an' pays ya back by deliverin' up a dead mouse. Not a mouse ya necessarily wanted, but a mouse all the same. Cat dunno. Ya see, Mr. Doll? Dumb cat. If it had any brain, it'd see ya didn't really want it."

"Who knew?" Doll asked. "The island? The coroner's inquest? Everybody but me?"

"Knew for certain?" Page tossed another pebble toward the water. "Only me. I made Jerry Lee tell me. Some others maybe guessed. The ones who knew about Jerry Lee's other trouble. Hard t' say how many a' those there are. Maybe none. Maybe a handful. Maybe, like ya say, the island. It's an answer I never really wanted to know."

Doll counted. There was Atkins and Ellis LeCates, and Page and Jerry Lee, and Doll himself—already too many. He turned to Page.

"I can't do it, Captain. Not even if I decided I wanted to. I can't put the cork back in the bottle."

"Well, now," Page said scratching at his chin, "I figure there are a lot a' reasons, but, for any one of 'em, I never really expected that ya could."

He looked at Doll, his eyes narrowed appraisingly, then turned away and spat a plug of spent tobacco onto the ground.

19

Dawn was orange in the eastern sky as Doll heaved his battered suitcase through the right side door into the narrow back seat of the VW. He felt tired. He'd slept little during the night, and, when he'd slept, he hadn't slept well. He hadn't gotten back to the inn until nearly one o'clock that morning. The state police in Easton had kept him that long.

The story hadn't made the morning papers, but the news had needed less than the night to cover the breadth of the island. Wesley Mowen had met him with it at the desk when Doll had gone to check out that morning. The innkeeper had begun tentatively, presenting his rendition from behind a studious neutrality. Only when Doll had confirmed its essential accuracy did Mowen offer an expression of sadness, although for whom the sadness was meant, Doll noticed, Mowen never made entirely clear.

Doll unbent from the back of the VW and locked the suitcase in. He worked his fingers to massage his burning eyes. As he opened them again, he saw the state police cruiser slowing out on the highway. He watched as the car turned into the drive, then swung into the parking area, and finally rolled to a stop behind the bug.

By then, Doll had recognized the driver. He waited while Corporal Unruh opened the door and got out. He stood against the side of the car, studying Doll incuriously, with his forearms folded casually on the top of the roof.

"You leaving us, Mr. Doll, at last?" Unruh asked. He offered a thin, cynical smile which, Doll gathered, was meant to suggest that the damage was already done.

"You said last night there wasn't any reason I couldn't," Doll answered.

"Still isn't." Unruh shrugged. "Not so far as I know. So, if you're through with your raisin' hell, guess you might as well go."

"With your permission, then, Corporal. . . ." Doll walked around to the opposite side of the car and opened the driver's side door.

"Thought you might like to know that we picked up Jerry Lee," Unruh said.

Doll stopped and turned. One look at Unruh's face told him that the announcement had produced its anticipated effect. The corporal waited for him to walk to the back of the bug before saying anything further.

"Hitchhiking. Trying to get across the Bay Bridge," the officer explained when he was satisfied. "Couldn't have stood out more if he tried. Worst way in the world to get off the shore and him with that jaw out there like the blade on a bulldozer."

"Is he all right?"

"Much as anyone can tell." Unruh curled up a corner of his mouth. "Right now, last I heard, he's still in the clam-up mode. Won't even tell them his name or where he lives."

"Where is he? What about a lawyer? He's got a right to one, even if he isn't smart enough to know it."

Unruh smiled his cynic's smile again. "Relax, counselor, we know the law. He's got to hear his rights, *and* he's got to understand them. He'll get a lawyer. He's up in Annapolis. They already got more than enough lawyers up there to go around."

"What happens to him, Corporal? How do things like this work themselves out here?"

"Depends," Unruh answered. "It's almost not a police matter anymore. Page gave a statement the same time you did. There's more than enough by itself in that. They don't really need anything else to get an indictment on Godfrey. At that point, in something like this, any judge that didn't buy his degree from a sign shop is going to order a full psychiatric. When that comes back, who knows what it'll say. It could go to trial. It's a murder. It probably will."

"Murder one?"

"The state will ask for that. They'll have to with that German thing." But Unruh shook his head. "The defense'll plea-bargain it. Or they'll get it reduced on mental incompetence. Jail or institutional confinement. It won't be any worse than that. The man can't take care of himself, Doll. It might be the best that could have happened. Suppose Page died. Where does he go then? Back to the sidewalks in Baltimore?"

"And what about Page?" Doll asked. "What happens to him?"

"Well, that depends, too. If what he said last night is true, then there's nothing anybody can do to him. It isn't a crime to wish somebody dead. If it was, we'd all be in jail. It isn't even a crime to say it, as long as you don't intend to have it carried out. But that'll have to wait till Jerry Lee decides to talk to someone. That's the only way that that whole thing is ever going to get straightened out."

"I don't see it," Doll said. "I don't see Page sending Jerry Lee out to do a murder. I can't believe he'd take the kid in for six years, only to set him up for the hard fall."

Unruh exhaled and tapped his fingers lightly on the roof of the cruiser.

"This is off the record," he said. "I can get in trouble for telling you this. I was there for part of his statement. Watermen are lousy actors." Unruh looked away. "And they're not supposed to cry."

"Thanks," Doll said.

"I never said it," Unruh answered. "Now you go on. Get your ass out of here." The officer pushed himself back from the roof of the car. "We may need you for more detail on your statement later, but aside from that, if I were you, I wouldn't be too quick to come back. There's at least one county coroner out there, who, just between you and me, would like to roast you in very small pieces, starting with your balls."

Unruh backed the cruiser up and retraced his path out the driveway. As the car regained the road, Wesley Mowen came out of the office of the inn. He carried a small piece of paper in his hand.

"Your receipt, Mr. Doll. I forgot t' give it t' ya before, and I didn't know but that ya might need it. Then I saw the police car, t' tell ya the truth, an' I figured I'd just better stay outta the way there for a while."

Doll took the paper and thanked Mowen for it, but the innkeeper hesitated as though he were disinclined to leave it at that.

"That's not the whole truth," he said at last. "That receipt there wasn't all what brought me out. It's George Page, an' Jerry Lee, an' LeRoy an' all. Course it had t' be. I reckon ya knew that. I thought ya might think folks around here might blame ya. Not so, Mr. Doll. I thought ya ought t' know that. What ya did, ya see, was kinda clear up a lot a' our consciences. I mean, it's awful easy sometimes just t' let things go along. Even when ya know ya shouldn't. Ya didn't let us, an' it's good ya didn't. Ya made come out a hurtful secret that surely never should've got kept."

Doll took the receipt and poked it into the pocket of his shirt. Mowen nodded and turned, starting out toward his office. Then, suddenly he turned back.

"Ya come back an' stay with us again," he called. "Some right good fishin' nine or ten weeks from now. Ya come on back, an' I'll set ya up with a finfish cap'n who knows right well where t' look."

"Maybe I'll do that." Doll waved. Mowen waved back. Doll drew in a breath and noticed that he felt a little less tired than before.

According to the plan Doll had formed, he'd stop first to see Elaine, then go on to close things out with LeCates. But, as it happened—and, he thought, as he might have expected—when he got to the Carrow house, he found Ellis LeCates' car in the driveway.

Doll found them in the kitchen, seated across the table from one another. Two untouched cups of coffee rested on the table before them. Elaine offered to pour one for Doll, but Doll declined on the less than honest excuse that he'd already had his quota for the morning. This time, though, she let him loose without offering any objection.

"We heard the news about Captain Page and Jerry Lee," she said. "At first I thought it had to be wrong, but it isn't." She framed the statement into something so close to a question that Doll had to answer that it wasn't wrong.

"So hard to believe." Elaine sighed. "But, of course, it always had to be someone we knew. But Jerry Lee and George! LeRoy sailed with them. In high school, Jerry Lee was Farron's closest friend."

"I heard that," Doll said. "I never figured out what it was they had in common."

"The island," Elaine answered. "The island boys stay together. The high school's over on the mainland. And both of them were badly picked on. Jerry Lee because of how he was and Farron because of LeRoy."

"I'm sorry for the way it turned out," Doll said.

"No." Elaine shook her head. "You didn't make it happen that way. And you gave us all the chances you could to call it off. We asked you to see it through, and you did. That's all there is." She looked away, out through the window and over the bay. "For the rest—for the memories of the other times, I can be sorry for Jerry Lee and George. Not for how it turned out. Ellis's name had to be cleared. So did Farron's. I can't be sorry for that."

"Then I'll leave the two of you alone." Doll took a step backward. "It's a long drive back, and I might as well get started. If I don't, it'll manage to waste the whole day."

"Ellis said that you made some suggestions," Elaine said, stopping him.

"I made them to Ellis," Doll answered, frowning. "I didn't expect to get the credit."

"But they're good, Mr. Doll." Elaine smiled. "Even if there's more than just a hint of deviltry in them. The job for Farron, I think, is the genius part. It gives him a way to make the money he'll need if he's going to fix up his father's boat—and, with him staying on the island now, it gives me a reason not to sell the house."

"You could find a job in Easton or maybe even closer," Doll suggested. "Even Easton isn't all that far a drive."

"And then the girls could stay in school where they are," Elaine added. "That'd be good for them. First, their father, then everything else. God knows, they've gone through enough change for now. They ought to have something the same to hold onto a little."

"However you work it out," Doll said. He returned Elaine's smile, then held out his hand toward Ellis LeCates. "Your luck's still holding, Ellis. Don't let it slide by," he said.

LeCates stood.

"I owe you, Doll. That's all I can say."

He shook Doll's hand and stared at the floor—a middle-aged man with his last, best chance of ending a ludicrously protracted adolescence. Silently Doll wished him well. There were some, maybe a lot of, chronological adults who were never able to end it at all.

Doll made the final good-byes as brief as he could. If he had his way, he'd remember the two of them as they were there, that morning, in Elaine Carrow's kitchen. Two people in a bubble of time, believing the best might still be ahead. Doll had no wish to be a further party to their future.

The last stop Doll made, he hadn't planned. He decided upon it only as he saw the masts above the trees and turned the wheel of the car at the final possible moment.

Alongside the wharf, the two skipjacks had been rearranged. The *Winston Mills* was now tied up outboard of Page's. Joely Edwards and Carroll Messick worked at some repair in the stern. Ornan Atkins was forward of the cabin, apparently pondering the mysteries of the dredge engine. When he saw Doll get out of the car, he stepped across to Page's boat and crossed the deck to the inboard rail.

He nodded good morning to Doll.

"Just thought I ought to let you know that I'm leaving," Doll said.

"Ya got no need t' report t' me. Figured ya would be, though," Atkins said.

"I wanted to say thank you."

"What for?" Atkins asked. "Didn't tell ya nothin' ya wouldn't've found out sometime for y'self. Like a boil, Mr. Doll. Like the kind the good Lord gave t' Job. Time comes, when ya got one, it's best that ya get the thing lanced."

"I'm sorry," Doll said, "about Page and Jerry Lee."

"If ya are," Atkins answered frowning, "then you're more of a fool than I take ya for. Sometimes life rolls us hard, other times gentle. We make our own ways, all a' us. George and Jerry Lee, just like the rest."

"Okay," Doll replied.

Atkins turned his head and nodded his chin toward the *Winston Mills*.

"We're 'bout set up t' go out," he explained. "Not drudgin'. Just sailin' her over to Crisfield. Captain over there's got some drudge parts that he's sellin'. We'll see how they fit up. Maybe we can use 'em." He looked at the sky. "Should be a nice run, if ya got the time t' come along."

"Not today. Some other time, maybe."

"Well, take ya choice," Atkins answered. He didn't offer to shake Doll's hand. It was, Doll speculated, perhaps the greater compliment that he didn't. "When ya come back sometime, I plan on bein' here," Atkins said. "I'd count it as a privilege an' pleasure t' have ya sail aboard."

Doll stayed to see the *Winston B. Mills* untie. He watched Joely Edwards handle the lines, while Carroll Messick fired up the refitted automobile engine that powered the skipjack's push boat. Standing at the oyster boat's helm, Ornan Atkins maneuvered the rudder and operated the long control cables that trailed over the stern and connected to the push boat's motor.

For a brief moment, the engine revved, breaking the inertia as the heavy hull nosed away from the side of its sister ship, then idled back as the skipjack edged ahead, into the curving channel and out on toward the open waters of the bay.

Doll watched the boat for longer than he planned. He followed her leadened progress past the last of the channel markers, and through a wide turn as Ornan Atkins brought the bow around to a heading into the wind.

Together at the foot of the mast, the two hands heaved the sails aloft, then set them, anticipating an initial course and wind.

At the wheel, Atkins took a long look around—at the rigging, the sea, and the signs of the moving air. Finally, he edged the helm over. The skipjack's bow fell off the wind. Her tall sails ceased their slapping and filled. The boom swung to leeward, then caught and stiffened.

Forward, slowly, a bow wave built, as the big boat heeled and her captain held her to course. For one more day in her nearly one hundred years, the *Winston B. Mills* rode the winds of the Chesapeake Bay.